Gary Wright

ISBN: 9798526137690

DEDICATION

Becoming a parent gave me the empathy I needed to be able to write this story. This is for my two little humans, Florence and Sully. Daddy loves you more than you'll ever know.

Content Warning: Please see note underneath 'About The Author' on the last page for content warnings.

Rip Current (Collins English Dictionary)

a strong current, esp one flowing outwards from the shore, causing disturbance on the surface

---

Rip currents can travel at speeds similar to an Olympic swimmer (4.5 mph) (source: RNLI)

In 2019 there were 78 accidental drowning deaths on UK beaches (source: National Water Safety Forum)

PROLOGUE

The water dragged him away, but not under. Panic was his greatest threat. Panic, and exhaustion. The rip was strong as the shore became distant.

He heard his name being called. His mother's voice. Loud in volume, trembling in tone. He wasn't the only one panicking. She was screaming, but with enough clarity for others to know what was wrong. When someone screams on a beach, people instinctively look out to sea.

Seven years old. He was just seven years old. He tried to fight the sea, to keep his mother's voice from dimming, but the more he tried, the fainter her calls became.

He had never had cause to contemplate death and the myriad of associated subjects. In the mind of this seven year old, death was abstract. Death was unknown. Death was unfathomable.

Despite waves crashing over him, he hadn't been under. The sea was trying to claim him and his resistance was wilting. His arms and legs, normally boundless in their capacity for energy, felt sapped and devoid of strength. His lungs, youthful and free of the excesses of adult life, burned with every breath. His will to get back to his mother, however, remained undiminished.

Still the waves came, silencing his mother's voice. A pattern of noise was established. The thunderous crash of a wave. The eerie silence that followed. The ominous, low grumble of the sea as it built it's strength. The crescendo reached as another wave crashed over him.

He fought to stay above water. Every sinew of him knew it was what he had to do. Instinct drove him to tread water until there was nothing left to give, until the pain of endlessly kicking his feet against the relentless resistance of the water beneath him caused him to stop. He couldn't do it anymore. Medical people would make reference to lactic acid in his muscles, but he was seven years old. All he knew was that it hurt too much to carry on.

Another wave pummelled him. This time, he went under. He scrabbled with his fingers to grab the surface of the sea but even his prepubescent mind knew that he wouldn't be able to get any traction. Gripping the edge of water was impossible. Hauling himself out was beyond the bounds of possibility.

The violence above surface contrasted with the calm below. The crashing sound of the waves was replaced with a melodic thudding. He knew he needed to breathe, and had wondered before what happened if you couldn't. He didn't feel pain. He didn't feel scared. He felt a strange feeling of acceptance, one that he wouldn't ever be able to explain.

Darkness consumed him before he closed his eyes.

30 Years Later

The trauma never left him. The mental wounds healed, but the scars remained. Still, he went to the beach. His wife and daughter loved it there, so much so that they had a beach hut. He accompanied them, but never went in the sea.

Saturday brought sunshine, which in turn brought a familiar sense of trepidation.

"We're leaving in 10 minutes," Sophie shouted upstairs.

"Alright mum," Maria replied. She had recently dispensed with 'mummy' and 'daddy', long before any child should. Six going on sixteen, they had said. Andrew secretly missed the innocence with which she had called him 'daddy'.

Their beach hut occupied a prime spot in the centre of Beachbrook beach. Beachbrook was a typical tourist town - packed to the rafters with holiday makers in the summer, but deserted and left for the locals in the winter. Local businesses prospered in the warm months but were shuttered in the cold. Saturday was one of the hot days that brought out the tourists and the locals alike.

Andrew sat, as he usually did, on his fold out chair on the sand outside the beach hut. He always remained fully clothed, never once changing into beach clothes and always watching. On a beach with no lifeguards, he felt even more on edge.

"Alright love?" Sophie asked.

"Yeah, fine," he replied. He didn't look at her. He was concentrating on watching Maria. She was becoming more independent by the day. With blonde hair and blue eyes, she was a typical free-spirited child who thrived on pushing parental boundaries. She was only about twenty metres away from him but he still couldn't temper his anxiety. He knew that she loved the water and that she was a confident swimmer but none of that mattered. He had experienced the violence of the sea first hand. Ability meant nothing. And now she was at the water's edge, dipping her toes into the sea. Andrew got up and jogged down to her. He stopped short of the water.

"Maria, what have I said about going in the sea without me or your mum being here?" He asked.

"You are here," she replied. "You were watching me weren't you?" Somehow, and in her own inimitable way, she had turned the tables and placed the burden of questioning onto him.

Andrew suppressed a smile. He shouldn't have been surprised and, in truth, he wasn't. His daughter meant everything to him. She had him hooked since the day she was born and that bond had only grown stronger through her formative years. Now, Maria had a little brother or sister on the way. Sophie was just starting to show a bump and people were just starting to notice. No-one had asked them about it yet and they had not publicly announced it. For now, it was their news.

"Of course I was watching you princess," Andrew said with a chuckle. She really did have him wrapped around her little finger. "New rules now though," he continued. "One of us has got to be here by the water if you want to go in. OK?"

Maria rolled her eyes. She did this a lot and it was something that Andrew and Sophie both hated, but they knew it was a phase and that she would grow out of it eventually.

"OK dad," she said.

She played in the water while Andrew watched, never going past her knees in depth. She was a boundary pusher but she also knew where to draw the line. She stayed in the water for about twenty minutes and when she came out she ran straight past Andrew and back to Sophie who was waiting for her with an open towel. He relaxed and slowly made his way back across the sand, watching the two women in his life. Sophie was busy drying Maria off and he could hear familiar protestations coming from his daughter.

"I can do it myself, mum." Maria took the towel from her mum and was swallowed up in it. Sophie knew better than to try to help her any more.

The rest of the day passed by on dry land. As the sun was on its slow descent to the horizon, Andrew, Sophie and Maria packed up their beach hut and made their way back to their car. Home was a mere five minutes away, but in that time Maria fell fast asleep. It had been a busy day. Andrew looked at her while she slept as he tried to lift her up quietly to take her indoors. Her skin was sun kissed with streaks of dried salt on it. Her hair was bleached and damp. She was gently snoring. Andrew carried her indoors, knowing that this danger nap meant that she would be up in the night. He didn't mind.

With Maria in bed, Andrew and Sophie sat in the garden as the sun disappeared behind the trees. The air felt cooler, but it was still warm. Andrew shut his eyes and felt he could've been sitting on a veranda in the Mediterranean.

"Let's have a chat about work, then," Sophie said, piercing the serenity of the moment.

Andrew opened his eyes. It was a conversation he had been hoping to avoid.

"Money's not too bad at the moment," he said. "We've got this month covered anyway. Something will come up. If not then I'll have a look around and see if there's anything going on any of the sites."

Andrew hated the idea of going back to work on the sites. He had managed to get away from that a few years ago and it really would be a last resort. Being self employed in the building game was difficult, but the independence was addictive.

"If the worst comes to the worst then I can always go back on the tools," Sophie said with a giggle. "I don't mind getting my scissors back out. I actually miss it sometimes." She hadn't gone back to hairdressing after Maria had been born. She had begun to make tentative arrangements to establish a new client list, but those plans had been scuppered by her falling pregnant.

Andrew smiled at her. He didn't want her to feel like she had to go back to work, especially now that she was pregnant. He would go back onto the sites before she had to do that. He didn't want to think about work and money. It was the weekend and he worried about it enough during the week.

"Beach again tomorrow?" He asked, changing the subject.

"Yeah," she replied. "Forecast isn't great but we might as well. Oh I meant to say, Joe is coming with us. Linda and Chris are both working."

Sophie and Andrew often looked after Joe, especially when his parents shifts clashed. Linda was a paramedic and Chris was a police officer. They both worked in Havington, the district next to Beachbrook. Sophie and Linda had met each other at ante-natal classes when they were pregnant with the children and they had soon formed a deep and lasting friendship.

Within weeks they had introduced their husbands to each other and the four of them had become an ingrained presence in each other's lives. The babies coming along only strengthened this friendship.

Andrew and Sophie spent a lazy evening in front of the TV. It was 10pm when Sophie went up to bed.

"Better get some sleep," she said. "Joe will be here at seven in the morning." Andrew rolled his eyes. He wasn't a morning person. "Unless you want to… you know…," Sophie continued.

Andrew's ears pricked up. He turned to Sophie and smiled.

CHAPTER 1

"Time to get up," Sophie called up the stairs. It wasn't clear who she was talking to as both Andrew and Maria were still in bed. "Joe will be here in a minute."

It had just gone 7am and Linda would be dropping Joe around before she went to work. Chris was already at work - his shift had started at 6am.

"Be down in a minute, love," Andrew called, forcing his eyes open. He looked next to him and Maria was lying there. She had managed to sneak in to his and Sophie's bed while he had been dozing without him noticing.

"Oi you, how did you get in here?" He said softly while gently tickling her in the ribs. She screwed her face up with stifled laughter but kept her eyes shut. She was very much a daddy's girl when it came to mornings. Neither of them liked to get up early and would use every excuse in the book to avoid dragging themselves out of bed.

"We'd better get up poppet, Joe will be here soon." Andrew had a lot of nicknames for Maria. Poppet, Sweetheart and Princess were the three he used most regularly.

The front door bell rang and Maria groaned. "It's too early, Dad," she said and rolled over.

Andrew looked at his bedside clock. It was 07:06. He climbed out of bed, scooped Maria up in his arms and, with her protestations ringing in his ears, carried her downstairs.

"Good morning Joe, how are you mate?" Andrew asked. Joe was already sitting in the kitchen eating some toast that Sophie had made. He was still wearing his pyjamas. He was comfortable in their house. He had been there so many times that it felt like a second home to him.

"Hello Andrew, hi Maria," Joe said with crumbs spilling from his mouth. "I'm good thanks, looking forward to going to the beach today."

Andrew looked out of the window. It didn't look like a beach day. There were thick dark clouds in the sky and he could see a wind whipping across the trees. If yesterday felt like the Mediterranean, then today felt decidedly Baltic.

"Are you sure you want to go to the beach?" Andrew asked. He already knew the answer, but asked the question anyway.

"YES," came the resounding reply from both Joe and Maria. They loved the beach, and were happy in each others company. Maria and Joe got on well. They were in the same class at school and argued like brother and sister. Maria dominated their young friendship and would often be caught leading Joe astray. Their basic traits were the opposite of each other. Maria was loud while Joe was quiet. Maria was outspoken while Joe was reserved. Put simply, Maria was a classic extrovert while Joe was a typical introvert. But they bounced well off of each other and that is what made their relationship thrive.

Andrew wasn't surprised and Sophie gave him a knowing look with a little smile on her face. There was no point encouraging them to do something else. He knew that he would be fighting a losing battle if he suggested it.

"OK, OK, beach it is," Andrew said. "Make sure you wrap up warm, though. It looks freezing out there."

Maria was wide awake now and, after breakfast, she and Joe ran up to her bedroom.

"We won't be long down there will we love?" Andrew asked Sophie. "It doesn't look particularly good out there does it?"

"Looks hideous," she replied. "But you know what they're like. If we go down there soon then we can get home for lunch."

Andrew leant in and gave Sophie a hug, then gently stroked her tummy. He tried to give her a kiss but she pulled away.

"Get upstairs and brush your teeth," she said with a giggle. Despite the rejected kiss, the flames of passion still burned brightly for both of them.

Andrew rolled his eyes and begrudgingly walked up the stairs to get ready. He put his ear to Maria's bedroom door and heard Maria and Joe playing. He couldn't work out what they were saying but it was clear who was in charge of whatever game they were playing. He chuckled to himself and knocked on the door.

"Who's there?" Maria shouted as Andrew walked in. "Dad, you can't just walk in here. It's my bedroom!"

"We're leaving in thirty minutes," Andrew said. "Maria, make sure you're ready. And give your room a little tidy, it's a tip in here."

Andrew walked out and shut the door. He put his ear back up to it and heard Maria telling Joe that the new game that they would be playing would be to tidy up. He smiled to himself then went into his bedroom to get ready. His phone was on the bedside table and he saw that Chris had sent him a message asking what they were doing today. Andrew replied that the kids still wanted to go to the beach but he wasn't sure if they were going to go or not. He looked at the bedside clock. It was 08:35.

The weather was just as bad outside as it looked from inside. As they left the house, Andrew was seriously considering putting his foot down and refusing to go to the beach in favour of another, more sensible pursuit for the day. There was no rain but the thick, moody clouds that had been building on the horizon were now overhead and threatening an imminent deluge. The wind was biting and penetrated the three layers of clothing that Andrew was wearing. He looked at Sophie. The edges of her lips curled up with the faint trace of a smile. He knew it would be futile to try to go back indoors.

Maria and Joe chatted the language of children in the back of the car on their way to the beach. Andrew was secretly pleased. He was aware of how fast Maria was growing up and, when she was with Joe, and while she dominated him, she still displayed the innocence of childhood.

"Are you OK back there kids?" Andrew asked.

"Fine thanks Dad," Maria replied.

And you, Joe?" Andrew asked.

"Yeah I'm fine thanks," Joe replied.

Andrew smiled. He had grown close to Joe through his formative years. There had been numerous sleepovers since he was born where Joe had fall-en asleep in Andrew's arms, and even more occasions where they had taken both Maria and Joe on days out. With the amount of time they all spent together, it was impossible for a bond not to grow.

They pulled up at Beach Road just as the first spots of rain started to hit the windscreen. Again, Andrew wondered whether he should just carry on driving and go back home. Again, he looked at Sophie and knew what the response would be if he attempted to do so. He had scarcely had time to put the handbrake on before Maria had thrown her door open and was running down to the beach with Joe in hot pursuit. Maria had learnt how to turn off the child lock in the car about a year ago and it was a running battle between her and Andrew about it being on or off. He knew that he'd have to speak to her about unlocking it later on, but for now he just shook his head with a smile and got out of the car. He looked at his watch. It was 09:20.

As they walked down the steps to the beach, Andrew and Sophie saw Maria and Joe chasing after each other on the sand. Unsurprisingly, the beach was deserted. The contrast between the two days of the weekend could hardly have been more stark. The wind was gusting and flurries of sand were swirling across the beach and out to sea. The holiday-makers had wisely decided that today was a day for indoor pursuits. There were several dog walkers braving the cold in the distance and all were wrapped up in winter clothes. Andrew thought about how warm and comfortable his bed had been only a couple of hours ago.

Sophie unlocked the beach hut while Andrew went to get some water from the beach tap so that they could boil the kettle and have a cup of tea. When he got back, Maria and Joe were both standing on the sand getting changed into their wet suits.

"You're kidding aren't you?" Andrew said. "You're not going in the sea when the weather's like this."

"I've already tried," Sophie said. "I told them that you would say 'no' as well but they didn't listen to me. Come on kids, wet suits off and let's get warm."

Maria scowled at Sophie, then turned to Andrew. "Please Dad," she said. "We'll only go in up to our knees."

Joe stood silently, impassive as Maria continued to work on Andrew. "What's the point in coming to the beach and not going in the sea?" She asked. "You can come in as well if you want."

There was no way that Andrew was going to go in the sea. He didn't go in on warm days, let alone on a day like this. But he knew that Maria wouldn't stop protesting until she got what she wanted, and the last thing that he needed was an argument setting the tone for the day.

"I'll tell you what," he said, "you can go for a paddle. That's what's called a compromise."

Maria rolled her eyes. "I know what a compromise is, Dad," she said.

Sophie had a little smirk on her face. She knew that Maria had Andrew wrapped around her little finger and that she had once again got her own way. Sophie helped Maria get into her wet suit and zipped it up at the back while Andrew did the same with Joe.

"You don't have to go in if you don't want to mate," Andrew said quietly to Joe, bending down and without Maria hearing. He could see a slight look of apprehension on Joe's face. "It's horrible out there. To be honest, we'd be better off going home, don't you think?"

Joe looked at Andrew and smiled. "Maria wants to paddle so I'll go with her to make sure she's OK," he said.

"Well as soon as you've had enough, come back and we'll go home. Deal?" Andrew said.

"Deal," Joe agreed.

They fist bumped each other. That was their special thing, a unified mark of agreement.

Andrew stood back up and looked at his watch. It was 09:30. "Right then, you've got fifteen minutes, then we're getting out of here," he said.

Maria and Joe ran to the edge of the water while Andrew and Sophie looked on from the beach hut. The rain drops that were in the air had turned into a fine drizzle by now, although Andrew was unsure if it was spray from the sea where the wind was so strong.

"I'll go down and keep an eye on them," Andrew said, even though they were no more than fifteen metres away as it was a high tide.

"They'll be fine," Sophie said. "You can see them from here and they're not going in. Try to relax." She knew why Andrew was so anxious. He had told her all about what had happened to him.

Andrew looked down at Maria and Joe. They were running at the water's edge and kicking water up at each other. The wind was whipping the sea into a violent frenzy behind them, yet despite this they seemed to be having fun. Andrew went into the beach hut and put on the big, thick coat that he kept in there for bad weather days such as this, then went back outside. He slid his phone, keys and wallet into the pockets of the coat and zipped them up for safekeeping. Maria and Joe were still playing in the same place.

Tea's up," Sophie said as she came out with two mugs. Andrew wrapped his fingers around the mug to get some warmth into them and took a big gulp. It was definitely tea weather.

"Thanks love," Andrew said. He didn't take his eyes off Maria and Joe. By now they'd run a bit further along the beach and were still kicking water up at each other and laughing.

"Not too far, you two," Sophie shouted. She was watching them as well.

"Hi Mum, hi Dad," Maria shouted with a big grin on her face. She was waving both hands and looked a picture in her little purple wetsuit against the backdrop of a raging sea with an impending storm brewing above it. Joe was wearing his oversized black wetsuit. He was waving as well, although not as enthusiastically as Maria.

"Are you done yet?" Andrew called out to them.

"No!" Maria shouted. Joe didn't say anything.

Sophie went into the beach hut and brought two fold up chairs out onto the sand. She sat on one and Andrew sat on the other. Both of them had finished their tea.

"Looks like we're here for a while," she said. I'll go and make us another cuppa." She took Andrew's mug from him and went back into the beach-hut.

The rain was heavier now. There was a rumble of thunder from far out at sea, but Andrew couldn't see any lightning. As he looked out to sea and scanned around the beach, he saw another dog walker in the distance to his left. He took strange comfort in the fact that they weren't alone on the beach, that some other foolhardy soul was also there.

Sophie came back out with two mugs of tea, steam billowing from the top of them. Maria and Joe were now at the very edge of the water.

"No further than that, guys," Andrew shouted. He looked at his watch. It was 09:40. It was nearly time for them to come back and get changed.

Maria again turned and waved, while Joe didn't respond.

"Time for them to come in now isn't it?" Sophie said to Andrew. The rain was getting even heavier and the thunder was rumbling even more ominously. Lightning was suddenly visible out at sea.

Just as Andrew was about to call out for them to come back and get changed, he heard a distant voice shouting.

"Lex, GET BACK HERE!" It was the dog walker that he had seen in the distance.

An excited black Labrador suddenly came bounding into view and ran up to Sophie. It jumped up at her while she was sitting on her chair, unaware. Andrew's immediate reaction was to jump up and protect his pregnant wife and as he did so he spilt his scalding tea over his hands. The dog owner was getting closer now.

"LEX, HERE," he shouted. Lex paid no attention and continued to jump excitedly up at Sophie, who by now was standing up as Andrew repeatedly tried to push the dog away. The dog squealed with excitement, overjoyed at the game that Andrew was playing with him.

"Come and sort this dog out mate," Andrew called in the direction of the dog owner.

"I'm really sorry," panted the dog owner who had run to get Lex. "He never normally does this." He took a lead from around his neck and attached it to Lex's collar. "Come on boy," he said, and they walked off on their way.

"Are you okay?" Andrew asked Sophie. His hands were beginning to sting now from where the tea had spilt on them.

"Yeah I'm fine," Sophie replied. "Are your hands alright?"

Before Andrew could answer, he looked around to check on Maria and Joe.

They weren't there.

"Sophie, where are they?" Andrew said with panic in his voice. He didn't wait for an answer. He turned away from her and ran down to the water's edge screaming their names.

"MARIA, JOE."

There was no reply, his words swallowed by the waves crashing in front of him.

Sophie was now by his side, also panicking and shouting for them.

"Andrew, there," she cried, while pointing out into the raging sea. Andrew looked and, just in front of the breaking waves, he could see Maria's purple wetsuit. It was barely visible and he couldn't tell if she was under the water. He couldn't see Joe.

"Go and call for help," Andrew screamed at Sophie. He knew that mobile phone signal was hit and miss on the beach. Then he was in the water without a thought. Maria was about twenty metres away from him. He fought against the waves initially and then, suddenly, was picked up by a rip current that pulled him in the direction of Maria. He was fighting to stay above the surface. Every ounce of him fought to get to Maria, to his little girl.

And then he heard her. "DADDY, DADDY," she shouted. He could hear how frightened she was, her words quivering with the distress of a fearful child. Inch by inch, foot by foot, metre by metre, he struggled to get to her. His heavy winter coat had filled with water and was weighing him down.

"I'm here sweetheart" he called. Suddenly he was with her. Joe was there as well. He was holding Maria's hand. Relief washed over Andrew. The children were both barely treading water, however, and Andrew was out of his depth as well. There was a strong current under them that was pulling them further away from land, no matter how hard they tried to fight it.

"Right kids, hold onto me and I'll try to get us out of this," Andrew said. He was trying to be calm but the panic in his voice was obvious.

"Thank you Andrew," Joe said quietly, his face almost expressionless. It was the first thing he had said since Andrew had got to them.

Maria clung onto Andrew's right arm and Joe held on to his left. He felt both of their faces pressing into the back of his shoulders. Any other time, it would have felt like the loving embrace of two children. Right now, it felt like they were clinging to him as though their lives depended on it. Andrew tried to swim against the current, but he was unable to do so. The weight of his coat, combined with both Maria and Joe was pushing him underwater. He struggled to get above the surface and strained every sinew to get both children safely to shore, but it was impossible. He was exhausted and they were being pulled even further out to sea.

"Can you swim against it?" Andrew asked Maria and Joe. They were both now white with fear, their eyes enlarged, and neither of them were responding to him. The sea, still fierce and menacing, had terrified them to the point of shock. "Maria, Joe, you've got to try," Andrew pleaded. Neither of them responded. They were exhausted now as well. "Come on," Andrew begged, but no matter what he said he couldn't get a response from either of them.

Andrew looked at Maria, then he looked at Joe. He knew what he had to do.

He had to make a choice. A choice that would define him. A choice that would shape the rest of his life.

He looked at Joe. A boy he had known since he was born. The only child of his closest friends. His daughter's best friend. His face was pale yet bore an expression of acceptance. At the tender age of six he was almost resigned to his fate.

"I'm sorry Joe," Andrew said quietly. "If you can swim against it then follow me." He knew there was no way that he could get them both safely back. He took hold of Maria under her armpit and turned towards the shore.

When he looked back, Joe was gone.

CHAPTER 2

It took every last bit of strength that Andrew could summon to pull Maria back to the shore. With every stroke he took he looked back desperately in search of Joe. In between mouthfuls of sea water he had screamed his name but received no response.

As soon as he was able to put his feet down on the sea floor and walk, Andrew had seen Sophie standing at the shore shouting his name.

"Sophie, come and get her!" He called urgently. Sophie waded up to her stomach and Andrew handed a shaking Maria over to her.

"I've called 999," Sophie shouted, her voice barely penetrating over the harsh noise of the waves crashing around them.

He turned around and then immediately made his way back into the sea. Rain was lashing down now. Lightning was piercing through the gloom around him and thunder was reverberating in the air. And he was exhausted. Absolutely drained beyond reason. He tried to swim but he couldn't force his arms to rotate. He took off his coat and cast it aside. He wondered why he hadn't thought to do that earlier. He could still just about stand on the floor, so he put his feet down and waited for the lactic acid that had built up all over his body to dissipate. Even now, while he was able to stand, there were fierce currents all around him, trying to pull him out to sea. He waited for about thirty seconds then tried to swim again but it was no use. He just couldn't do it. The exertion of getting Maria back to shore had proved simply too much for him. Yet still he knew that Joe was out there somewhere. All on his own.

"JOE!" He shouted as loud as could. "JOE, WHERE ARE YOU?" His cries were consumed by the noise of the waves. He stood there for as long as he could, neck deep, calling out for Joe. His calls weren't answered.

He didn't know how long he had been standing there before he heard the distant sound of helicopter rotors whirling. He turned to his right as the noise grew louder and saw a powerful search-light shining down onto the sea. The helicopter drew closer to him and soon he was blinded by the light as it bathed him in brightness. He gestured frantically that it was not him that they needed to be searching for, but his waves of protestation merely exacerbated the situation and made it look like he was in trouble and needed assistance. He knew that, all the time he was in the water, they would be focussing on him and not looking further out to sea for Joe. Begrudgingly, he turned to the shore and made his way back on to the beach.

When he got back to the shore he saw that there was a lot of activity now occurring. Lifeguards from a neighbouring beach were in attendance and were making their way on surfboards into the sea. He saw a parade of blue lights flashing at the top of the steps near to where his car was parked. His eyes were stinging with sea water, but he could count at least three police cars, two ambulances and a fire engine.

What he couldn't see anywhere was his wife or daughter.

He ran from the shore, but didn't know where he was running to.

"Excuse me," a voice shouted. Andrew turned around and saw a Policeman beckoning him over.

"My wife and daughter, where are they?" Andrew shouted.

"They're in the Ambulance," the Policeman shouted back, while running towards Andrew. "They're okay. Is the boy still out there?"

"Yes," Andrew said. The policeman was standing next to him now. A range of emotions suddenly hit him. Up until this point, everything had happened so quickly that he hadn't had chance to even think about the gravity of the situation. But now it dawned on him. Maria was in an ambulance and had experienced something that would traumatise her for years to come. And Joe was missing. Andrew was supposed to have been looking after him. His best friends had trusted him to look after their son and he had failed. Even worse, he had made a conscious decision to sacrifice Joe to save his daughter. He suddenly felt very, very sick.

"He's still out there somewhere. He's wearing a black wetsuit. Tell the helicopter, please." Andrew sounded desperate. The helicopter was overhead now and not over the sea. The crew were unaware that Joe was still missing.

The policeman immediately relayed this information on his radio and, within seconds, the helicopter had rotated and headed back out over the sea to resume the search for Joe.

"I've got to get to my daughter," Andrew said to the policeman. He turned and ran towards the steps. When he got to the top of them he saw that one of the ambulances had its back door open. He hurried over to it and clumsily made his way inside.

"Is she alright?" He asked, breathlessly. Maria was sitting on the stretcher in the ambulance. She was covered in blankets wrapped in a foil blanket and had a large oxygen mask over her little face. She was still white and was shaking.

"She hasn't said anything yet," Sophie said. Her eyes were red. She had been crying.

"Maria, princess, are you okay?" Andrew asked, begging her to answer him. Maria just stared straight ahead, her eyes not even flickering.

"We need to get her into hospital," one of the paramedics said. "She'll be fine, we just need to get her checked over. She's not got hypothermia so don't worry about that. They'll look after her."

"Why has she got that mask on?" Andrew asked.

"We think she swallowed a bit of water. It's just a precaution in case of aspiration."

The paramedic stood up and indicated that he wanted to leave straight away. Andrew noticed that there was someone else in the ambulance, someone who hadn't said anything yet. Until now.

"Andrew, isn't it?" The voice said. A woman in a smart suit stood up. "I'm Sue Willmott, a DS from Beachbrook Police Station. Can I have a word outside?" She spoke politely but firmly, and made her way towards the rear exit of the ambulance.

"Yeah, of course," Andrew replied. "I'll just be outside, okay darling," he said to Maria as he also climbed out of the ambulance. Maria didn't reply.

They stood in silence for a moment, as Andrew looked around and took it all in. The whole area was now alive with emergency service personnel. Many police cars had been abandoned with their lights still flashing. There were three additional ambulances and two fire engines. The helicopter was still hovering over the sea, its search light still shining brightly. Distant sirens cut through the air as more first responders made their way to assist in the search for Joe. A small crowd was gathering on the road opposite where Andrew was standing. He felt anonymous, yet incredibly visible at the same time.

"Press will be here soon as well," DS Willmott said. Andrew looked at her. She was in her early forties, with short, dark hair and glasses. She looked every bit the career detective that she was.

"I don't care about the press, is there any news on Joe," Andrew replied abruptly. He knew that Maria was safe. All of his focus now turned to Joe.

"You're shaking," DS Willmott said softly.

Andrew looked down at his hands. She was right. He was shaking uncontrollably. He was soaked through and, with all of the adrenaline coursing through his veins, he hadn't been aware of how his body was reacting to everything that had happened. He suddenly felt very cold and faint.

"Let's get a medic over here please," DS Willmott shouted. Andrew had gone deathly pale and looked like might pass out at any second.

Two paramedics came running over and laid Andrew down on their stretcher.

"I'm fine," he protested weakly as they lifted him into the back of an ambulance. As they did so, he saw the other ambulance pull away. The one in which Maria was being treated. "I want to go with her," Andrew said as he tried to get off the trolley.

"Calm down mate," one of the Paramedics said. "Let's get you right first." Andrew felt too weak to argue. "First things first, let's get these clothes off. You're soaked."

The paramedic cut through Andrew's clothes with a surgeon's precision, and wrapped him up in a traditional blanket, then a foil blanket, and then finally another traditional blanket over the top. In a blanket sandwich, the foil was the filling.

"Here, drink this," the other paramedic said. He handed Andrew a cup of tea in a paper cup. "Just going to take your temperature mate," he continued.

Andrew felt a thermometer in his ear.

"35.6," the Paramedic called. "Well you're not hypothermic, but it's close," he said to Andrew. "Let's keep you warm and we'll see where we go from there, alright?" He shut all of the ambulance doors and turned the heaters in the ambulance up to maximum output.

Andrew heard some activity outside. A car screeched to a stop and he heard a voice shouting "wait up mate." He wondered if someone had found something.

Andrew forced himself to drink the tea, but all he could think about now was Joe. He was out there, somewhere, alone. He looked to his right and saw that DS Willmott was sitting in the ambulance. She was looking at him. He couldn't work out her expression. It was something between sympathy and contempt.

"Anything on Joe, anything at all?" Andrew said to her. She gently shook her head.

"What happened out there?" She asked. Again, her voice was soft but firm.

"I couldn't get them both in," Andrew began to say, his voice cracking with emotion. He felt his eyes fill up with tears. He bowed his head and the tears flowed.

"We're going to need to go through this in a lot more detail, Andrew. I'm sure you understand that," she said to him, making notes as she spoke. "But right now, we need to focus on finding Joe. Did you see him go under?"

"No," Andrew replied, quickly. It was true. He hadn't seen him go under the water. But he knew that he had. "He drifted away from me and I couldn't get to him." Again, this wasn't a lie. But it wasn't the whole truth either.

The paramedic came back over and took Andrew's temperature again.

"36.1," he said. "You'll be fine." Andrew was feeling a very long way from fine. Something was consuming him, something that he had never before experienced. The only way he could even think to describe it was active grief. A feeling of pain so raw that it overwhelmed his very being; of loss so deep that it hurt to breathe.

"We've got everyone we can out there looking for him," DS Willmott said.

"What can I do?" Andrew asked.

"Honestly?" DS Willmott replied. "There's not a lot you can do. We've got all of the beaches covered. The helicopter is up and the Lifeboat is out. They've put a call out to any fishing boats nearby to come and help as well."

Andrew was now openly sobbing.

The paramedic came and took his temperature again.

"36.5," he said. "You're good to go if you're feeling okay." Physically, Andrew felt a lot better now than he did when he had got into the ambulance. He had stopped shivering and his body temperature had risen to an acceptable level. Mentally, he was struggling.

"The best thing for you is to get home and get some clothes, and get up the hospital to see your daughter," DS Willmott continued. "I'll get someone to give you a lift."

She left Andrew in the ambulance while she went to find a police officer to give him a lift home. Five minutes later, she returned with the local PCSO. Andrew recognised him from the town, but didn't know his name.

"Andrew, this is PCSO Rivers. He covers Beachbrook Town Centre. He'll give you a lift home. I'll be in touch." With that, DS Willmott disappeared.

"Hi mate, I'm John," the PCSO said. "Come on, I'll give you a lift home."

Andrew didn't say anything as he climbed out of the ambulance. He didn't know how long he had been in there. Time seemed to be an abstract concept at the moment, both so important in the search for Joe, but so irrelevant to his current state of mind. He looked around and noticed that the crowd had swelled in numbers and was now formed of rows of people rather than merely numbers of people. He also noticed that a camera crew was setting up by them. DS Willmott had been right. The rain was falling steadily now. The wind had dropped and the clouds were low and settled.

There was an empty police car now in the space where Maria's ambulance had been. It had been parked there in a hurry and both the driver and passenger door had been left open, such was the seriousness of the situation.

"Car's over here mate," PCSO Rivers said. He led Andrew over to his police car, which was parked in the long row of those abandoned earlier. Andrew was still cloaked in the foil blanket and was naked underneath. He didn't know if he was exposing himself in any way as he followed PCSO Rivers, stumbling as he did so.

His mind had, for now, checked out. In the sea, when it had been a physical case of fight or flight, he had fought with every fibre of his existence to save Maria and Joe. Now, mentally, he had taken flight.

The journey home was a blur to Andrew. He sat in the back of the Police Car in silence, although the noise inside his head was deafening. So many questions to answer, both to himself and to others. Could he have done anything differently? Why did they go to the beach? Why did he allow them to go in the sea? No, wait. Why DID they go in the sea? These questions swirled and swirled around his head.

"We're here mate." Andrew's internal wrangling was interrupted by PCSO Rivers. They had pulled up outside Andrew's house and he hadn't even noticed. He got out of the car and shut the door without saying anything. PCSO Rivers watched as Andrew walked unsteadily up the path, then got out when Andrew stopped suddenly.

"All alright mate?" PCSO Rivers called.

"Keys," Andrew said quietly. "I haven't got my keys."

His keys were in his coat that he had taken off in the sea, along with his phone and wallet.

"Has anyone else got any?"PCSO Rivers asked.

Andrew pointed to the house next door, without saying anything. Their car was on the drive. PCSO Rivers went and knocked on their door. Andrew heard a muffled conversation but didn't hear the actual words. Two minutes later PCSO Rivers was back with him, with the keys to his front door. He opened it for Andrew.

"Do you want me to wait?" He asked. I'll gladly run you up the hospital when you're ready."

Andrew shook his head and walked inside. "No, I'll be fine thank you. I'll take Sophie's car," he replied vacantly. "Her keys are here somewhere."

He shut the door without saying goodbye to PCSO Rivers and went into the front room where he collapsed onto the sofa. He sat there in contemplative silence. The questions were repeating themselves in his head. An image was indelibly stained on his mind, the image of Joe's face as Andrew chose to save Maria over him. He couldn't shake it. He would never shake it.

He didn't know how long he had sat there for, when the silence was broken with the sound of the house telephone ringing. Andrew hadn't heard it ring for a long time. Everyone used mobile phones now.

He stood up and the foil blanket fell off him. He was naked. He walked to the phone which was in the hallway and picked it up.

"Hello," he said. His voice was shaking, but he was relieved to hear Sophie's voice on the other end of the line.

"Andrew! I've been trying everywhere to find you. Are you okay?" She said.

"Joe's still out there," he replied.

"I know," Sophie said. Her voice trailed off. "Are you coming up here? Maria has been asking for you."

"I'll be there soon, I promise," Andrew replied. "Tell her that I'm on my way. Bye love." Andrew put the phone down without waiting for a reply from Sophie.

He went up to the bathroom and stood under the shower for a long time. It was scalding hot but he didn't feel any pain. He just felt numb. He tasted the salt from the sea as water dripped from his hair down his face and into his mouth, and whenever he shut his eyes, the image of Joe's face there, staring at him. It didn't matter how long he stood there. It was an image that wouldn't wash away.

He got out of the shower and looked at himself in the mirror. He didn't recognise the man staring back at him. This was a man who had allowed two children to play on the beach in a storm. A man who had taken his eyes off of those children and they had somehow got themselves into terrible danger. A man who had gone in the sea to get them and had only come out of the sea with one of them. A man who had made a conscious choice to let one of them go.

Again, he was consumed by internal questions. Why did he place the protection of his wife above his duty to watch the children? Why did they go in to the sea? Why hadn't he taken his heavy coat off when he was with Joe? Would he have been able to bring them both to shore if he had done so? These were questions that would haunt him.

He went to his bedroom and got dressed, and went downstairs to find Sophie's car keys. They were on the mantelpiece where they always were. He went out to the car and made his way to the hospital. He was running on autopilot. He relied on basic and instinctive motor functions to get him there. He nearly crashed several times but he made it, physically unscathed.

He walked in to the Accident and Emergency Department and went up to the counter.

"I'm Maria Wicks' dad," he said to the receptionist. He didn't recognise his own voice. It sounded hoarse and guttural.

"Aah yes, they're expecting you," the receptionist replied. "They're just through there in Room 18," she continued, while pointing to a side door.

Andrew made his way through the door, down a long corridor, and found Room 18.

"Daddy," Maria cried out as Andrew opened the door.

Daddy. Andrew closed his eyes briefly. She had been screaming 'Daddy' when she was in the sea. Not 'Dad'.

He looked at Maria, who was lying on a hospital bed. She didn't have the oxygen mask on any more and the colour had returned to her face. She was, however, inexpressive. Andrew had never seen her with this look on her face before. It was as if she was incapable of processing the events of the morning. Sophie was sitting next to Maria and was holding her hand. He noticed that Sophie's eyes were still red.

Hi Princess," Andrew said as he closed the door behind him.

"Your voice sounds funny," Maria said. The sea water that he had swallowed must have done something to his vocal cords, he thought. "Where's Joe?" She asked.

Andrew didn't have an answer to this at the moment and he hadn't thought of what he would say to Maria when she inevitably asked about Joe. Before he could say anything, however, he heard the voices of people walking along the corridor outside. He could hear two, distinctive male voices.

One of them said "I just need to talk to him," as the door opened.

It was Chris.

CHAPTER 3

Linda was in a deep, peaceful sleep when she was awoken suddenly.

"Mummy, mummy," Joe called from his bedroom. She looked at the clock on her bedside table. It was 02:02. She knew that it was going to be a long night. She lay there for a while, hoping that Joe would go back to sleep but she knew that he wouldn't. "Mummy, mummy," shouted Joe again, louder this time. Linda rolled over and looked at Chris who was lying asleep next to her, snoring. He didn't show any signs of being disturbed by Joe. Linda sighed. Joe had been waking up more and more frequently at night over the past few months and it was always her who went in to settle him. It was exhausting her. She was working a full time shift pattern which was bad enough at the best of times. Add a sleepless child into the mix and the result was tiredness to the point of debilitation.

Linda got out of bed and heard the wind howling outside. The weather had changed since she went to bed. She made her way into Joe's bedroom, hoping that he was talking in his sleep. No such luck. He was sitting up on his bed, wide awake.

"Mummy," he said with a smile on his face. He always called for mummy because it was always her who came during the night.

"What's going on Joe," Linda said wearily. She was rubbing her stinging eyes. "It's the middle of the night, you should be asleep."

"Can we play?" Joe asked.

Linda knew that this was going to take a while. "How about we read a book and try to get back to sleep?" She said.

"Yeah, book time!" Joe said excitedly. He had always loved to read with Linda and Chris.

"Go and choose one then," Linda said as she lay down on his bed. She was feeling a bit more awake now but she knew that she would pay for it later when she was at work.

Joe chose his favourite chapter book and Linda read it with him three times, cover to cover. He still wasn't showing any signs of tiredness. She looked at the clock on his night light. It was now 03:20.

"Right then Mister, it's definitely time for sleep. You've got to be up in a few hours time to go to Maria's house," she said, this time with more authority. "Come and lie down and let's snuggle."

She lay on her side in Joe's bed and he cuddled into her, his back against her stomach. Linda shut her eyes. As much as she hated to get up in the night, she secretly loved it when she was cuddling her son like this. After about half an hour he was asleep. Linda always knew when he was asleep because he had made a unique noise. It wasn't quite a snore, but it was louder than heavy breathing. She waited five minutes to make sure that he was in a deep sleep, then quietly made her way back into her own bed. Chris was still snoring. He was still in the same position that he had been when she had left the room. She knew that he would be getting up in about an hour's time and then she would be awake for the day. Linda shut her eyes and slowly drifted into a restless sleep.

She woke up with a start to Chris' alarm blaring. She had asked him so many times to turn it down but he wouldn't because he wasn't sure that it would wake him up if the volume was any lower. He told her that he would go and make them a cup of tea. She would rather have gone back to sleep for another hour, but she didn't say anything. Chris left the bedroom and she heard him walk into Joe's room. She could tell he was trying to be quiet but he was very heavy footed. She really didn't need him to wake Joe up now. About a minute later she heard Chris walk out of Joe's room and, to her relief, she didn't hear anything to suggest that Joe had woken up. She knew how ratty Joe would be if he didn't get enough sleep.

Linda was awake enough to be unable to get any kind of meaningful sleep now, so she dragged herself out of bed and went to the bathroom where she splashed water over her face. She looked in the mirror. A shattered woman looked back at her.

She went downstairs. Chris was just getting ready to leave. They had a conversation where he said that he would help more with Joe at night time, but Linda was so tired that she couldn't remember exactly what they had discussed after he had gone. She picked up the mug of tea that he had made her, went into the lounge and looked at the clock on the mantelpiece. It was 05:20. There was potentially another hour's sleep for her right now. She put her tea on the table and collapsed onto the sofa where she fell into a deep sleep within minutes.

"Mummy?" Linda shook herself from the depths of slumber. Was she dreaming? "Mummy?" She opened her eyes and tried to orientate herself. She was on the sofa in the lounge and Joe was standing in front of her. "What are you doing down here mummy?" He asked. She sat upright and looked at the clock. It was 06:30 and she had to drop Joe off at Andrew and Sophie's house in half an hour.

"Quick, upstairs to get ready," she said to Joe. She very rarely overslept and didn't like to rush, especially at this time in the morning. She scooped Joe up into her arms and rushed up the stairs. She tried to simultaneously brush both of their teeth but it would've been quicker if she had done them individually. She threw her paramedic uniform on and grabbed some of Joe's clothes and put them in a bag. She'd have to take him to Sophie and Andrew's house in his pyjamas, and ask if he could have breakfast there as well.

They were out of the house by 06:55 and arrived at the Wicks' house just after 7. Linda knocked on the door and Sophie answered and Joe ran inside.

"I'm so sorry," Linda said, flustered. "I overslept. He's got some clothes here but he hasn't had breakfast yet. Is it alright to give him some?"

Sophie looked at Linda. She looked completely drained. "Are you alright Lin," she asked. She was the only one who called her Lin. "You look done in."

"Joe was up in the night," Linda replied. "I'm alright, nothing a lie in won't cure." She smiled. "Come and give mummy a kiss goodbye," she called out to Joe. He ran from the hallway and wrapped his arms around her.

"Love you mummy," he said as he kissed her on the lips. He then ran back inside.

"Thanks so much for this," Linda said. "What have you got planned?"

"Well, we were thinking of the beach, but the weather looks rubbish, we'll see," Sophie said.

"Yeah, I don't think it's getting any better later is it," Linda replied. "Let me know what you get up to and make sure he behaves himself. Sorry but I've got to dash, I'm running late love. I'll see you about six all being well."

"Yes of course, get going," Sophie said. 'Have a great day and be safe out there."

Sophie shut the door as Linda hurried down the garden path and back into the warmth of her car. She had left it running to keep the heater on. She looked at the clock in the car. It was 07:10. She needed to be at work by 07:30 for handover, to start at 08:00. It normally took her twenty minutes but the driving conditions were awful. She pulled away in a hurry.

The roads were empty as she made her way to Havington Ambulance Station, following the route that Chris had taken a couple of hours earlier. She thought about what the day would bring. She had been in the paramedic world long enough to know that wind and rain usually led to car crashes. She pulled up at the Ambulance Station just before 07:30 and ran inside. She had made it just in time.

"Morning Linda," Sam called. He was her regular crew mate and was sitting at a table, drinking a cup of coffee. "You alright?" He asked.

"Yeah all good thank you," Linda replied breathlessly. "Thought I might've been late this morning. Bad night with Joe."

"Go and get sorted," Sam replied. "I'll make you a coffee and sort out the handover." Early shifts had been like this for a while now. Linda had always made it in on time but the sleepless nights with Joe were taking their toll on her, and Sam was really beginning to notice it.

"Thanks love," Linda said to Sam. She got on really well with him. He was in his early twenties and was wise beyond his years. He was a technician and Linda loved working with him. He had only been doing the job for a few months but she knew that he would be brilliant at it and she had taken him under her wing. She walked into the locker room and relaxed, knowing that he was sorting out the handover. She looked at herself in a mirror. The bags under her eyes were still there but she looked and felt better than she had done in the bathroom at home earlier. After kitting up she went and found Sam who had already completed the handover and had a cup of coffee waiting for her. Black, strong and no sugar. He knew how she liked it.

"You look like you need it," Sam said sympathetically.

"Yeah, he was up again in the night," Linda replied. "All okay with the handover?"

"Yep fine," Sam said. "No issues."

They drank their coffee and then went out to their ambulance.

"I'll drive today if you like," Sam said. Linda wasn't going to argue. "We're call sign AM 21 today," Sam told her.

Sam drove out of the Ambulance Station and went and parked up in Havington High Street. This was a central spot in the district and meant that they were in a good position to be able to respond to calls within the set response times. Linda checked her phone. There a message from Chris asking if everything was okay. She replied that she was alright but that she was exhausted and that a bit of help at night time would be appreciated. She flicked her phone onto silent mode and put it in the glove box.

While they waited for their first call they heard a few other crews being sent to elderly, homebound patients who had fallen overnight. These calls usually came in early in the morning as carers were on their rounds and were the ones who found them. Linda and Sam weren't needed for any of these calls, however.

"So what happened with Joe last night then?" Sam asked.

"Oh, the usual," Linda replied. "He's been playing up recently with his sleep and I was up with him for a couple of hours again."

"Can't someone have him for you one night just so you can get a good night's sleep?" Sam asked.

The truth was, there wasn't anyone who she felt she could ask to do this. She had no family in the area and both of her parents had passed away years ago. She couldn't ask Sophie and Andrew as Joe slept at their house enough as it was to help out when she and Chris were working night shifts. She had never met Chris' parents. His mum had died when Chris was in his twenties and he had fallen out with his dad before he had met Linda. She didn't know anything about him other than he lived somewhere in Beachbrook. She wouldn't have known him if he had walked past her in the street.

"Afraid not," Linda said despondently. "I'll just have to kick Chris out of bed to do him one night."

Sam laughed. "How's Joe doing, anyway?" He asked.

"Apart from not sleeping? Yeah he's good," Linda replied. Despite the tiredness, nothing in the world was more important to her than Joe. She had been addicted to him ever since she had found out that she was pregnant nearly seven years ago. She was an excellent mum who put Joe before anything else in life, and she felt guilty on days like these when she had to drag him out of the house so early and leave him with others while she came to work. She regularly had thoughts of stopping shift working so that she could spend more time with him, but there was little chance of doing this while still being a frontline paramedic.

They sat on the High Street, watching Havington wake up and people start to go about their daily lives. Linda looked at the clock on the radio. It was 08:39. She was about to message Sophie to see what they were up to when they got their first call of the day.

"Control to AM21, please attend Hollingwood Tunnel, northbound. Reports of a two vehicle injury RTC. Police on scene. No update on injuries yet."

Sam and Linda looked at each other. He rolled his eyes. They had been to several car crashes in Hollingwood Tunnel recently and they both knew that it was a nightmare for communications.

"Received and en route," Linda replied to the Operator. "We'll be out of comms while we are in there."

Sam flicked on the blue lights turned on the siren and drove north to Hollingwood Tunnel. It took them about twenty minutes to get there. Despite the fact that there wasn't much traffic on the roads, the approach to the tunnel was backed up with vehicles. It was a dual carriageway so Linda guessed that the crash had blocked both lanes. Sam navigated a path down the centre of the two lanes that was already in place. The police must have already been through here, thought Linda.

The crash had occurred about half a kilometre into Hollingwood Tunnel, which was about the midway point of the tunnel itself. Sam parked the ambulance next to the police car that was already at the scene. One of the vehicles had substantial damage to the front end. The other was facing in the wrong direction with damage to the rear. Sam went to the vehicle facing in the wrong direction while Linda ran over to the vehicle with damage at the front. She spoke with one of the police officers who was talking to the driver, who was still in the vehicle.

"Hi Linda," the police officer said. Linda knew her as she was on the same team as Chris. Her name was Tasha.

"Alright Tasha," Linda replied. "What's going on?"

"This is Drew," Tasha said calmly. "He's forty-five, and has got some pain in his neck and back. We haven't tried to move him yet but he's starting to feel light headed. He's got his seatbelt on still. We've got a fire crew on their way to help get him out if needed." She stood up and moved back while Linda manoeuvred herself into a position where she could speak to Drew. The driver's door was damaged to such an extent that it wouldn't open. Linda knew that he would need to be cut out of the car.

"Hi Drew," Linda said. "I understand you've got some pain?"

"Yeah," Drew moaned. "My back and neck are killing." His eyes were shut and he sounded in genuine pain.

"We don't want to move you at the moment then," Linda said. She could hear the distant sound of sirens as the fire engine was fighting its way through the traffic to get there to assist. Sam was by her side now.

"All okay with my patient," Sam said. "Can I help?" Sam hadn't dealt with a patient trapped in a car before, but Linda was confident that he could do so. She took him just out of earshot of Drew.

"This is a good one for you," she whispered. "Fancy taking the lead on it?"

"Yeah, great," Sam replied.

Linda stayed in the background while Sam dealt with Drew. She was close enough to intervene if needed, but far enough away to give him the authority to make decisions as necessary. He was doing a good job, she thought. He co-ordinated well with the fire fighters and the police officers during the extrication process and his treatment of Drew was first class. She assisted with loading Drew onto their trolley when she became aware of another ambulance crew arriving at the scene, along with another police car. This confused her. They hadn't asked for another ambulance to attend and there was no need for them to be there.

The ambulance parked next to Tasha, who spoke to paramedic on board. Linda didn't recognise the paramedic - it was a crew from a different district. She could see from their faces that something was very wrong.

"Are you alright a second Sam, I'm just going to check something out," she said.

"Yeah, all good," Sam replied.

Linda walked over to Tasha and the paramedic. Tasha's eyes were wide and her cheeks had gone white.

"Linda, you need to get to Beachbrook Beach right now," Tasha said. "Jump in my car and I'll drive you."

Beachbrook Beach? Joe? "What the hell has happened?" Linda shouted.

"Something has happened with Joe," Tasha replied. "He's been in the sea and they can't find him. Chris is there but he can't get hold of you on your phone. Get in and I'll take you." Tasha only knew as much as the paramedic had told her.

The tunnel reverberated with a guttural scream. Tasha had to take hold of Linda and physically help her to the Police Car. She helped to sit her in the front passenger seat and ran around to driver's side. When she got in, Linda was rocking forwards and backwards and moaning gently.

"I'll get you there as quickly as I can," Tasha promised. Linda didn't reply.

Beachbrook was about twenty-five minutes from the Hollingwood Tunnel. As Tasha drove out of the tunnel the roads were quiet, but the weather was atrocious. A wall of rain hit their windscreen as they emerged into the natural world. There was no traffic to navigate because of the crash that they were leaving behind them and Tasha made good progress. Linda remained almost catatonic next to her. Tasha didn't want to interfere in her private thoughts so remained silent.

Linda was struggling to process the thought of Joe being alone and lost at sea. She needed answers about what had happened. How it had happened. Why it had happened. She tried to speak to Tasha, to ask her to get an update, but no words would come.

Tasha sensed that Linda wanted to know what was happening.

"Do you want me to try to get an update before we get there," Tasha asked gently. Linda nodded. Tasha was still tuned into the Havington radio frequency and contacted the control room.

"Control from Hotel Victor 25," Tasha said.

"25, go ahead," came the reply.

"Hotel Victor 25, I'm away from the RTC and conveying PC Jamieson's wife to Beachbrook. Please can we have an update, over," Tasha said.

The radio went silent for about five seconds, then came the reply. "Control to 25, last update from DS Willmott at scene. Female child out of sea, male child still not accounted for. Major search operation is ongoing. No further information, over." The operator's voice cracked with emotion. She remained professional yet knew who was listening. It would have been impossible not to have been moved by the circumstances.

Linda shut her eyes as the message was relayed. This was a scenario not even played out in her deepest, darkest nightmares. She slipped back into a state not quite at full consciousness, an internal protective mechanism. She was still moaning gently, but was unaware of it. Time passed without her realising, and she was brought back to reality as if waking up from a dream. This was not a dream, however.

"Linda, we're here," Tasha said softly. She had parked in Beach Road at the RVP.

Linda bolted upright and sprang out of the car. She knew where she was, but she didn't know where Joe was.

"Where is he?" She screamed. Her eyes hurt. She had been crying and hadn't even realised it. Everyone around her stopped and looked sympathetically. They knew who she was.

"It's Linda isn't it?" A Sergeant asked. He had been standing nearby. "My name's Mike and I work with Chris. I brought him here. He's just down the steps on the beach."

Linda didn't wait to answer him. She ran for the steps and sprinted down them, screaming Chris' name.

He was at the bottom of the steps, looking out to sea.

CHAPTER 4

Chris' alarm had gone off at 05:00 that morning. He slipped quietly out of bed and sat on the end of it, rubbing his eyes. He loved being a police officer, but he wasn't keen on the early mornings. Linda stirred next to him.

"Morning," she said, wearily. She had work herself in a couple of hours and had been up in the night with Joe.

"Morning darling," Chris replied. "I'll get ready and make us a cup of tea."

Chris liked to be organised. He always had a shower the night before an early shift so that he could just brush his teeth, have a quick wash and be out the door after a quick brew. He found it saved him twenty minutes in the mornings and that twenty minutes was precious time spent sleeping. He had laid his uniform out the night before as well. More minutes saved.

After getting ready he quietly crept into Joe's bedroom. The room was gently illuminated by Joe's nightlight. Joe had never liked to sleep in the dark and the nightlight was recent progress from having the main light on all night. Chris tiptoed over to Joe's bed, being careful not to make a noise. Joe was a light sleeper and he didn't want to wake him up. Chris looked down at his little boy. He had fair hair and freckles on each cheek. Chris had always loved Joe's freckles. He felt they gave his face character. Joe was lying on his back and snoring quietly. Chris gently kissed him on the forehead.

"Have a great day, mate," Chris whispered to Joe. Joe grunted and turned over. Chris smiled and softly walked out of his room.

He went downstairs to the kitchen and put the kettle on. He looked out of the window. The wind was whipping up and it looked cold outside. As the kettle boiled he heard Linda walking to the bathroom upstairs. He made two cups of tea - Linda's was in a mug, and his was in his travel cup. He would drink his on the drive to work. Linda came down just as he was getting ready to leave. She looked shattered with large bags under her eyes.

"Bad night?" Chris asked.

"Yeah, he was up for two hours," she replied. "Didn't you hear him?"

"Nah, I was out like a light," Chris said. He felt guilty. He rarely heard Joe in the night as he was such a deep sleeper and it always seemed to be Linda who bore the brunt of the sleepless nights that were becoming more and more frequent over recent times.

"I'll do tonight, I promise," Chris said. Both he and Linda knew that was unlikely.

"It's alright, I really don't mind," she said, but her expression betrayed the sentiment of her words. "I'll get him up in a while, I've got to drop him to Sophie and Andrew's house at 7."

Chris gave her a kiss goodbye and made his way out the front door, closing it quietly behind him. It was a twenty minute drive to Havington. He liked driving there. It was a good time to turn off from his personal life and switch into work mode. It was especially good on weekend early shifts as the roads were so quiet, but today the weather was horrible. There were some exposed roads on the way there and Chris felt the effect of the wind on the car as he was driving down them. Dawn was breaking and Chris could see thick clouds all around. He knew it would be a day for car crashes and fallen trees at work.

He arrived at the station at 05:40 and went to the locker room to get kitted up before the 05:45 briefing. Most of the team were there.

"Morning all," Chris said. Sleepy greetings were exchanged all around. No matter how long anyone had worked shifts, it was still a horrible time to be awake and at work.

"Good morning team," Sergeant Adams said as they all sat at the briefing table. There were ten constables along with Sergeant Adams. Someone had made a big pot of tea which Chris poured out into mugs.

"Aren't you getting a bit old for this, Chris?" Jim Croft, one of the probationary PC's, joked. Chris smiled and raised his eyebrows. Jim had a point, though. At forty-one, Chris was the oldest on the team by over ten years. He was also the only one who had a child. Generally speaking, most officers had moved on to specialist roles by the time they passed into their forties, but Chris still enjoyed the challenges of being out on the streets.

He was well thought of by his team, and particularly by Sergeant Adams, who at thirty-eight was closest in age to Chris. His approachability and relative maturity meant that many of the team had gone to Chris with problems in the past, and he was an effective conduit between Sergeant Adams and them.

The briefing only lasted a few minutes. Not a lot had changed since the day before. - briefings were rarely updated at weekends. Sergeant Adams read out the crewings for the day and allocated various tasks and enquiries to different Officers. Chris hadn't been giving a crewing for the day.

"Have you forgotten me Sarge?" He said at the end of the briefing.

"No mate, you're riding with me today," Sergeant Adams replied. "I need to talk to you about a few things." Chris was confused, but Sergeant Adams's face didn't give anything away.

"Anything to worry about?" Chris asked with a nervous grin.

"Not unless you've got anything to worry about?" Sergeant Adams replied, pokerfaced. He then burst out laughing. "No mate, nothing to worry about," he said. Chris smiled wearily. He was tired and the day had barely begun. Matt had been right earlier. He was getting too old for this.

Chris went and got his kit, then went to get the Sergeant's car ready. He'd never crewed up with Sergeant Adams before and didn't have a clue what he wanted to speak to him about. Five minutes later Sergeant Adams came to join him.

"I'll drive mate, you look knackered," Sergeant Adams said.

"Whatever you like Sarge," Chris said. He was an advanced police driver but he didn't mind when other people volunteered to do the driving. They could always swap later in the shift.

Sergeant Adams got into the driver's seat and set his driving position. He had only been with the team for about six months, and had moved there on promotion from the Beachbrook District. Chris didn't know him well but he already had a lot of time for him.

"So what did you want to talk to me about Sarge?" Chris asked as they drove out of the Police Station gates.

"It's Mike in here, mate," Sergeant Adams replied.

"Okay Mike," Chris said. They sat in silence for a few seconds. It was strange for a Sergeant to allow a Constable to address them by their first name, but Chris wasn't going to argue.

"I want to talk to you about your career plans," Mike said. "I've been here about six months now and, I've got to say, you're a brilliant copper. The team all look up to you - probably more than they do to me! Have you thought about promotion at all?"

Chris sat there thinking for a few seconds about what Mike had said, because a lot of what he had said had struck a chord. Chris knew that he was a good and able police officer, and it was true that the team did all look up to him. Promotion wasn't something that had ever really thought about but he knew that it was a logical and natural progression.

"It's just that we need an acting sergeant on the team when I'm not here," Mike continued. "You know how much they keep moving me about to cover other things at the moment and the chief inspector wants someone from our team to step up rather than having to shuffle all the other skippers about. Would you be up for it?"

An acting sergeant was a constable who assumed the duties of sergeant when a substantive one wasn't available. There wasn't currently one on Chris' team as all of the constables were either too young in service, weren't suitable or hadn't expressed an interest.

"I've never really thought about it, to be honest Mike," Chris said. "But I suppose I could give it a go." He didn't want to seem too keen in case it didn't work out, but inside he was quite chuffed to have been asked.

"That's great mate," Mike replied. I'll get all that sorted out tomorrow then. You can do some shadowing with me, starting today. That's why I wanted you to come out with me."

It made sense to Chris now. In the six months that Mike had been with the team, he hadn't ever crewed up with anyone to go out for a shift. Chris knew that the rest of the team would be gossiping at the moment and wondering if Chris was in trouble for something. He let out a little smile.

"Weather's foul isn't it," Mike said. It was raining heavily in Havington and the streets were empty.

"Yeah, my boy was supposed to be going to the beach today. Don't suppose they'll be doing that now," Chris replied.

"I hope not," Mike said. "It's just the one you've got isn't it?"

"Yeah, one and done!" Chris said, laughing. "You've not got any have you?"

"Nah, not me mate," Mike said, also laughing. "None that I know of anyway."

They drove around Havington for a while but didn't see anyone about.

"You live over this way, don't you?" Chris asked Mike.

"Sure do, just in town," Mike replied. "You're in Beachbrook aren't you? Good place to work, that was. Nice and quiet but a few decent jobs. Have you got much family that way?"

Chris went quiet. He was an only child and his mum had died when he was only twenty-three. Cancer had got her. He had fallen out with his dad about ten years before and he hadn't spoken to him since. He had never met Linda or Joe, and Chris didn't even know if he was aware that he had a grandson. The argument itself was over something really trivial, but they had both said some things that were unforgivable and, as a result, they had never got over it. This came at a stage when Chris was just floating through life. He was in his early thirties and living at home. He couldn't hold down a meaningful job for any length of time and was out drinking every weekend. He couldn't even remember what the argument was about, that's how trivial it was. The argument itself wasn't the problem, however. It was the aftermath of the argument that caused the estrangement. His dad had told him that he was ashamed of him and that he was wasting his life. Chris had told him that he had never really liked him. And that was that. He packed his bags that very same day and left the house, never to return. Chris sofa surfed with friends for a few months until he managed to find a flat of his own to rent. His dad still lived in Beachbrook but he was now quite reclusive and, surprising as it may seem in a small coastal town, Chris had never bumped into him. He had frequently thought about taking the first step and going to see him. His dad only lived ten minutes away from him. But his pride had always prevented him from doing so. One day he would, he always told himself. One day.

"My dad lives there but I don't really see him," Chris replied. His tone of voice indicated that he didn't wish to discuss this any further.

They continued to patrol in silence for a few minutes. Chris looked at the clock on the central console of the car. It was 07:15. Linda would've dropped Joe off by now, he thought. He sent her a text message to check that everything was okay, but knew that she wouldn't reply until she got to work.

"Any patrol available for a three car injury RTC, London Road, Havington?" The radio came to life. There wasn't anything going on anywhere else so the whole team made themselves available.

"Fancy it?" Mike asked Chris. Chris smiled and flicked on the blue lights.

They made their way to the incident at speed, but it transpired that the three car injury RTC was actually a two car accident with no injuries. There were already two crews at the scene so Chris and Mike left them there to deal with it.

"Got to be the weather that caused that one," Chris said when they were safely back in the car. The rain was now beating down on the windscreen and the wind was howling outside. It wasn't the weather to be going out for a Sunday drive, nor was it the weather to standing at the roadside dealing with a car accident. Chris thought that he could get used to the privileges of being a sergeant after all.

"Fancy a brew?" Mike said to Chris. "I've got a few bits of admin to tidy up at the nick. You can listen out and fill in for me while I'm doing that if you want?"

Chris nodded. "Sounds great," he said with a hint of anticipation in his voice at the prospect of a couple of hours being the acting sergeant.

As they pulled into the police station, Chris looked at his watch. It was 08:27. He quickly checked his phone and saw that Linda had replied to him. She said that all was fine but that she was exhausted. He knew that he was going to have to get up with Joe if he woke up in the night. He sent a text message to Andrew to see what they were up to with the kids. About 10 minutes later Andrew replied.

"They still want to go to the beach but I'm trying to talk them out of it," was the message. Chris laughed to himself. He knew that Andrew wouldn't take them when the weather was like this. "OK, let me know what you get up to. Weather is foul," he replied. He didn't receive a response.

Just as Chris had made a cup of tea for Mike and himself, there came a call over the radio from the operator.

"Any patrol available for a two car injury RTC, Hollingwood Tunnel?" Hollingwood Tunnel was on the outskirts of Havington and had recently been opened as a relief tunnel for access to the motorway leading to London.

"Hotel Victor 25, show us attending," said Tasha, one of Chris' colleagues. "Please let the sergeant know that we will be out of comms while we're dealing with it." This was one of the problems with dealing with incidents in the tunnel. There was not yet the infrastructure in place for outside communications either via radio or telephone due to the lack of network signal in there.

"Received that," Mike said over the radio. "PC Jamieson is taking the reins for a while. Any problems please go through him." Chris swelled with pride at this radio message. Apart from the two car crashes, though, nothing else was happening. The odd vehicle check aside, it was a quiet morning.

About an hour later the radio burst into life. The operator's voice sounded urgent.

"Control to Sergeant, are you receiving?" The operator only ever asked for the sergeant if it was something serious.

"Control from PC Jamieson. I'm acting for a couple of hours. How can I help?" Chris replied.

"Control to PC Jamieson, have you got some patrols we can send over to Beachbrook? We've got a potential major incident over there," the operator said. The urgency was still apparent in her voice. Chris knew something serious was happening.

"I think everyone is free Control," Chris replied. "Take who you need."

"Control to PC Jamieson, thank you," the operator replied. "Control to Hotel Victor 26 and 27, please make your way on immediate status to Beachbrook Beach. Change radio channels to Beachbrook frequency for further details."

Chris' ears pricked up. Beachbrook Beach. "What's going on over there, Control?" He asked anxiously.

"Control to PC Jamieson, something has happened on the beach. Details are sketchy at the moment but it looks like some kids have been washed out to sea," came the reply.

Chris' blood turned cold.

CHAPTER 5

Chris got up from his desk and ran into Mike's office.

"Mike, MIKE," he screamed. "Joe was going to the beach, did you hear on the radio?" Tears were streaming down his face and his words came out so fast they were almost incomprehensible.

Mike had turned his radio down so that he could concentrate on his admin, so he didn't know what Chris was talking about. "Calm down mate," he said. "What's happened?"

"We've got to go. We've got to go now," Chris shouted. "Some kids have been washed out on Beachbrook Beach. Joe was supposed to have been going there."

"Chris, come on mate," Mike said reassuringly. "We don't know if it's him. Who was he with?"

"Andrew and Sophie Wicks," Chris said. His voice was full of fear.

"Let me check," Mike said. "Control from Sergeant Adams, can I have a bit more detail on the Beachbrook job? Who was the informant please?"

"Control to Sergeant Adams," came the reply. "Informant is a Sophie Wicks. Very distressed but said her husband had gone in to the sea to try to rescue their daughter and a friend. No other information available at the moment."

Mike looked at Chris and saw the colour draining from his face. "Control, show myself and PC Jamieson attending," he said quietly. "Please inform the Duty Inspector that one of the children involved is the son of PC Jamieson."

The radio went quiet for a few seconds. "Received and will do," was the eventual response.

Chris bolted from the Sergeant's Office, closely followed by Mike. His mind was racing, full of questions that he was unable to answer. Why had they been at the beach in that weather? Why had they been in the sea? What had Sophie and Andrew been thinking? His mind ached with the conscious sense of uselessness.

They got into their police car and Mike illuminated the blue lights and activated the siren. They made their way out of the police station gates at speed. The high and low pitched wails of the siren filled the air. The rain was getting heavier and was irradiated in the blue lights. The driving conditions were treacherous, but Mike pushed the car to the limits of its potential.

Chris sat there, trying to remain calm but unable to do so. Every part of him was willing them to get there quicker. He took out his telephone and - in a moment of clarity amidst the chaos - tried to call Andrew. The phone line wouldn't connect. He tried to call Sophie but it rang straight through to answerphone. And Linda. What would he say to Linda? Maybe she already knew and was at the scene? He tried to call her. It also rang through to the answerphone.

"We'll go straight to the beach when we get there," Mike said to Chris. He was driving expertly and making good progress. The roads were still quiet.

Chris tried again to call Andrew, Sophie and Linda but was unable to get through to any of them. Despite the speed and skill with which Mike was driving, the journey felt as if it was going in slow motion for Chris. Time, as an irreversible constant, seemed to be being warped. Seconds felt like minutes. Minutes felt like hours. His mind drifted back to earlier in the morning when he had kissed Joe goodbye. Why hadn't he stayed with him? Why hadn't he woken him up to tell him how much he loved him? These were questions that he couldn't answer but that would plague him. He thought about his earliest memories of Joe, when he was born two weeks before his due date. Chris and Linda had joked about how he couldn't wait to meet them. He thought about how scared they had both been when they brought him home. Their own little boy, someone completely and overwhelmingly dependent upon them both. He thought about the deep and intense love he had for his baby. His little boy. And then he thought about him now. The connecting road between Havington and Beachbrook winds along the coast. Chris looked out to the sea. His boy was out there somewhere. Tears fell freely from his eyes.

"Control from PC Jamieson, is there any update in Beachbrook?" Chris asked. His voice was cracking with emotion.

"Control to PC Jamieson," came the reply, "have you got your phone with you? I'll give you a call." Chris confirmed that he did have his phone with him and seconds later it started ringing.

"Hi Chris," the operator said. Her voice was calm and sympathetic. "Patrols are at the scene now and the coastguard helicopter is overhead. Updates are coming in all the time but it looks like one of the kids is out of the sea. One of them is still out there. It hasn't been updated with any other details at the moment."

The inner turmoil that had been eating away at Chris boiled over. "Who's still out there?" He shouted down the phone.

"It doesn't say on the log," came the reply. The operator didn't have the answers that Chris desperately needed.

Chris hung the phone up without saying goodbye. He tried to call Linda again. It went straight through to answerphone. As he was doing so, Mike was retuning the car radio set to the Beachbrook frequency. Chris wondered why he hadn't gone onto this channel straight away to get the updates as they happened.

As soon as the radio was tuned into Beachbrook, they heard an update. "Control from DS Willmott, an update for you. Can confirm that the female child is out, repeat, out of the sea. Male child is unaccounted for. Rendezvous Point for further patrols is Beach Road. Will give further information when available. Over."

Mike turned to Chris. He saw that his face had contorted with a mixture of pain, anger and helplessness. They were about five minutes away now and Mike pressed the accelerator a little harder. He could make it in four minutes flat out.

They eventually arrived in Beach Road and screeched to a halt just as an ambulance was pulling away with blue lights on. Chris correctly guessed that Maria was in there. She was the only person who would need medical attention. Mike parked next to the one remaining ambulance, which had all of the doors shut. It didn't look like anyone was in there.

Chris threw his door open and went to take his seatbelt off. He hadn't even put it on. He jumped out of the car and ran silently towards the beach steps without closing the door. Mike jumped out and chased after him, also neglecting to close his door.

"Wait up mate," Mike shouted. Chris didn't look back at him. He raced down the steps and onto the beach where he was met by a scene showing a flurry of activity. The Coastguard helicopter was over the sea with a powerful searchlight looking down into the raging waters. Lifeguards were out on surfboards fighting against the large, breaking waves in their search for Joe. Police officers were fanned out on the beach at regular intervals for as far as Chris could see. He saw that everything that could be done was being done, but still it wasn't enough. He ran up to the nearest police officer that he could see. He knew a lot of the local officers in Beachbrook but didn't recognise this one.

"What's going on?" Chris shouted at him. He was wide eyed and hysterical.

"Calm down mate," came the reply. The officer didn't know that Chris was Joe's dad. "The dad got the girl out but we don't know where the boy is. Probably too late by now if you ask me. Parents must be going mental."

Chris saw red. He was normally mild mannered and rational, but now clenched his right fist and swung at the officer, catching him flush on his left cheek. The officer went down just as Mike caught up with Chris.

"Chris, move away," Mike shouted as the officer scrabbled to his feet. His cheek was red and swelling already.

"What the hell was that?" The officer yelled with pain in his voice. Chris was agitating to get at the officer but Mike was holding him back.

"It's his son," Mike was shouting. He guessed that the officer had said something about Joe to provoke Chris.

The commotion had attracted the attention of other officers in the vicinity and they ran over to see what was happening.

"Get back to your posts," Chris screamed. He knew that if they were dealing with him then they were not looking for Joe.

"He's right," Mike said. "Back to your posts please. I'll deal with this." The officers all saw Mike's sergeant stripes and followed his orders. "Right then mate," he said, addressing the officer who Chris had struck, "this was either an accident where you fell over and banged your head on a rock, or we can investigate it… beginning with anything inappropriate that you might have said. What's it going to be?"

The officer looked at Chris, still being held back by Mike. He knew that what he had said to Chris was wrong and had no desire to be caught up in the middle of an internal investigation. "Rocks are dangerous around here Sarge," he said. "Really sorry mate," he said to Chris. Chris didn't reply but his tensed arms relaxed a little.

"Get yourself off and get sorted out," Mike said, and the officer disappeared up the steps, still rubbing his face.

Chris ran down to the shoreline. He wanted to get closer to where Joe was. Mike was following close behind him, and stopped Chris just as he was about to run into the sea.

"You can't go in mate," Mike said calmly. "They've got professionals out there doing their thing. If you go in then it's going to be you who needs rescuing."

Chris knew he was right. He stood at the shoreline with water coming up to his shins. His feet were soaked inside his heavy duty work boots but he didn't feel a thing. He looked out at the sea. It was savage out there. The lifeguards were struggling in the waves and the helicopter was being blown around in the sky. Chris stood there, just watching. His son was out there somewhere, alone. He agonised at the thought of not being able to do anything. Mike stood beside him, his feet also soaking, and didn't say anything. His arm was around Chris. He didn't say what was obvious to both of them, that the chance of Joe surviving was slim.

"I've got to get hold of Linda," Chris said eventually. He still didn't know if she was aware of what was happening or where she was. He looked at his phone. No signal. Reluctantly, he slowly made his way back up the beach and up the steps where his phone regained network coverage. He tried to call Linda again but again it diverted straight to answerphone. He looked around and saw Mike on his telephone.

"Chris, I've just spoken to Ambulance Control," Mike said as he hung up the phone. "She's at the RTC in the tunnel and hasn't got any signal. I've told them what's happening and another ambulance is on the way to take over from her. She'll be on her way here as soon as possible."

"Thanks Mike," Chris replied weakly.

Chris and Mike stood amidst all of the emergency service vehicles as people bustled all around them.

"Chris?" came a voice from behind him. Both he and Mike turned around. It was DS Willmott. Chris and Mike both knew her well having worked on several jobs with her in the past.

"Hello Sue," Mike said. "Is there any update?"

"I'm not sure what you know at the moment," DS Willmott replied. "Maria has gone off to hospital but she will be fine. Andrew brought her in. I'm really sorry, Chris, but there's no news on Joe yet. We're doing everything we can."

Chris knew that everything that could be done was being done, but still it didn't feel enough.

"Did you know they were coming to the beach today?" DS Willmott asked him.

"Andrew mentioned it but he said he was trying to get out of it," Chris replied. "I never thought they'd actually come." Now that he'd said it out loud, it was a question that he needed to get an answer from. "Where's Andrew?" Chris asked.

"He's just gone home to get changed then he's going to the hospital. Have you spoken to him?" DS Willmott asked.

Chris shook his head. "I tried to call him and Sophie but couldn't get through," he said. He had been so preoccupied with his concern for Joe that he hadn't given a moment's thought to Sophie and Andrew. Now, though, he started to feel an anger grow inside him, more powerful than he had ever felt before. "Why were they here?" He asked rhetorically.

"I really don't know," DS Willmott replied, her voice tailing off.

"I take it you'll be arresting them?" Chris asked, referring to Sophie and Andrew. "It's blatant child cruelty."

Child cruelty was something not dealt with much by response officers, but Chris had recent experience of a particularly harrowing case where a couple of children had nearly died as a result of neglect by their parents. He remembered that the law relating to child cruelty made reference to a person over sixteen years of age [Sophie and Andrew], who has responsibility for a child under that age [Joe], wilfully exposing him in a manner likely to cause him unnecessary suffering or injury to health. The wording of the offence seemed to fit the circumstances here in Chris' mind. By allowing Joe to go into the sea during a storm, it was obvious that they had wilfully exposed him to harm. The extent of that harm was as yet unclear and Chris didn't yet want to contemplate anything more serious than child cruelty.

"We don't know the full set of circumstances yet," DS Willmott said gently. She could see that Chris was not going to be placated by this. "Everything is under review until we've established exactly what happened here. Let's concentrate on finding Joe and then we can sort everything else out."

Chris grimaced. He wanted answers and he wanted them straight away. "Either you find out, or I will," he said, then turned around abruptly and made his way back down the steps and onto the beach. He stood there, just staring out to sea. So many different emotions were washing over him. Time again seemed to be a malleable concept. He felt like he had been there for a long, long time as thoughts of Joe enveloped his mind. His voice, his smile, his laugh. His face. His handsome, cheeky little face. Chris tasted salt on his face. He couldn't work out if it was spray from the sea or if it was the tears that were now again flowing from his eyes.

"Chris!" He was brought back to reality by Linda screaming his name. He turned around and she was running down the steps to him. He ran towards the bottom of the steps and they embraced. Her eyes were red and puffy and she was shaking with maternal apprehension.

Before they could speak about what had happened, they heard a shout from one of the officers located on the shoreline.

"There's something out there," was the call. They could barely make it out over the crashing of the waves and the thudding of the helicopter rotors. Both of them ran to the officer, who was pointing at a dark object in the sea, about ten metres from the water's edge. It was about the right size to be Joe, and it was dark in colour. One of the lifeguards out at sea had noticed some activity as well, so paddled over to them. The waves were pummelling her as she did so. The object appeared inanimate, showing no signs of life. Chris both hoped it was Joe and prayed that it wasn't. The lifeguard eventually reached the object and struggled to lift it.

It was a dark coat. She heaved it onto her surfboard and brought it to shore. DS Willmott and Mike had by now arrived and were standing with Chris, Linda and the officer.

"Lay it there, search it and get CSI down here now," DS Willmott instructed the officer, who obeyed the command. He gently lay the coat down on the sand, safely away from the shore. He put a pair of gloves on and searched the pockets. He found a set of keys, a mobile phone and a wallet with the driving licence of Andrew Wicks inside.

Chris and Linda looked crestfallen. Joe was still out there. Chris turned away and strode up the beach, closely followed by Linda and Mike.

"Where are you going mate?" Mike asked. He was worried about Chris. He knew that he was, understandably, on the very edge of a mental collapse.

"Just give me a minute," Chris replied. He walked up the steps and went and sat in the front passenger seat of their police car. Linda joined him, sitting in the back seat. Mike thought it wise to leave them alone and just keep an eye from a distance.

"What the hell happened?" Linda asked. "What were they doing here?"

"I've been asking myself the exact same thing," Chris replied. "Andrew messaged me earlier to say that they wanted to come but he was trying to talk them out of it. Look at this weather. It's just insane that they came here." The rain was still lashing down. The wind was still howling.

They sat in silence for a while, both mentally exhausted by their own inner agitations. Chris suddenly opened his door and summoned Mike over. He felt useless just sitting there without being able to do anything. He needed to do something, anything.

"I've got to talk to Andrew," Chris said to him. "Can you take me to see him?" His voice was measured.

This put Mike in an invidious position. He didn't have children, but he been a police officer long enough to sympathise with the paternal instincts that Chris was displaying to get the facts about what had happened. On the other hand, he had seen Chris assault someone earlier and was worried about what would happen when Chris saw Andrew. He weighed it up in his mind and decided that Chris would find a way to confront Andrew at some point. It would be better if he was there to intervene if needed.

"I'll take you, but you've got to promise that it won't kick off," Mike said to Chris.

"It won't," Chris said bluntly.

Mike got into the driver's seat and started the engine. He looked around. Linda was sitting silently in the back seat, slowly rocking. Chris was staring straight ahead. His arms were tensely lying on his legs and his fists were clenched so tightly that his knuckles were white.

"Belts on please guys," Mike said. He didn't really care about the seatbelts, he just wanted to break the silence and to make Chris move his arms. "You'll have to direct me Chris, I don't know where Andrew lives."

They pulled up outside Andrew's house five minutes later. Chris got out of the car and went and knocked on the door, with Mike close behind him. There was no reply. Linda was still in the back of the car, wrapped up in her thoughts.

"The cars aren't here," Chris said faintly. "I guess they'll be at the hospital. Can we go there?"

They got back into the car. Chris turned around to Linda. "We're going to the hospital, love," he said to her. We'll get some answers there". She didn't reply.

Mike attempted some small talk on the way to the hospital, but Chris and Linda weren't receptive to it. There was only one conversation that Chris was fixated on having and it wasn't with Mike. Mike had guessed this and was still unsure if it was wise for him to be facilitating this meeting, but he was still of the opinion that it was better for Chris to have the protection of him being there to stop things getting out of hand than it would be without him there. He was sure that Chris would have gone in search of Andrew regardless. This was the lesser of two evils.

As they pulled up outside the hospital, Mike reminded Chris of their agreement. "Remember, you're here to talk to him. This isn't a shouting match. I can't protect you like I did on the beach if things get out of hand."

"I know, and I appreciate it," Chris said calmly. "Linda, are you coming love?" He asked. She quietly opened her door and climbed out without saying a word.

They made their way into the Accident and Emergency Department. All three of them knew this area of the hospital very well. The receptionist saw Linda. They knew each other, Linda having spent many, many hours in A & E.

"Linda, sweetheart, are you okay?" The receptionist asked. Linda's face spoke the story of maternal grief. She didn't reply.

"We're looking for Maria Wicks and her parents, please," Chris asked impassively.

"Yes of course," replied the receptionist. "They're in Room 18. The dad only got here two minutes ago."

Chris and Linda turned away without saying anything and made for the side door. Mike thanked the receptionist and followed closely behind them as they walked through the side door and into the long, narrow corridor. They walked quickly.

"Chris, Linda, remember we're in a hospital and there's going to be a scared little girl in there," Mike said seriously. Suddenly this didn't seem like such a good idea. They were now outside Room 18.

'I just need to talk to him," Chris said as he opened the door.

CHAPTER 6

Chris and Linda stood motionless in the doorway with Mike standing closely behind them. Sophie and Andrew looked at them as a deafening silence filled the room. The only noise was the distant beeping of medical monitors. A range of emotions emanating from those present amplified the tension to breaking point.

"Hi Chris, hi Linda," Maria said quietly.

Chris had been fixated on Andrew. He hadn't blinked since he had laid eyes on him and his eyes were wide and fiery. Maria's words broke his tunnel vision. He shook his head and looked around the room. Sophie was next to Maria who was lying on a hospital bed. It was clear that she had been crying. She was half sitting and half standing, unsure as to whether she should have got up when they came into the room. Maria had a confused and dazed look on her face. Chris wasn't surprised. At six years old, how could you process the gravity of the situation?

Linda had been looking at the floor, unable to bring herself to look at Chris or Sophie, afraid of what her response might have been. Since she had first got into the police car she had been locked in a private grief so intense and acute that she had not yet had time to consciously acknowledge their role in Joe's disappearance. Instead, she looked at Maria. She was innocent in all of this. But how had she escaped to safety when Joe hadn't?

Andrew saw the pain etched on Chris and Linda's faces, pain that was likely to manifest itself in anger. He was prepared for it. In truth, he felt he deserved it, but he didn't want Maria to be exposed to it. Feelings of guilt still ravaged him.

"Let's go outside if you want to talk," Andrew said firmly.

"I think that's a good idea," Mike said in agreement.

Chris and Linda turned around without saying anything and strode back along the corridor while Mike waited at the door to Maria's room.

"Daddy will be back in a minute, okay Poppet? Andrew said to Maria as he walked towards the door. "I've just got to go and talk to Chris and Linda about something. Won't be long. Mummy will stay with you."

Maria didn't reply. She had seen the look on the faces of both Chris and Linda and didn't know what was going on.

Andrew walked out into the corridor and saw that Chris and Linda had already disappeared from view. "I'm Sergeant Adams," Mike said. He didn't offer his hand for a formal handshake. "I'm Chris' supervisor. He's on edge as you'd expect so that's why I'm here with him."

Andrew appreciated having someone there. While he was always confident in his ability to defend himself if he needed to, he knew that this situation was potentially volatile. "Thanks," he said. "It all just happened so quickly," his words trailed off.

"They need to hear it more than me," Mike said, gesturing Andrew to walk up the corridor.

Andrew slowly turned and walked in the direction of the exit. Mike walked a couple of paces behind him, keen not to engage him in conversation. He had observed at first hand the impact of this incident on Chris and Linda and felt that Andrew was responsible. The only reason he was here was to protect Chris, not Andrew.

Chris and Linda had made their way outside and gone to the garden area that was adjacent to the A&E entrance. It was where smokers congregated, even though smoking was banned on all hospital grounds. It was still raining and the garden was empty. They sat on a bench and Chris held his head in his hands while Linda sat next to him, staring up into the sky and letting the rain drops slap her on the cheeks. Andrew approached them with Mike close behind him. He didn't know what he was going to say. He knew there was no way to placate them but he felt he owed them some kind of explanation.

Chris looked up at him. "Well?" he asked. One word, but the venom in his voice was toxic.

Andrew didn't reply immediately.

"What the fuck happened?" Linda asked forcefully. Chris looked at her. He had never heard his wife swear like this before.

Andrew didn't have the answers that they wanted to hear. He knew how reckless it had been to let them be near the sea to start with. How could he even begin to explain that he had chosen to sacrifice the chance of rescuing Joe in order to get Maria to safety. To them, he thought, it would seem inexplicable in the cold light of day.

"I don't know how they got in the sea," he said weakly. "They were just playing. I told them they could paddle but not to go any deeper and they weren't even doing that. A dog ran and jumped up at Sophie and because she's pregnant I tried to get it away from her. When I looked back they had gone."

Chris and Linda didn't know that Sophie was pregnant but neither of them even noticed that Andrew had disclosed it.

"So you went straight in after them?" Chris asked. Once again, his eyes were staring intently at Andrew.

"Of course I did," Andrew replied. "But I'd put that big coat on after they'd gone to play, you know the one I keep in the beach hut. It just weighed me down."

"Did you get to them?" Linda asked. A solitary tear rolled down her cheek from her right eye. Andrew didn't notice because of the rain on her face.

He looked at the anguish on their faces and the anger that was brewing inside of Chris. He tried to put himself into their position, to recognise the strength of feeling he would have if the roles were reversed and he was asking these questions about a missing Maria. It was hard to be rational when looking at decisions that were demonstrably irrational. Why hadn't he just taken the coat off to start with? Would he have been able to save both of them? Again, the questions flooded his mind.

He knew that, in all likelihood, Joe was dead. He hadn't dared to think it until now but he had not yet been rescued and Andrew knew uniquely how powerful the grip of the sea had been. Now, he had clarity in his thinking.

Now, he knew what he had to do to protect Maria from a lifetime of people asking why she was more important than Joe. Now, he knew what he could say to allow Chris and Linda to believe that Joe hadn't suffered. And now, subconsciously, he knew what he had to say in the interests of self preservation.

"I only saw Maria," he said quietly. "I didn't see Joe at all. He had already gone under."

Linda screamed hysterically. Chris held her head tightly against his own as the rain, seemingly sensing the occasion, came down even harder. Mike stepped forward and placed his coat over Linda. As he did so, Andrew noticed that something on Mike's utility vest was flashing red. It was the 'record' function on his body worn camera. Mike had activated it to record their conversation.

The colour drained from Andrew's face. He was now trapped by his words, a prisoner to his fabrication that Joe had disappeared without a trace. He tried to think logically but the clarity that had been present previously was now gone. He had never intended to deceive Chris or Linda, it had just happened. But now that it had happened, could it be refuted? Maria had seen Joe. She had seen Andrew try to rescue him. How would he explain that away? How could he ask his traumatised, six year old daughter to lie for him? Waves of questions kept crashing over him and he felt his hands shaking uncontrollably.

He wondered if he should try to change his words, if perhaps there was a way that he could take them back and explain what he had said in a different way. It was not too late, he could still dig himself out of the hole he had created, he thought. He was trying to think of a way to reframe his words when Mike's phone rang and he stepped away, out of ear shot. Andrew didn't want to say anything without it being recorded. If the damaging words were on the camera then their immediate retraction should also be on there. He would wait until Mike came back and he would explain that, when he had said that Joe had already gone under, this was AFTER he had tried to rescue him. They might not accept or understand why he had made the decision he had, but it would be much closer to the truth. All thoughts of self preservation and the justifications he had given himself to lie to such an extent were now out of his mind. He knew that Chris and Linda deserved better than that.

Mike returned, his face ashen. "That was DS Willmott on the phone," he said, his voice trembling with emotion. "I'm sorry. I'm so, so sorry."

CHAPTER 7

Most of the emergency services personnel had been stood down from Beach Road as Mike's police car screeched to a halt at the RVP. The crowd had swollen in size, however, and there were several more media outlets at the scene. It seemed that word had spread quickly that something significant had happened.

Chris and Linda jumped out of the police car. They both had an overwhelming need to get to Joe, to be with him and to hold him. They both ran to the steps where they were met by a police officer holding a scene log, and crime scene tape withholding access to the beach. DS Willmott was halfway down the steps on her phone when she heard the commotion coming from Chris and Linda, both remonstrating with the police officer who wasn't allowing them to go any further. She quickly made her way back to the top of the steps.

"Chris, Linda, I'm so sorry," she said. She had a daughter who was a similar age and couldn't even begin to imagine what they were going through. "Joe is down there and someone is with him," she continued. "I can promise you that he isn't on his own and we'll take good care of him."

"I just need to see him," Linda cried. Her maternal urges blinded her to the policing protocols in place.

DS Willmott looked at her sympathetically, then looked at Chris. "You know we need to keep the scene secure, Chris," she said. "If there is any evidence of a crime then we can't risk losing it." She looked back to Linda. "You have my word that we'll look after him." Chris and Linda collapsed into each other's arms and held each other tightly, their world completely shattered.

Mike sidled up to DS Willmott. "We've just seen Andrew at the hospital," he said quietly. DS Willmott looked taken aback.

"What do you mean?" She said.

"Chris was desperate to see him so I took him. I didn't want there to be any trouble later on so I thought I'd be there just to make sure there wasn't," he explained.

"Mike, I'm running an investigation here," DS Willmott said, clearly annoyed. "You know better than to do things like that."

"Yeah I know, it didn't seem like such a good idea when we got there to be honest," Mike said. "Anyway, I recorded everything on my body camera if you want it. Probably isn't much on there that you don't already know. Andrew said that he didn't see Joe at all and just went in the sea to rescue Maria. I'll get it downloaded for you."

"Okay thanks. I need to get him in for an interview anyway, but that'll help," DS Willmott replied. She could see where Mike was coming from and why he had taken Chris to see Andrew. "Where is Andrew now?" She asked.

Mike didn't know where Andrew was. As soon as he had broken the tragic news to Chris and Linda, the three of them had rushed back to Mike's car and made straight for the beach on blue lights. They had left Andrew standing there in the garden area outside the A&E Department. As far as Mike knew, Andrew was still at the hospital.

He was right. Andrew was still at the hospital. He was still in the garden and was struggling to process the news that Joe was dead. He was slumped across the bench that Chris and Linda had been sitting on and hadn't moved since they had rushed away. His mind was racing. An internal conflict was raging between the grief that was threatening to engulf him, and the need to maintain his fabricated version of events. He wondered if there was any way that he could now row back on what he had said. That had been his intention, after all, before Mike broke the news that Joe had died. He thought about what he had actually said. "I only saw Maria, I didn't see Joe at all." It was damning, he thought.

He sat there in the pouring rain, agonising over what he should do next, when Sophie interrupted his thoughts. He had been gone for over an hour and Sophie had become so worried that she had left Maria's side to go and look for him.

"Andrew, what's going on?" She asked. "Maria is asking for you." She walked towards Andrew and reached out to hold his hand as he stood up.

"He's dead, Sophie," Andrew whispered. She instinctively squeezed his hand, then pulled hers away, her eyes widening before filling with tears.

"No… he can't be," she said hesitatingly. She was fumbling for the words to express herself. "He… No. No Andrew."

Andrew pulled her close to him in an embrace. "We need to get back to Maria," he said. "She's on her own in there." He didn't want Maria to be alone. He also wondered what she remembered of the incident. What would she remember about being in the sea? Would her six year old brain deem it too damaging and repress it all? Would she remember Joe being there? He knew that questions would be asked of her at some point, in some way.

Andrew took hold of Sophie's hand. It was shaking. He led her out of the garden and back towards the A&E entrance. She walked falteringly. As they were about to enter, her phone started to ring. She took it out of her pocket and looked at the screen. It was an unknown number.

"Can you answer it Andrew?" She asked, handing him the phone. She didn't feel up to talking to anyone, but knew that it could be an important call relating to what had happened. DS Willmott had taken her number and told her that any unknown calls would likely be from her.

"Hello," Andrew said, his voice still hoarse.

"Hi Andrew" DS Willmott replied. She recognised the hoarseness. "Sergeant Adams told me that you've seen Chris and Linda and that you're aware of the tragic, tragic news?"

"I am," Andrew replied after a pause. DS Willmott could hear that he was struggling to get his words out.

"You'll appreciate that I need to get to the bottom of what happened here, Andrew," she continued. "I'll need to speak to you and Sophie about it, and

Maria as well when she's up to it. Can you come down to the station today if possible?"

Andrew swallowed hard. The immediacy of the request shook him, but he thought that to refuse might make it look like he had something to hide.

"Yeah of course," he replied. "I just need to check on Maria then I'll make my way there."

They ended the phone call and Andrew took a deep breath.

"Was that the police woman?" Sophie asked.

"Yeah, I've got to go there in a bit to speak to them about it all," Andrew replied. "I think they'll need to speak to you as well at some point. And Maria when she's better."

Andrew and Sophie made their way back to Maria's room where they found her asleep and a nurse sitting by her bedside.

"She's just gone off so I thought I'd sit with her until you got back," the nurse said. "She shouldn't really be left on her own after such a trauma." Sophie's eyes, only just dry from the news of Joe, began to fill up with tears again.

"I'll go to the police station now," said Andrew. "I'll be back as soon as I can." He turned and walked out of Maria's room and made his way back to the car. Clarity of thought had now returned to him. What had happened to Joe was tragic. It was the most unimaginably devastating thing that could ever have happened and the sympathy he felt for Linda and Chris knew no bounds. However, he was now tied to an alternative version of events, one of his own creation, and he would have to stick to that. No-one apart from Maria knew any different and - even if she did remember anything about Joe in the sea - it could easily be explained away as a frightened child with an unreliable memory. Andrew knew that he was a good man. He knew that he had tried his very best to rescue Joe but that he had made a decision to save his daughter. He also knew that - given the same set of circumstances - he would make the same decision. With his mind now clear on how he was going to approach the situation, he got into Sophie's car and began the short drive to Beachbrook Police Station.

DS Willmott was still at the beach when Andrew arrived at the police station. She hadn't expected him to arrive there so quickly and was surprised when she got a radio message from the front counter staff that he was there.

Following her conversation with Andrew on the phone, she had spent some time on the beach with Joe. He had been found in the sea, not far from where he had gone missing. He had been brought to shore by one of the lifeguards on their surfboards, where he had been gently and carefully laid on the beach. A windbreak had been erected next to him to allow him some dignity in death - it was the only means of doing so in a storm.

DS Willmott had sat alone with him. She had instructed that undertakers attend the scene and knew that they would be there soon to take Joe to the mortuary where he would await a Post Mortem examination. She looked at Joe and felt a wave of emotion flood over her. She was a mother and, at that moment, she felt the maternal instincts of love and compassion wash over her. Joe looked perfect. He looked asleep. DS Willmott was a strict professional but couldn't help but be moved by the circumstances of this case. Any death of a child is tragic, but the circumstances of this one were beyond tragic. It was truly devastating.

"I promise you, I'll find out what happened," DS Willmott said softly to Joe. She stroked his head just as she saw two men in black suits trudging across the sand towards her, carrying a stretcher between them. The undertakers had arrived.

With a promise to Joe to keep and a steely resolve to do so, DS Willmott strode away from the shoreline and instructed the duty sergeant nearby to allocate an officer to attend the mortuary with Joe. She didn't want him travelling alone. She walked up the steps and saw that Mike's police car had now gone. She had asked him to take Chris and Linda home and it looked like they had complied. She found her car and got in. She looked at herself in the rear view mirror. Though her eyes were filled with tears, she had never felt more determined to successfully resolve a case. Many questions needed answering.

She drove off in search of those answers.

CHAPTER 8

Andrew waited impatiently for DS Willmott to return from the beach. He wanted desperately to get back to Maria and Sophie and every minute spent waiting was a minute he wasn't with them. He paced up and down in the interview room where he had been asked to wait, his clothes still drenched from where he had been sitting in the garden outside A&E in the pouring rain. He was now clear in his mind what his version of events was and what he was going to say to DS Willmott when he was asked.

DS Willmott, on the other hand, was in no rush to speak to Andrew. She was waiting for Mike to download his body camera footage for her to review prior to interview. He had told her that there wasn't anything on there that he thought was of evidential value, but she was a meticulous detective who liked to have everything in order before proceeding.

Mike had returned to the police station shortly before DS Willmott. He had taken Chris and Linda home where he had escorted them inside. He had tried to make them a cup of tea and to make small talk but his presence at their house hadn't seemed particularly welcome. He felt that they needed time alone to begin the grieving process. He knew from his experiences in the police that it was going to be a long and drawn out affair, and that the investigation and inquest was likely to take its toll on both Chris and Linda. He had naturally told Chris that he was to take as much time off work as was needed and that there would be no question of him being asked to return until he felt fully able to do so. He had left his personal phone number with both Chris and Linda and made his way back to Beachbrook Police Station.

"I've got the download here, Sue," he said to DS Willmott. "Do you want a look?"

DS Willmott viewed the footage and made a couple of notes in her Day Book. "How were they both?" She asked.

"Not good if I'm honest," said Mike. "What do you reckon? Child neglect?"

"It's a bit thin to be honest, but we'll see what they've got to say for themselves," she replied. "Andrew's here waiting. I'd better go and get his account."

She made her way to the Front Counter area and took a deep breath before entering the room where Andrew was. He looked at her as she entered. She had a look of grim determination on her face.

"Hello, Mr Wicks," she said. No pleasantries now, Andrew thought.

"Hi Sue," he said, trying to bring some informality back to proceedings.

"DS Willmott, if you don't mind," she replied. No such luck.

They sat in tense silence while DS Willmott loaded a DVD disc into the recording equipment and completed a few pieces of paperwork prior to the interview commencing. Andrew thought about trying to make small talk, but chose against it. A short time later the interview commenced.

DS WILLMOTT: "Thanks for coming in Mr Wicks. You're here because a child has died and I'm investigating the circumstances of that death. This interview is just to get an initial account from you, but I do need to advise you that you are being investigated on suspicion of child neglect. Therefore, I need to caution you. You do not have to say anything but it may harm your defence if you do not mention when questioned something you later rely on in court. Any thing you do say may be given in evidence. You are NOT under arrest and you are free to leave, and as you're here at a police station you may have a solicitor advise you free of charge. Would you like a solicitor?"

Andrew was bewildered. He had come to the police station thinking he was there to just tell her what happened and all of a sudden he was being read his rights. He felt a fog set about his conscious state. He needed to stall for time before he gave any answers.

ANDREW: "That's thrown me to be honest. Do I need a solicitor?"

DS WILLMOTT: "I can't advise you on that I'm afraid. What I can say is that it is an ongoing right and that if you decide you don't want one now, you can always change your mind later."

ANDREW: "Oh okay then, in that case I don't see why I'd need one." He was still reeling from having heard her caution him.

DS WILLMOTT: "Mr Wicks, tell me what happened today." Her voice was strong.

ANDREW: "Well, we were at the beach. That's me and Sophie with Maria and Joe. We were looking after Joe because his mum and dad were at work and we often look after him when they're working. The kids were adamant that they wanted to go to the beach but the weather was awful. I keep wondering why I didn't just put my foot down and tell them that we were staying at home." His voice trailed away. It was still deeply affecting him that he hadn't made better decisions earlier in the day.

"DS WILLMOTT: "What happened at the beach, Andrew?" Her voice seemed softer now, a classic police interview technique. Start strong, develop a relationship.

ANDREW: "They were playing by the sea, Maria and Joe. The weather was awful, so bad that I had to go and put on my coat that I keep in the beach hut. Really, really bad. Anyway, a dog came and jumped at Sophie. She's pregnant you know. We haven't told anyone but she's four months along. So I was trying to get the dog away and then I looked around and they weren't playing there anymore, they had gone." A solitary tear fell down his cheek. It was a tear borne of genuine guilt and remorse.

DS WILLMOTT: "Gone where, Andrew?" Her questions were short, but they worked perfectly for someone willing to provide answers. It had become the fashionable thing for people to simply go 'no comment' in interviews. It was a nice change to actually interview someone who was answering questions, she thought.

ANDREW: "I don't know. I ran to where they were and it's all a bit of a blur really." He didn't want to do it. He didn't want to fully commit himself to the fabrication.

DS WILLMOTT: "I've reviewed some footage given to me by Sergeant Adams. He was with you when you had a conversation with Joe's parents earlier. Maybe if I introduce the content of that, it might help you to recall what happened?"

Checkmate, Andrew thought. He had no wriggle room. No way out. She knew what he had said. It was unambiguous. He had clearly said on camera that he hadn't seen Joe. He sat in a reflective silence.

Eventually, he spoke.

ANDREW: "Well, I saw Maria. She was wearing a purple wetsuit, you see. She was about twenty metres out. I dived straight in and went right to her, but I was panicking. I hadn't taken off my coat or anything and it really weighed me down. I don't know why I didn't just take it off to start with, I really don't. Anyway, I got to her and I managed to get her in. Then I went straight back out to try to find Joe."

DS WILLMOTT: "But you took your coat off at some point, didn't you?"

ANDREW: "I did, but it's a blur. I just can't remember when or why." This was the truth.

DS WILLMOTT: "So did you see Joe at all when he was in the sea?" This was the one question that Andrew didn't want to answer. He closed his eyes. The vision of Joe's face in the sea stared at him.

ANDREW: "No," he whispered without opening his eyes.

The rest of the interview passed in a haze for Andrew. DS Willmott went into the finer points of detail on what he had told her, but the fundamentals had been established in those early exchanges. She wrapped up the interview when she was satisfied that she had all of the information that Andrew could give her.

"Thanks Andrew," she said after she turned the tapes off. The informality had returned. Andrew wondered if this tactic had been a ruse that she had created to try to engage better with him. If it was then it had worked. "I'm going to need to speak to Sophie and Maria as well in due course," she continued. "I'll be in touch to arrange it. In the meantime, I've got your wallet, phone and keys here. The phone probably won't work but the wallet and keys should dry out okay."

"Okay," Andrew said, grabbing his things and putting them in his pockets. His brain was completely scrambled and he needed fresh air. He left the interview room quickly and ran outside where he gulped down litres and litres of air. He stood there thinking about the interview and his responses to the questions. He had decided before that he was going to give those answers, but the process of doing it had made him feel sick. He wondered if DS Willmott had believed him. She had no reason not to, he thought. He collected his thoughts and slowly made his way back to the hospital.

DS Willmott returned to her office after the interview. Mike was still in the CID office, talking to one of the DCs about the day's tragic events. A lot of the Police Officers at Beachbrook knew Chris and he was universally liked.

"How did it go," Mike asked.

"I'm not really sure," replied DS Willmott. And she really wasn't sure. There had been something in the interview that hadn't seemed quite right. Nothing that she could particularly put her finger on. Andrew had said the right things at the right time, had shown remorse in the right places and did seem to feel genuine guilt over what had happened. She just had the feeling that there was something amiss. She had a nose for this kind of thing. She looked through her notes and bit her bottom lip. Something wasn't right. She was sure of it.

Then she realised what it was. She immediately picked up the phone.

"Is that CSI?" She asked. The answer came in the affirmative. "That coat from the sea… I need it forensically examined as soon as possible."

CHAPTER 9

Chris and Linda sat in their front room. Mike had just left them and a cold, reverberating silence filled the air. Linda's undrunk cup of tea from the morning sat on the table. It seemed like a lifetime ago to her that Joe had woken her up as she overslept on the sofa. What she wouldn't give to go back to that moment, to call in to work sick, to take Joe back up to bed and lie there with him and read all of his favourite books. To have him nestle his head into her chest, to feel the warmth of his body as he slowly fell asleep against her. All she felt now was a numbness, the dawning of a grief so vast and profound that she didn't want to contemplate it. How could she continue, she thought. How could she navigate life without her boy? Did she want to?

Chris sat next to her. Close physically, maybe, but so far away in his own thoughts. Why hadn't he told Chris not to take them to the beach? The weather was appalling, why hadn't he made clear that it was a terrible idea? So many questions that couldn't be answered and would remain unresolved. He felt alone, as if in a desert without a compass and with barren, endless horizons in every direction.

Both of them had dealt with the loss of a child in their working lives. Neither of them had ever contemplated being on the other side of the investigation, of the unrelenting anguish it brought, of the feeling of guilt at taking a breath of air when Joe couldn't.

They sat there until late afternoon, still in silence, each of them still wrapped up in their own, private turmoil. The sudden sound of Chris' mobile phone ringing jarred them both from their semi-conscious state.

A withheld number.

"Hello?" Chris said. His voice was that of a broken man.

"Chris, it's Sue Willmott. How are you holding up?" As soon as she asked it, she knew it was a stupid question. Chris didn't reply so she followed up quickly with her reason for calling. "I'm wondering if we can get hold of Joe's toothbrush if possible? We need a sample of his DNA."

Chris' ears pricked up. "Why do you need his DNA?" He asked.

DS Willmott had prepared for this question. She didn't want to arouse any suspicion in Chris of foul play because she herself didn't know if there was anything amiss yet. She was simply working off a hunch, a gut instinct that something wasn't quite right with Andrew's story.

"It's just a formality, just to make sure that we have every verifiable means of identifying Joe that we can. Just for the inquest, that's all."

The inquest. Chris hadn't thought that far ahead. He hadn't thought beyond the present.

"Okay, I'll get that arranged for you," he said. If he had been thinking with a clear mind he might have told DS Willmott that identification wasn't an issue and there was no need for her to have Joe's DNA, but in his crushed state he didn't have the clarity of thought to do so. "What's happening? Tell me what's going on Sue," he asked.

DS Willmott paused. "I've interviewed Andrew," she said slowly, trying to decide what she should be telling Chris. She was mindful that he was both a colleague but also the father of the potential victim of a crime, and that the boundaries between these two things should not be compromised. "At the moment, there is no evidence that it is anything other than a tragic accident, but you know that I'll leave no stone unturned to work out what happened. I give you my word on that, Chris."

Chris had stopped listening at the point she had said "tragic accident."

"How can someone let a child go in the sea in a raging storm and it be a tragic accident?" He shouted. "They might as well have put a gun to his head." The venom in his voice was palpable. "I'm not putting up with this shit," he screamed and hung the phone up. His heart was racing and his police shirt was wet with sweat.

"What's happened?" Asked Linda.

"They're talking about it being an accident," Chris told her.

Linda's eyes filled up. She didn't feel that it was possible to cry any more but the injustice of the initial assessment left her devastated.

"It's not an accident though, is it Chris?" She asked meekly. "I mean, they knew that he wasn't a strong swimmer. He should never have been there, should he?" She pulled a cushion into her face and wept.

Chris stormed out of the room. He was normally a mild mannered man but he could feel a rage brewing inside. He went out into the garden where it was still and calm. The rain had stopped and a thin layer of cloud was now overhead. There was no wind and no noise. Just silence. He shut his eyes and took some deep breaths, trying to slow down his heart rate. He appreciated the peace, although this was disturbed shortly after by a noise coming from inside the house. Linda was wailing.

Chris made his way inside and up to Joe's bedroom where he found Linda on Joe's bed, curled up in the foetal position and apparently inconsolable. He tried everything. He tried to cuddle her, to kiss her, to talk to her, to shake her, but nothing could rouse her from her anguish. He felt a failure as a father and a failure as a husband. He quietly walked out of Joe's bedroom and shut the door behind him, leaving Linda to face her grief as he went to confront his own.

He spent a long and restless night in their bed, alone. Linda didn't come to join him. Sleep was a distant prospect. Besides, he didn't want to sleep anyway. Waking up would just bring the revelation all over again that Joe was gone. He wondered if Joe might visit him in a dream, but then thought of the nightmare that reality would bring when he woke. Chris thought of the holidays they had shared, of the short life that Joe had experienced, of the life that he would never get to live. He wondered what kind of man Joe would've become. Would he have joined the police, like his dad? Would he have become a paramedic like his mum? Would he have lived a long and happy life, getting married and having children along the way? Chris felt robbed. Not only had Joe's life been stolen but Chris and Linda had also been robbed of a future of happiness with the blessings of grandchildren. Mother's Day and Father's Day were now reasons for commiseration, not celebration. Exam results days would bring pain, not satisfaction. Birthdays and Christmases? Pointless. To lose a child, he thought, was to lose your reason for living.

Despite her grief, Linda fell asleep several times in the night. Her body, already physically exhausted by the repeated nights of broken sleep, was now also broken down mentally. Her sleep was punctured by nightmares of Joe, alone and submerged in the sea. Several times she jumped violently, awaking herself in the process. The thought of her little boy being by himself as he drew his last breath, struggling against a merciless force of nature in a futile battle, left her desolate. Was he scared? Did he suffer? Would he have known what was happening and what was about to happen? Did he call for his mummy? She tortured herself with these questions, knowing that she would never find the answers to them.

Morning came. The storms that had battered Beachbrook yesterday had given way to sunshine. Chris had seen the early breaking of dawn back in the garden, having given up on the idea of sleep. He sat on the garden swing, still in his police uniform that he had been wearing the day before, quietly reflecting. There were things that needed to be arranged. Joe's funeral. How to arrange a funeral for a child? He knew that he would have to take the lead. Linda was unlikely to be able to help, given her precarious mental state. And Linda. What help would she need, going forward? And he thought of himself. How would he cope with this? He had dealt with bereaved families before and knew of the basic stages of grief. Denial. Anger. Bargaining. Depression. Acceptance. Yet while he knew that they were universally recognised, he felt that acceptance was a distant and unrealistic notion.

He went back inside and creeped upstairs. Linda was sleeping on Joe's bed. Joe's favourite books were on the bed with her, one of them opened and Linda's hand propping the page up. Chris knew how many hours of sleep Linda had lost in here with Joe recently. Hours lost but memories gained. He knew that memories were what they both needed to rely on to get them through the coming minutes, hours and days. He gently closed the door and left Linda to sleep.

The day passed much as the night had. Linda spent the day in Joe's bedroom, silent and consumed by grief. She didn't eat or drink anything until Chris went up late in the afternoon and gave her a cup of tea with some biscuits. She just sat on his bed, silently thumbing through his favourite books and remembering the happy times that she had spent reading them with him. She slept the night in there again.

Chris spent the day reflecting on everything that had happened. His anger had calmed but had by no means subsided. He thought of a dormant volcano. Calm on the exterior, but with the potential to erupt. He would never forget what had happened and who had caused it to happen. The day had been punctuated by a detective arriving to collect Joe's toothbrush. He hadn't explained to Linda what was happening with that. It was just another detail that he felt she didn't need to complicate things at the moment.

He did manage to sleep that night. Hours of deep sleep were interspersed with nightmares of Joe suffering, nightmares that he awoke from to find that the reality was worse than the dream. He slept through until after the sun had come up and made his way downstairs. Day two without Joe.

He knew that life was never going to be the same again. That much was a given. But he also knew that he couldn't spend days and weeks holed up in the family home. There were reminders of Joe everywhere. Photos on the fridge. Books on the shelves. Stains on the carpets. He needed to try to get some kind of routine back into his life.

He looked at his phone. He had turned it onto silent mode when he had hung up on DS Willmott a couple of days before, not wanting to speak to anyone. He saw five missed calls, three of them from a withheld number yesterday, shortly after he had turned it on to silent. He correctly assumed that it was DS Willmott trying to get back in touch with him. The other two were from Mike's personal phone, both from that morning. He cleared the call log and saw that he had two answerphone messages as well. He dialled his voicemail.

"Hi Chris, it's Sue again. I completely get your anger. I've got a little one as well and I know how I'd be feeling. Really, I understand. I just want you to know that I will be doing everything I can to work out exactly what happened and why. I know how important this is to you, believe me I do. I just want you to know that it is very important to me as well. If you need anything then please call me."

She could wait, he thought.

"Hi Chris, it's Mike. Just checking in before briefing. Sorry it's so early but I have been thinking about you guys all night. Anyway, I'm here if you need anything mate."

Chris pressed the call return button which dialled Mike's number.

"Hi Chris," Mike said. "How are you doing mate?"

"Bearing up," said Chris. "Linda is struggling. I'll get onto her Occupational Health department later for some advice."

"Do you need anything?" asked Mike. He genuinely wanted to help if he could.

"We're okay thanks Mike," Chris replied. "Just need some time to let it all sink in." He shut his eyes and immediately hated his choice of words. "Mike, I'm going to go crazy at home. I know you said to take some time out but I'm going to come back at some point soon."

"I was actually discussing all this with the Inspector this morning," Mike replied. He had anticipated this. He knew the kind of man that Chris was and that he needed to be busy. "When you're ready, and ONLY when you're ready, if you'd like then we will get back to some light duties shadowing me. Does that sound okay?"

"Sounds good," replied Chris. It didn't sound good, but it would be a start. Nothing would sound good again for a long time, he thought.

They continued to talk for a few minutes, until Chris heard footsteps on the stairs. Linda was at the bottom of the stairs. Chris hung up the phone and looked at Linda. She was still wearing her paramedic uniform from work two days ago. Dark shadows circled her bloodshot eyes and her cheeks looked red and raw.

"I'll get you a cup of tea," said Chris.

Linda nodded and went into the front room. Her mug was still there from when she had overslept. That seemed like a lifetime ago, a time when she was happy to be exhausted. She dropped onto the sofa and Chris brought her a cup of tea. She wondered how he was coping so well. She wasn't bearing up at all well, yet she had heard Chris on the phone arranging to go back to work. How was that possible? Did he really need to go back so quickly? Was he grieving still or had he got over Joe already? She knew that was impossible. She knew that he and Joe had shared a close and profound bond. She closed her eyes.

"How are you doing love?" Chris asked softly.

"Struggling," Linda said. It was the first thing she had said for days. "You know what the last thing he said to me was? Love you mummy." Her voice broke up as Chris sat next to her. "I heard you talking about work on the phone," she said.

Chris looked at her. He loved his wife desperately and to see her in such pain only exacerbated his own. "I've just got to get back to it," he said quietly. "I'm struggling as well. I feel everything. I'm angry, so so angry. All the time I'm sitting here I'm just watching the walls and thinking about it. I need to just do something, anything. Does that make sense to you?"

It did make sense to her. She knew Chris and how he was wired. "I get it darling," she said. "I'm just going to take a bit longer I think."

They slipped into each others arms and held each other. They didn't let go for a long time.

CHAPTER 10

Andrew walked into Room 18 in the hospital and found Maria sitting on Sophie's lap on the chair at the side of the bed. She was dressed in clothes that he didn't recognise, but the colour was back in her cheeks and she had a small smile on her face.

"Daddy," she shouted. She jumped off Sophie's lap and ran to him, wrapping her arms around his legs and embracing him. Still Daddy, was Andrew's first thought. "You're not going again are you Daddy?" She asked.

"No Princess, I'm not going anywhere now," he replied, smiling at her.

"Apart from home," said Sophie. "The doctor has just been round, she's good to go home now."

Andrew looked at Sophie. He had been at the police station for a few hours and when he had left her she had just found out that Joe had died. He wondered why he had gone. He should have waited with them, to be with the two most important people in his life when they needed him most, he thought.

"How are you doing?" he asked Sophie.

"I'm alright," she replied. Her eyes betrayed her words. She was not alright. She was still reeling from the revelation that Joe had died and yet she had not had time to deal with it internally as she had been tending to Maria ever since. Maria hadn't asked any questions about Joe yet, but Sophie knew that it would be only a matter of time until she did. She hoped that she would have the right answers for her.

They drove home in Sophie's car. The rain had stopped now and the wind had calmed. Andrew and Sophie didn't say anything to each other and the only noise came from Maria, making up stories involving the dolls on the back seat with her. She hadn't played with dolls for a while, Andrew thought. She had grown out of them about six months ago. Now she seemed content being a child again.

"We're home, poppet," Andrew said to Maria as he pulled up on the driveway. He had forgotten about his car which was still parked up in Beach Road. He'd have to collect it tomorrow, he thought. And the beach hut. It was still open and exposed. Would any of the police officers have thought to close it? He didn't want to go back down there now. He would go down there first thing in the morning. If anything happened to the beach hut overnight then so be it. He would deal with it tomorrow.

Andrew opened the front door then went back to the car to get Maria. He scooped her up in his arms. He closed his eyes as a memory burned into his consciousness. He had held her like this when he brought her in from the sea. Joe's face appeared. That helpless, yet accepting, face. Would it ever fade from view?

He carried Maria into the house and laid her on the sofa. "Do you want anything princess?" He asked.

"Milk please Daddy," she replied. A drink she hadn't drunk for months.

Andrew went to the kitchen to get her a glass of milk. He looked at the table and shuddered. Joe's pyjamas were folded up neatly on there. He remembered that Joe had been in his pyjamas when he had seen him eating his toast at the table that morning, and that Sophie had got him changed. Should he return the pyjamas, he wondered. He picked them up and felt the guilt rising within him. He closed his eyes and pressed them to his face. They smelt of a child. Of Joe. Tears began to fall. Big, remorseful tears. Sophie was at his side now, holding his hand and crying as well. They both suppressed any noise so that they wouldn't alarm Maria.

"Daddy, have you got my milk?" Maria called.

Andrew blinked several times and wiped his tears away on Joe's pyjamas. He handed them to Sophie and she expertly folded them and placed them back on the table. He gazed into his wife's eyes. "We'll get through this," he whispered to her. She nodded without speaking as he turned away to get Maria her milk.

Andrew and Sophie lay side by side that night but neither of them slept. They didn't discuss what had happened, instead each of them silently reflected on their own role in the events of the day.

Sophie was thinking of Linda. She wondered how she was coping with the loss of Joe. She knew that their friendship would never recover from this. How could it? She just hoped that in time Linda would come to see that it was an accident. An awful, tragic accident, but still an accident nonetheless. She tried to put herself in Linda's position, to try to work out the impact that it would be having on her but the thought of losing Maria was just too much to contemplate. And she thought about Joe. About his freckly, smiley face and what a good foil he was for Maria. She knew that there were going to be tough times ahead with Maria. Her best friend had died and it seemed that she hadn't understood what had happened. Maria was the only one who knew why it had happened, though. Why had they gone into the sea, Sophie wondered. Why had they gone in?

Andrew was lying there with his eyes open, afraid to close them. The image of Joe was haunting him. He knew that his lies were a betrayal of Joe and he didn't know now why he had committed to that version of events. He could only have saved one of them and most people would've understood why he chose to save Maria. Chris and Linda would never understand. He got that, and he felt awful for them, but a father's love for his daughter trumped everything. He again tried to close his eyes and still the image of Joe plagued his mind.

"MUMMY, DADDY!" Maria screamed. It was just past midnight. Sophie and Andrew both jumped out of bed and ran into her bedroom, where they found her sitting bolt upright against the headboard of her bed, sweating profusely and crying hysterically. Her eyes were rolling. Sophie grabbed hold of her and held her tightly. Maria was kicking and thrashing about as Sophie and Andrew tried to calm her down.

"Come on sweetheart, we're both here," Andrew said calmly. Inside, he felt anything but.

Maria suddenly fell limp and opened her eyes. She was shaking, but didn't seem to understand what was happening. She began to cry. It was her 'normal' cry, with the familiar whimpering noise that Andrew and Sophie both knew well. Compared with the hysterical screams that she had been emitting just before, it was a welcome relief to hear.

"What happened darling?" Sophie asked.

"I don't know Mummy," Maria replied, still snivelling. "I think I had a horrible dream."

Andrew walked out of the room to compose himself. Seeing Maria like this had upset him and he was pretty sure he knew the content of her dream. There was no way that she could be asked to relive what had happened in the sea, he thought. Who knew what psychological damage would be inflicted on her if she was to go through all of that again? He wondered whether DS Willmott could compel Maria to give a statement, but he would fight tooth and nail to protect her from having to do so.

"Andrew, I'm going to take Maria in with me," Sophie said. "Are you alright to sleep in here tonight?"

"Yeah of course," Andrew replied. He picked Maria up and carried her into his bed, with Sophie following closely behind. Andrew laid Maria down on his side of the bed. "It's still warm, princess," he said to her as he kissed her on the forehead. She had stopped shaking now and looked happy that she was going to sleep with Sophie. "I'm just going to go and have a drink," he said to Sophie. "Try to get some sleep."

He walked downstairs and put the kettle on. There was a plate in the sink. It was the plate that Joe had eaten his toast from the previous morning. Andrew shuddered at the little reminders everywhere. He washed the crumbs away and dried the plate, putting it back in the cupboard. He took his cup of tea into the living room where he sat for the rest of the night, all alone with only his guilty conscience for company.

Sophie came downstairs as the sun came up.

"Have you slept," she asked Andrew.

"Not a wink," he replied. "You?"

"Bits and pieces," Sophie said. "Maria was fine after she came in."

In the midst of all of the chaos, Andrew had remembered that it was Monday. He was supposed to be at work that morning finishing off an extension on a bungalow. He only had a few days left on the job but he couldn't face going to do it. Not so soon after what had happened.

"I'm going to take today off, love," he said to Sophie. "Don't really feel up to it to be honest."

"That's fine with me," said Sophie. She didn't want to be on her own anyway.

They sat and attempted to make small talk, both desperately trying to avoid discussing the looming shadow hanging over them. The awkward silences that punctuated the conversation finally made them confront the events of the previous day, however. Sophie was the first to bring it up.

"I don't even know what to say about yesterday," she began. "It doesn't seem real, does it? I keep wishing I could go back to this time yesterday and change it all."

"Exactly the same here," said Andrew. He was slowly shaking his head. "Why did we go there? It just doesn't make sense when you look back at it, does it?"

Sophie's eyes had filled with tears but, now that they had begun the conversation, she was determined to have it. She needed it. "It just all happened so fast didn't it? The dog and all that, I swear we didn't take our eyes off them for more than a second did we? Have you worked out what they were doing in the sea yet?"

"I don't know," Andrew replied. "I just can't think of why they went in. They knew they weren't supposed to. But, I'll tell you what, there's no way I'm letting the police near Maria. You saw how she was last night. They're not making her go through all that again just to get a statement from her."

Sophie nodded in agreement. "You're right," she said. "I don't care what anyone says, we've got to protect her now. Tell me you'll do what it takes to protect her, Andrew."

"You know I will," Andrew replied. He was so glad that Sophie agreed with him. While his intentions were pure in terms of protecting Maria, it also preserved the story that he had told. Maria was the only one who could contradict it. By not allowing her to give a statement, there was no way of proving that he had seen Joe in the water. Waves of guilt again flooded over him. How could he even be thinking like this, just a day after the death of Joe? Was self preservation really that important, he wondered. On the other hand, he thought, he was determined to protect his daughter. If his self interests were served as a by-product of this, then who was he to argue against it?

"Did you not see Joe at all in there?" Sophie asked. A cold shiver shot down Andrew's spine. It hadn't occurred to him that this would be up for discussion. Could he bring himself to lie to his wife? Could he confide in her and trust her with the awful truth? He had a split second to make his decision.

"No," he said quietly. "There was only Maria there. Joe had gone." He was fully committed to the story now, both publicly and at home. He had no-one he could confide in, no-one to share the burden of his guilt with.

It was something that he would take to the grave with him.

CHAPTER 11

"Hi everyone," Chris said as he walked into the briefing room just before the night shift began. The whole team were there. Only Mike was missing. All of them sat in silence just looking at him. Seconds went by without anyone saying anything.

"This was a mistake," Chris thought. The truth was that none of the team had children so they couldn't relate to the joy of having one, nor the utterly wrenching pain of losing one. They just didn't know what to say or how to say it.

Finally, Tasha jumped up and ran over to Chris. She wrapped her arms around him and pulled him in tightly to her. He appreciated the gesture more than he would ever have been able to explain to her.

"Good to have you back, Chris," Mike said breathlessly as he walked through the door. He was angry at himself that he hadn't been there when Chris had turned up. He had actually been waiting for him in the locker room to escort him into the briefing room, but Chris hadn't yet gone to get kitted up. He had walked straight in from the car park.

"Thanks Sarge," Chris said. "Do you mind if I say a few words to the team before briefing?"

"Of course not," Mike replied. "It's all yours."

"Thank you," Chris said. He had been off work for five days now and had been rehearsing what he would say to them when he came back. The words flowed exactly as he hoped that they would.

"You all know what happened the other day. Truth is, it's knocked me massively. I've been at home ever since and it still doesn't make any sense to me. I know there's an investigation going on but that's all over in Beachbrook. I needed to get back to work. Linda is still really struggling and I almost didn't come back in but she told me to come. Anyway, I just wanted to tell you that I'm back. The Sarge has got me shadowing him for a while but please just treat me like normal. It's the only thing that will make me feel anything like normal, if that makes sense?"

Chris sat down at his chair around the briefing table, hoping that they had listened to him and had taken on board what he had said.

"In that case, you can make the teas then," Jim Croft said. Chris smiled. Jim was still a cheeky probationer, but it was exactly what Chris needed to hear.

"Okay, I'm on it," Chris replied, walking out to the kitchen to make a pot. He heard the normal small talk return to the briefing room as he left and breathed out in relief. He had been dreading coming back in and speaking to the team but he had done it. He made the tea and went back into the briefing room just as Mike was completing the crewings for the shift.

"Chris, you're with me tonight as discussed," Mike said. "Go on then everyone, off you go and be safe out there tonight. Any problems then you know where I am."

The briefing room emptied, leaving just Mike and Chris in there. They had spoken several times in the week to arrange Chris' return to work, but this was the first time that they had spoken face to face since Mike had taken them home from the beach.

"Occy health have been on to me," Mike said. "They don't really want you back at work mate. I'm sure you know that. They told me to put you in touch with them as soon as possible. Do us a favour and give them a bell on Monday will you?"

"Yeah of course," Chris replied. He knew that Mike had stuck his neck out for him to facilitate his return to work, and he appreciated it.

"We've got to go through a couple of bits, orders from the boss," Mike said. "Risk assessments and all that. We'll get them done before we go out. How are you though mate, really? And Linda?"

Chris took his time to answer. The last few days had both flown by and been the longest days of his life. The dark cloud of grief had inhabited their house for five days without showing any signs of retreating and it had taken its toll on both him and Linda. Chris had focussed on returning to work as his escape, his sanctuary from sorrow. Linda had no such focus. Depression had utterly devoured her. She had been prescribed various medications by their doctor to try to keep it at bay, and they certainly helped her to sleep, but the loss of Joe had rendered her almost vegetative when awake. If it wasn't for the random bouts of hysteria, Chris would have thought that she was completely detached from the world.

"Linda is struggling, Mike, that's the truth," Chris said. "I'm being honest when I say that this is the best place for me right now, familiar people and routine and all that, but Linda is just not with it at all. If she's still like it next week I'm going to get her seen properly by someone."

"Well you just let me know if there's anything I can do, anything at all," Mike said. "I spoke to Sue Willmott earlier, she said she's tried to call you a couple of times this week but hasn't been able to get through to you."

Chris had purposely been avoiding her calls. He had managed to keep a lid on his anger since he had spoken to her previously and didn't want to speak to her until he felt ready to do so.

"Yeah I'll speak to her this week," he said, without committing to a time or date.

"Well she told me to pass on to you that she's still working on it. She told me that you got upset with her the other day, and I completely understand why. I've got to tell you that she's been trying to get Maria in for a video statement but Andrew and Sophie are refusing to allow it at the moment."

Chris felt his anger rising. His cheeks turned red and his eyes opened wide. It was obvious to Mike what Chris was thinking, so he tried to placate him.

"They're just trying to do what's right for Maria at the moment, mate," he said. "I'm sure they'll come around once the initial shock has gone. I know it's really hard to hear but she's only Joe's age and it's going to be really hard on her as well. I know you're going to be angry, but all I'd ask is that you bring that anger to me rather than taking it elsewhere, if that makes sense?"

There were so many things that Chris wanted to say. How dare they? How dare they not let Maria tell them what had happened? She was the only one who knew why they were in the sea, how could that information be protected? And after Andrew and Sophie had let his son die, the least they could do was give him the answers that he needed to put him on the pathway to closure. Instead, he suppressed these thoughts. He would revisit them another time, he thought.

"Yeah, thanks Mike," Chris said calmly.

"That's okay mate," Mike replied. "Right, let's get on with these risk assessments then shall we?"

Mike had been given strict instructions from the Inspector about managing Chris' return to work. He was not allowed to attend any incidents involving death or children. That was a given. The Inspector was also keen for him to avoid all contact with the public until he had been assessed by Occupational Health, but he was happy for this to be managed by Mike. The Inspector had delegated Mike to be Chris' official Single Point Of Contact in relation to any welfare issues. Mike had already unofficially assumed the role, but it had now been rubber stamped and officially confirmed.

When all of the administration had been completed, Mike and Chris sat alone in the Sergeants Office drinking a cup of tea. The radio was alive with the usual incidents that a Friday night shift brings - fights, domestics, drink drivers. Nothing out of the ordinary was happening.

"Fancy going for a spin?" Mike asked. He'd always liked night shifts. They were a chance to put all of the admin to one side, get out of the station and be a proper copper again. He loved being a sergeant but sometimes felt that he was a glorified paper shuffler.

"Yeah, I'm game," Chris replied. He was keen to get out. He thought that telling the team about Joe might lighten the mental load, but it hadn't. He just wanted to take his mind off everything and working was the best way he could think of doing that.

They kitted up and got into the sergeant's car. Chris looked around. The last time he had been in here was when Mike had dropped him home from the beach. He closed his eyes and tried to push the memory out of his mind, to replace it with a happier thought. He had been trying to adopt this as a technique for dealing with the aftermath of the previous weekend. It was a technique that he had been developing while at home, where there were powerful reminders everywhere of Joe. Of course, he didn't want to forget Joe. He just wanted his memories of him to be a happy place to visit, not a place plagued by his tragic demise.

Mike drove again. He wanted to find something to test the water, to see how Chris would respond to dealing with a routine incident. Mike was worried that Chris was back out on the streets far too soon, but again he was trying to balance Chris' wishes with any potential issues. He thought it was a similar scenario to when Chris had met Andrew and Sophie at the hospital. At least he was here with Chris to supervise and make sure that he could intervene if needed. He was sure that it wouldn't come to that, though. He trusted Chris and was sure that he wouldn't put him in that position.

The Havington district covered a large area. Not only did they have a busy town centre, but there were also a few rural villages that were policed as part of the district as well. Mike drove out of the town and parked the car up on a rural road that dissected some of these villages. They were hidden from view from traffic coming in both directions. It was a great place to find a drink driver. Sure enough, within twenty minutes of being parked up there a white van drove past them at speed. White vans on a Friday night were a great source of drink driving arrests. Mike drove off after the van. No words were exchanged and none needed to be - both Mike and Chris knew that the driver was a likely candidate. The van driver seemed to hesitate before pulling over. He knew that the game was up.

"Good evening," Chris said to him. "Been anywhere good?" He smelt the alcohol straight away.

"Just had a couple after work," the driver slurred. He was bang to rights. His couple was actually about eight pints. He'd stopped counting after a couple.

The driver failed the roadside breath test.

"It shows you're about three times over the limit," Chris said. "You could kill someone, you know?" His voice was raised but he was still in control of his emotions. Mike edged slightly closer to him.

"Wasjusst trying to get home officer sir," the driver replied. He was no longer coherent. "Bit sneaky of yous isn'ttit though, hiding like that?" He stumbled forward towards Chris, his hands raised.

Chris didn't see red. He didn't lose his temper. He saw with great clarity a man who had put others in harm's way, who was drunk and potentially unpredictable, and who was now stumbling towards him. In a split second, Chris had taken the man to the floor. He had him in cuffs and arrested before Mike could even get involved. Mike called for a van to attend the location to escort the driver to custody. He didn't fancy having to clear up any sick from the back of his police car, and he wanted to have a long talk with Chris about what had happened anyway. The driver was safely loaded into the van and Mike followed them on the journey back to the custody suite with Chris.

"What happened there Chris?" Mike asked. He had seen clearly and unambiguously that the driver had lost his footing and stumbled. His hands were raised as a means of balancing himself, not as a sign of aggression. From his perspective there had been absolutely no need for him to be taken to the floor.

"He was coming at me Mike," Chris replied. He genuinely felt that he was in danger of being attacked.

Mike sighed quietly. This presented him with a dilemma, one that he had hoped he wouldn't have to confront. It was clear to him that Chris wasn't ready to be out on the streets. Who could blame him? It hadn't been a week yet since his world had been turned upside down. Mike knew, however, that he had a responsibility not only to Chris, but to the public as well. He didn't want to detach Chris from the team and he wanted to keep him close so that he could still manage him and his return to work effectively, but he was now sure that it would have to be a an office based job. He also knew that the conversation with Chris that he would need to have about it would not be a pleasant one.

"We'll talk about it after you've booked him in," Mike said. The rest of the journey passed in silence.

Chris' head was swimming. He thought that all he'd done was perform his job to the best of his ability. He'd followed his training and restrained the driver in a safe and effective manner. It's not like he'd hit him with his baton or pepper sprayed him, he thought. Mike would surely see that when they went through it all later, he thought. He completed all of the custody processes and the driver was placed in his cell. The driver wasn't complaining about how he had been treated. In truth, he couldn't even remember what had happened or why his clothes were covered in mud. Chris and Mike went back to the Sergeant's office where Mike closed the door.

"Right then Chris, tell me what happened mate," Mike said. He didn't want this conversation to be confrontational.

"You saw what happened, didn't you?" Chris replied. He was still confused about why they were even discussing this. Would Mike have been discussing it with any other member of the team if they'd done what Chris had, or would he have accepted their version of events and trusted them. "He came for me and his hands were raised, so I put him down and cuffed him. It's standard police work."

"He didn't come for you," Mike said quietly. "He slipped and he was trying to balance himself. That's why his hands were in the air."

"He was going for me," Chris replied curtly.

"I don't think you're ready for this yet, mate," Mike said. He couldn't say it any other way.

Chris' cheeks went red. He walked out of the office without saying a word and went out to the car park where he took some deep breaths. He was trying to maintain his composure, but was struggling. Mike had misunderstood everything that had happened. He had not done anything wrong, yet he felt that he was under a microscope because of what had happened to Joe. He took his phone out and tried to call Linda. She didn't reply. The sleeping pills had probably kicked in, he thought. He sent her a message, apologising if he had woken her. He waited in the car park for a while. Everyone was still out at various incidents and it was peaceful.

"Alright mate?" Mike said. He had waited a while before going to find Chris, just to give him time to calm down.

"Not really Mike," Chris replied. "To be honest, I feel like I'm being done over everywhere at the moment. This was supposed to be me trying to get a handle on everything and now you're going to take me off the road. What else have I got left to lose?"

He was still holding his phone, which vibrated in his hand as he was talking to Mike. It was a message from Linda.

"Sorry Chris. I love you. Goodbye."

CHAPTER 12

Chris looked at his phone. He couldn't comprehend what he was reading. Six words arranged in three abrupt sentences.

"Sorry Chris. I love you. Goodbye."

He began to shake. An agonising yet familiar feeling began to creep across him. A feeling similar to when he first heard on the police radio that something had happened at Beachbrook beach. That had seemed like a lifetime ago but the feelings were still raw.

He dropped the phone.

"What's happened mate?" Mike said. He could tell that something was very, very wrong.

"The phone," was all that Chris could say.

Mike bent down to pick up Chris' phone. The screen was shattered from where it had been dropped but he could still read the message. It took his breath away. Six words. Just six words. But the meaning and intention behind them was obvious.

Mike knew that he had to think and act quickly. He immediately called up on his radio and arranged for Beachbrook patrols to attend Chris' home address. They were to force entry if necessary and to search for Linda. He asked the control room to arrange for an ambulance to attend.

"Come on Chris, we're going mate," he said to Chris after he had given his instructions. He couldn't even begin to imagine the inner turmoil that was plaguing Chris. He moved quickly towards the police car but Chris stood rooted to the spot.

"I can't face it Mike," Chris said quietly. "I can't do it again." He was feeling numb, his grief for Joe exacerbated by those six words.

He was breaking the words down in his head.

'Sorry Chris.' An apology? What was she sorry for? Why was she apologising? What had she done? And could it be reversed?

'I love you.' This love was reciprocated. His love for her was without boundaries and he knew that hers was the same for him.

'Goodbye.' A farewell that spoke for itself. The implication was clear.

"Chris, you've got to come mate," Mike said louder, unintentional panic creeping into his voice. "You know you've got to. We don't know what's happened and we might be able to get there in time if she's done something, but we've got to go right now."

Chris knew that Mike was right. Somehow he forced himself to move and walked awkwardly to the police car. Mike was speeding off before Chris had even had chance to close his door.

The journey was cruel. It was the same route, in the same car, that Mike and Chris had navigated not even a week before. On that occasion it had ended in tragedy. Chris couldn't bring himself to think about the outcome of this journey.

"Control to Sergeant," the radio operator said.

"Go," came the reply from Mike. He had no time for pleasantries, his concentration being on getting to Beachbrook as quickly and as safely as possible.

"No signs of life at the property," the radio operator said. "Entry being forced."

"Is there a car there?" Chris suddenly shouted into the radio.

"Standby," came the reply. Then thirty seconds later, "negative. No car at scene."

"She's not there," Chris said to Mike.

"Control, I need a live cell site trace on the following phone number," Mike said urgently into the radio. He gave them Linda's phone number.

"Received, will do," came the immediate reply.

Chris had tried desperately to call Linda several times but it kept going straight through to her voicemail. He finally left her an answerphone message.

"Linda, love, I got your text. I know you're struggling at the moment. I should've been home with you. I'm so sorry. Please, please don't do anything. I'm coming to find you and we'll work this out together. I love you." He hoped that the noise of the sirens hadn't drowned out his voice.

"We'll go to your house first," Mike said. "You'll know if anything is out of the ordinary." He was trying to think logically but he was still feeling stunned. Any thoughts about Chris' return to work had been rendered entirely redundant by the unfolding events.

"Control, any update on cell site analysis please?" Mike asked the operator.

"Negative at the moment," the operator replied. "Are you able to go over to the Beachbrook frequency, they are running the incident on that channel."

Chris frantically retuned the car radio set. He didn't know where Linda would have gone. She had been so erratic recently that she could have been anywhere. He would never have thought that she had the capacity to plan anything like this, let alone to carry it out. He had been scanning his mind for clues or hints that she might have given him to suggest that she was planning something, but he came up with nothing. Should he have seen this coming? Was it possible that this was going to happen? The loss of Joe had destroyed her. Perhaps it was inevitable that it would come to this, Chris thought. He should never have come back to work. His priority should've been Linda and he had completely and utterly failed her.

The Beachbrook radio frequency was active with lots of radio communications.

"Control from Havington Sergeant," Mike called up. "I'm on my way to the home address. I have PC Jamieson with me. He is the husband of the Misper."

Linda was now being referred to as a missing person. Because of the nature of her text message, she had been instantly assessed as high risk which meant that a lot of resources were put in place immediately to try to locate her. One of those resources was the night duty Detective Sergeant, who would be coordinating the investigative side of the incident until other, more senior, officers attended.

"Control from DS Willmott, I'm the night duty DS. Please advise Sergeant Adams and PC Jamieson that I will meet them at the home address."

Neither Chris or Mike knew that Sue Willmott was the night duty DS that night. It seemed appropriate, Mike thought, that she would be there. She was well acquainted with the circumstances surrounding Linda's depression and she was a good investigator.

"We'll meet Sue there and work out a plan," Mike said. They were nearly at Chris' house.

Chris didn't say anything. He was staring out of the window, trying to forge some kind of subconscious connection with Linda. "Where are you?" He whispered faintly under his breath, so quietly that Mike didn't hear him. The only place that she would have gone to in a crisis would have been Sophie's house, but that was the last place that he would now expect to find her. "Talk to me Linda, where are you?" He was desperate to reach out to her, for something to come into his mind. The only place she wanted to be was with Joe, he thought. He was shaken from his thoughts by Mike shouting at him.

"Chris, we're here. Come on mate."

Chris shook his head and brought himself back to reality. He got out of the car and looked at his house. The front door was hanging off its hinges and there were blue lights illuminating the whole road. He looked around. It was normally a quiet road and something major was happening. Neighbours were peering out their windows, trying not to be seen but unable to resist the urge to look. Chris and Mike both walked quickly to the front door where they were signed into the house by a police officer holding a scene log. A crime scene. Chris closed his eyes and made his way inside.

He looked around. Nothing out of the ordinary downstairs. He cautiously made his way upstairs. His bedroom was exactly how he had left it a few hours earlier. Then he walked into Joe's room. The last time he had seen it, the room had been a tip. Linda had been living in there night and day and hadn't cleaned it once. Now, it was spotless. In showroom condition, Chris thought.

"Joe's room has been cleaned," Chris said to Mike. He heard footsteps walking up the stairs as he was speaking. It was DS Willmott.

"Chris, I can't even begin to imagine what you're going through," she said. She was holding a hand held radio, that was tuned to the Beachbrook frequency. The personal radios that Mike and Chris were carrying were still tuned to the Havington frequency. DS Willmott's hissed into life.

"Control to DS Willmott, we've had a ping on the cell site analysis. Mobile phone was last active on the Beachbrook Beach mast. Repeat, Beachbrook Beach mast. Phone no longer switched on."

Chris again began to shake. "She's gone to Joe," he whispered.

The three of them quickly made their way downstairs.

"Sign us out," DS Willmott shouted at the officer with the scene log as they ran out of the house.

"Sue, jump in here," Mike called to her. She had come to Chris' house in an unmarked police car that wasn't fitted with emergency lights and a siren. It would've taken her twice as long to get to the beach if she didn't go with them.

The air was filled with blue lights and the wailing of sirens as Mike raced to Beach Road. The immediate plan was to flood the area with patrols and hope that someone would come across Linda. The police helicopter had been requested and was making its way to perform coastal searches. Specialist search and rescue teams were also en route, as well as dedicated dog handlers and coastguard crews. A huge police operation was now swinging into action.

Mike parked on Beach Road. Chris felt debilitated by the familiar feelings of angst that were crashing through him. Last time he had been here with Mike, his boy had died. This time, he was unsure of the fate of his wife. He slowly got out of the car, unsure if he wanted to be there, unsure if he wanted to know what was going on. He wasn't sure if he could go on himself without Joe, but to lose Linda as well? He knew that he wouldn't be able to without them both. He managed to open the door and get out. Linda was here, somewhere, he thought. Her phone was here so she must be here.

"Chris, is that Linda's car?" Mike asked.

It was. It had crashed into a lamppost and had significant front end damage. The front door was open and the car was empty.

"Chris, stay here," Mike shouted, as Chris began to run over to the car. "Sue, get on the radio and get a dog unit here now. They'll be able to track her."

CHAPTER 13

Linda had developed a deep and yawning depression over the course of the five days since Joe's death. She had been sleeping in Joe's bedroom and had become more and more separated from reality as time had progressed. Bouts of hysteria had been commonplace. On more than one occasion Chris had needed to physically restrain her, fearing for her safety as she thrashed about in a manic state.

She couldn't recall when it was that the doctor came, but she knew that it had been dark outside. She had become hysterical and Chris had held her tightly as she wailed and lashed out at him. Maybe it had been two nights before, maybe it had been three. She couldn't remember the conversation that she had with the doctor. She didn't even know if there had been one, or if Chris had done the talking for her and explained what had happened. All she remembered from the doctor coming was the sleep that followed. He had prescribed her something. She hadn't even looked at what it was, she had just taken it as instructed and had fallen into a long, deep and peaceful sleep in Joe's bed, undisturbed by the horrors of the present.

Waking up the morning after had been the worst moment of her life. It had been worse than finding out the news that Joe had died initially, as she had woken up happy. For a moment she wondered why she was in Joe's bed and where he was. The sudden realisation that he was gone had hit her hard. She felt guilty for having slept, for having left him on his own until she awoke.

While Chris was talking of returning to work, there had been nothing further from Linda's mind. The thought of having to interact with others left her feeling nauseous. She had not been in contact with anyone from work and had no intention of doing so. A couple of messages that Sam had sent her had been left unanswered.

The passing days added to her misery. She didn't speak. Chris had tried, but couldn't engage her in any meaningful way. Friday evening came and Linda was still lying in Joe's bed clinging to his books, the edges of which were now frayed. Chris came into the room and told her that he was leaving to go to work. He tried to kiss her but she recoiled. She couldn't handle physical contact. And then the front door closed and there was silence. Chris had gone. She was now totally alone.

She crept out of Joe's room and went downstairs.

She knew what needed to be done.

But first she needed some memories to take with her.

Chris had laughed at her when she had made traditional photo albums. He had told her that everyone stored them on the computer or in the cloud now. She took them out of the sideboard in the dining room and absolutely immersed herself in them. Each photo represented a moment in time, an image from the past, a snapshot of a happier place. A memory.

Joe as a baby. He was always smiling, rarely crying and gave cuddles to anyone. Linda had wanted an album with pictures covering every aspect of his first year so that she would always have that to look back on. It had all of the normal photos that would be expected, but she had wanted to include everything. There were photos of her breastfeeding, of Joe covered in food, of explosive nappies, of the bags under her eyes from the sleepless nights. She had wanted it all documented. She looked at the photos and closed her eyes, trying to relive the moments, willing the images to form movies in her mind. The movies never came.

Joe as a toddler. His freckles fully formed. His smile broad, his teeth crooked and his eyes wide. He was baby model material, Linda thought. She wanted to reach into the album, to be a part of the photos again. She looked at a picture where Joe was asleep on her shoulder. She could feel him there now, the way he used to breathe heavily on her as he slept. He used to pinch her skin gently to comfort himself. She could feel it now, the delicate squeeze of a toddler.

Joe's first day of school. A whole album dedicated to it. His hair parted down the centre, his blue blazer, white shirt and grey shorts. His tie far too big for him. His smile still blazing across the image, stealing the scene like it always did.

A photo of Maria next to Joe. Linda shuddered. Why had they gone in the sea? Why was Maria saved and not Joe? Questions that had been repeating themselves on a loop.

A photo of Sophie and Linda with Maria and Joe. Linda shut her eyes and closed the album. She didn't need those memories.

She walked into the kitchen and took out her phone. The battery had long since died. She plugged it in and waited for it to boot up, then listened as notifications flooded in. She didn't want messages, she didn't need condolences and she didn't require attention. All she now wanted was to be with Joe.

She closed the front door quietly as she left the house. She had made Joe's bed and tidied up his room. She was carrying his favourite book with her, the last one that she had read to him. She climbed into her car and drove on autopilot, her instincts guiding her to her destination.

She pulled into Beach Road and crashed her car into a lamppost by the steps. It didn't matter. It was only a car. She felt calmer now. Closer to Joe, she thought. She wanted to go onto the beach first, to try to find the spot where Joe had been brought in from the sea. And she was about to, but her phone started to ring. She looked at it. Chris. She couldn't answer - she was too far gone now, too wrapped up in the moment.

The phone stopped ringing. It was time to send the messages. The first was to Andrew's phone.

"You are responsible for this. For all of this."

Her phone beeped. A message from Chris. "Sorry if I woke you love, just checking in. Hope you're sleeping now."

She would be shortly, she thought.

She followed the cliff path for about fifty metres and stopped abruptly. This was the place, she thought. It was about here that Joe was pulled in. She sat down and listened to her breathing. It was calm. The weather was so peaceful, not a breath of wind in the air and the moon lit the sky like a beacon. Perfect, she thought.

She looked at her phone, at the message from Chris. She loved him deeply. Her commitment to him was eternal and binding and she felt unspeakably bad at how she would be leaving him. But she needed to be with Joe. Maternal grief had manifested itself in her and she could no longer be without her boy.

She looked over the cliff edge. Rocks. The tide didn't come this high. It would be quick, she thought.

She agonised over what to say to Chris. Several messages with explanations got deleted. In the end, she settled for a simple message. An apology. A declaration of love. A farewell.

"Sorry Chris. I love you. Goodbye."

Not perfect, but it would do, she thought. She pressed send. No going back now.

She looked all around. She felt sorry for the person who would find her. She hoped it would be a professional, someone who had dealt with this before. She prayed that it wouldn't be a child tomorrow morning. Chris would get her found, she thought.

No more thinking. She was on the edge now, tilting herself forward, willing herself to have the courage to do it.

Then she was free. Her mind came to life. Colourful, vivid memories flooded through her, triggering an overwhelming state of euphoria. She truly felt released from the grief that had consumed her.

"I'm coming, Joe," she whispered.

Then, darkness.

CHAPTER 14

DS Willmott sat in her office on the morning after Linda had died. She was now responsible for the investigation into the death of Joe as well as the circumstances surrounding the suicide of Linda. She had attended the scenes of both of them as the primary investigator and had developed a deeply personal interest in the case. She had made a promise to Joe that she was going to find out what had happened to him and now his death had been the catalyst for another tragedy. She had been with Chris when Linda had been found and had witnessed him completely break down. He hadn't been shouting and swearing or hysterical, he had just shut down. Mike had taken him away from the scene and had taken responsibility for ensuring all of his welfare needs were addressed. DS Willmott was tired, having been up for the majority of the night, but her resolve to work out exactly what had caused this tragic chain of events was strengthened.

Linda had been removed to the mortuary the previous night. Joe was still there. DS Willmott had put a request in to the mortuary staff that they be laid next to each other until their bodies were released by the Coroner for their funerals. She had been to see Linda before she made her way into the office and the contrast between Linda and Joe in death had been stark. Where Joe had looked peaceful and as if he was sleeping, Linda bore the violent wounds of the impact into the rocks. There was no way that she could be made presentable for Chris to visit her, DS Willmott had thought.

While the investigations into Joe's and Linda's deaths would run parallel to each other, they needed to be treated as two completely separate incidents. Joe's death could still produce a criminal outcome, whereas there were no suspicious circumstances surrounding Linda's demise. Her main responsibility with regard to Linda was to provide the Coroner with enough information that they could determine an outcome at inquest.

Linda's phone had been seized from her pocket. Remarkably, it was still intact. DS Willmott had been able to get the password to unlock it from Chris before he had left the scene, and she had it on her desk in front of her. For evidential purposes it would require a full download, but just so she could determine if there was anything on there of preliminary interest, she picked the phone up and unlocked it. It felt strange, that this had been the phone of a tormented woman, who less than twelve hours ago had sent a message from this very device indicating her intent to die, and that she had carried out this act with this phone in her pocket.

DS Willmott scrolled through the recent call list. The only thing of note was the missed call from Chris on the night before. DS Willmott closed the call register and opened the 'Messages' tab. The last message sent was the one to Chris. "Sorry Chris. I love you. Goodbye."

DS Willmott scrolled down to the next message. It was to Andrew. "You are responsible for this. For all of this."

She read it, and then read it again. She was a seasoned detective but it sent a chill down her spine. She knew at that very instant that there would be no chance of rapprochement between Chris and Andrew. She knew that this message would form a central plank in her investigation. Chris would inevitably become aware of it, either during the investigation or at Linda's inquest and she feared how Chris would deal with it.

As she was formulating her investigation plan, her mobile phone started ringing. It was Andrew.

"Hello Andrew," she said.

"Hello," Andrew replied. "I'm a bit worried about a message I got in the middle of the night from Linda. I was hoping I could tell you and you could see if everything is alright."

DS Willmott closed her eyes. Andrew didn't know yet.

"I know about the message she sent you," she said quietly. "I've got her phone here in front of me. Look, Andrew, it's not easy to do this over the phone but I'm sorry to say that Linda died last night. I know how this will make you feel bearing in mind what was said in the message."

The line went silent for a few seconds.

"Are you still there, Andrew?" DS Willmott asked. She could hear heavy breathing on the other end of the line before the phone line went dead. "Shit," she said quietly to herself. Her day had just got a lot more complicated. She would have to visit Andrew to speak with him in person and to get a statement about receiving the text message. Complicating the matter was the fact that he was still under investigation for Joe's death so any information relating to that investigation needed to be obtained under caution. She felt a headache developing.

She tried several times to call Andrew back but his phone rang straight through to answerphone. She sighed and rubbed the back of her head.

"Fancy a coffee sarge?" DC Tom Harris said, poking his head into her office.

"I need one, thank you," DS Willmott replied. She leaned back in her chair and rubbed her temples, trying to work out the correct course of action.

Her phone rang again. This time, it was a withheld number.

"Hello?" she said.

"Sue? It's Bob in the CSI Office here," came the reply. "I've got the results on the forensics for the coat that you asked for last week. Shall I email them to you?"

"Oh yes, thank you so much Bob," DS Willmott replied. Her weariness had given way to a sudden burst of adrenaline. She had wondered how long the results would take to come in.

It took about five minutes for the email to land in her inbox but it felt like a lot longer than that. She wondered why she hadn't just asked for the results over the phone, and was just about to call Bob to get them verbally when her email notification pinged.

She opened the email and read the results. She read then again to confirm what they said.

"No way," she whispered to herself, just as DC Harris walked into her office with her cup of coffee. "No time for that drink, Tom," she said jumping out of her chair. "I need you and Amy to come with me now. Come on, you're driving."

DS Willmott directed DC Harris as he drove to Andrew's house. DC Amy Flanagan sat in the back of the car, unsure why she was there or what was going on. Despite the tragic events of the past week, DS Willmott felt happy that her hunch had paid off. When they arrived she marched up the driveway with a spring in her step. She was on her way to fulfil her promise to Joe.

Andrew answered the door. His eyes were red and glazed, and he looked surprised to see DS Willmott at the door.

"I'm sorry I hung up on you," he said. "It was just a lot to take in. Do you want to come in?"

"Yes I do," DS Willmott replied. She walked in to the front room where Sophie and Maria were sitting and playing a board game. Sophie's eyes looked red as well. Andrew had presumably told her what had happened, DS Willmott thought.

"Can we speak in private please Andrew?" She asked. He pointed her down the hallway to the kitchen.

"What's going on," Andrew asked as he closed the door quietly. He still didn't know why a personal visit was necessary. "I was going to call you back as soon as that news had sunk in," he added.

"It's not a social call, I'm afraid," DS Willmott replied. "Andrew Wicks, I have received further information relating to your possible involvement in child neglect. Therefore, I am arresting you on suspicion of that offence. You do not have to say anything but it may harm your defence if you do not mention when questioned something you later rely on in court. Anything you do say may be given in evidence."

She could see the blood drain from Andrew's face.

"I…I…I don't understand," he stuttered. "I told you everything I could the other day."

"Don't say anything now please, Andrew," DS Willmott replied. "Save it for when you're on tape please. Would you like to go and tell Sophie what is happening or do you want me to go and speak to her?"

"No, I'll do it," Andrew said quickly. He didn't want Sophie to know what was happening. He had just broken the news to her that Linda had died.

He didn't want to completely overwhelm her, especially given the fact that she was pregnant and had suffered enough stress over the past week.

"I'm just going with DS Willmott, love," he said to Sophie as he walked into the front room. "Got to help them out with a couple of bits. I'll be back as soon as I can."

Sophie looked at him. She knew that something was wrong. He was deathly pale and his voice was trembling. "Are you alright?" She asked. "Can't it wait, we've been through enough this week haven't we?" Her question was said to Andrew but was clearly aimed at DS Willmott.

Andrew gave her a kiss. "It'll all be fine, love. Maria, look after your mum for me until I'm home will you?"

"Will do Daddy," Maria squealed. She was still calling him Daddy.

Andrew turned and walked out of the front room, and followed DS Willmott and there two DC's out of his house. He sat in the back of their car and they drove back to the Police Station. Andrew tried several times to engage them in conversation but each time he was advised that it was better for him not to say anything. He was nervous. He wondered what new evidence DS Willmott had. Was there a witness who had seen him with Joe in the sea? He had been trying to avoid replaying the events of the previous Sunday in his mind, but he now revisited his memory to see if there was anything that he had missed. He couldn't think of anything.

We're here," DS Willmott said as DC Harris pulled into the rear yard of Beachbrook Police Station. "I know you haven't been arrested before so I'll explain everything to you as we go, okay?"

Andrew nodded, but remained silent. He got out of the car and walked into the Custody Suite. The first thing he noticed was the smell. The only thing he could think of was mouldy, festering socks. Then, the noise. Someone was banging on a cell door and someone else was screaming blue murder.

"You get used to it," DC Harris said. He could see that Andrew was in unfamiliar surroundings and that he was uncomfortable.

DC Harris searched Andrew and logged his belongings, then Andrew was introduced to the Custody Sergeant. DS Willmott outlined the circumstances of the arrest. It was a whirlwind of information for Andrew to comprehend and he struggled to understand exactly what was happening.

"Do you want a solicitor?" The Custody Sergeant asked gruffly.

"I don't think so," Andrew replied. "I didn't need one last time. Do I need one now?"

"That's a no then," the Custody Sergeant said. "Let me know if you change your mind."

Andrew nodded. DS Willmott took him down a long corridor to a cell where he was told to leave his shoes and belt outside. The last week had seen two deaths with links to Andrew and the police were taking no chances with him.

"I'm just going to get a few things ready then I'll be back to get you for interview," DS Willmott said to him as she shut the door. She didn't want a reply. She was saving any conversation for when it was recorded and permissible as evidence in court.

In truth, she was ready there and then to get him into interview. She knew exactly what she wanted to ask him and she was eager to get on with it. She was employing the age old tactic, however, of making him wait. Give him an hour to sweat on it, she thought to herself. It was a strategy that she thought would work on someone like Andrew.

She was right. Andrew was pacing up and down in his cell, desperate to know why he was there. He was still reeling from the news about Linda. He had thought several times over the course of the past few days about getting in touch with either her or Chris, but what would he say? What could he say?

He hadn't received the message from Linda until he had turned his phone on that morning and he felt winded when he read what she had sent to him. "You are responsible for this. For all of this." He knew that he was responsible for everything, but to have it laid out to him in such stark fashion had left him shaken. He had agonised over what to do with the message. He hadn't told Sophie. He was trying to protect her as much as possible from everything that had been going on. Instead, he had called DS Willmott quietly. That was when she had broken the news to him about Linda.

DS Willmott opened the cell door. An hour had passed and Andrew had noticeable beads of sweat on his forehead. DS Willmott saw them and smiled internally while still remaining pokerfaced on the exterior.

"Let's crack on then shall we," she said to Andrew.

She led him down the corridor, past the Custody Sergeant and into an interview room. He noticed that the banging had stopped and that an eerie silence had descended on the Custody Suite.

He sat in his chair opposite DS Willmott and looked at her as she arranged her paperwork.

'What do you know,' he thought to himself. She looked up and he immediately averted his gaze.

"Right then," she said. "It'll be the same process as before. Are you ready to go?"

Andrew nodded anxiously.

DS Willmott loaded the DVD discs into the Digital Interview Recorder and pressed record.

She looked Andrew up and down. She knew that he hadn't told her everything in that first interview, and that he bore some responsibility for the tragic events that had occurred over the past week.

'It's showtime,' she thought to herself.

CHAPTER 15

DS WILLMOTT: "Mr Wicks, you have been arrested on suspicion of child neglect after further evidence has come to light relating to the investigation. For the avoidance of doubt, this is in relation to the investigation into the death of Joseph Jamieson. Before we begin is there anything that you would like to tell me that might differ from the account you have already provided to me?"

ANDREW: "I don't think so, no. I'm confused about why I'm here to be honest. I told you everything last time." He was feeling weighed down by the pressure of the situation. He was sure that DS Willmott had managed to find a witness who had seen him in the sea with Joe. What else could there be?

DS WILLMOTT: "I'd just like to clarify some of the details from the first interview, if I may?" She didn't wait for an answer. "You went to the beach last Sunday. The weather was awful but the children were adamant that they wanted to go. Is that right so far?"

ANDREW: "That's right."

DS WILLMOTT: "Joe and Maria went down to the water's edge. You then went and put on your coat from the beach hut because the weather was so bad. A dog jumped up at you and you took your eyes off the children, then…"

ANDREW, interrupting: "No, the dog jumped up at Sophie. I was protecting her because she was pregnant, you see."

DS Willmott had laid a trap and Andrew had walked straight into it. She had known that the dog had jumped up at Sophie. She wanted him to correct her on this fact, and he had. What he hadn't done was to correct her on the timing of him putting the coat on. It was such an important part of her interview strategy and it had worked perfectly.

DS WILLMOTT: "My apologies. You're right, the dog jumped up at Sophie and you tried to get the dog away. You then looked around and the children weren't playing any more. They had gone. You ran down to the sea and saw Maria. You went into the sea and managed to get to her, but you were weighed down by your coat. At some point you took the coat off and at no point did you see Joe. Is that about right?

ANDREW: "Yeah, that's about right." It still seemed surreal to him. He had tried to compartmentalise it in his mind when at home with Sophie to try to avoid thinking of it or talking about it. This interview was reigniting the aching pains of guilt and remorse within him. His eyes filled with tears.

DS WILLMOTT: "Are you okay to continue?" She had seen the tears brewing but any sympathy she felt for Andrew had long since passed. Her only thoughts now were of tying him up in as many knots as she could with the evidence she had.

ANDREW: "Yes, I'm okay thank you." He wiped his eyes and took a deep breath.

DS WILLMOTT: "There are just a few things that I need to go over in a bit more detail. When you got to the beach, where did Maria and Joe get changed?

ANDREW: "On the sand. I helped Joe with his wetsuit and Sophie helped Maria with hers." He was taking his time to think about the answers he was giving, fearing that anything that he said might be used in some way to incriminate him.

DS WILLMOTT: "Did either of them go into the beach hut at all?"

ANDREW: "No, they got changed on the sand and then went to play by the sea." He couldn't see where this line of questioning was going, but it seemed innocuous enough to him.

DS WILLMOTT: "When was the last time that Joe had been in your beach hut?"

ANDREW: "A while ago, Got to be a few weeks, maybe more." Again, he was more than happy to answer questions such as this.

DS WILLMOTT: "The coat that you were wearing, please can you describe it to me?"

ANDREW: "Of course. It's dark brown and made of cotton I think. It's just a scruffy one that I keep at the beach hut in case the weather is bad. It's the kind that takes on loads of water when it gets wet though, like what happened when I was in the sea. It got really heavy and weighed me down."

DS WILLMOTT: "And you had your keys, phone and wallet in the pocket of it when you went in to the sea?"

ANDREW: "Yeah, you gave them back to me last time you interviewed me."

DS WILLMOTT: "That's right. Now I just want to go over what happened when you were in the sea in finer detail. When interviewed last time, you said that it was all a blur. Now that a bit of time has passed, have you had a chance to think of anything else that might help me with my investigation?" She purposely left the question open, giving him a chance to tell her a different version of the truth. He took his time before he answered. He knew that this was moving into much trickier territory.

ANDREW: "Well, like I said, I saw Maria and went in to get her. My coat was weighing me down but I managed to get her in. Then I went back out to try to find Joe, but I couldn't see him anywhere."

DS WILLMOTT: "So you had your coat on when you got Maria in, then?"

ANDREW: "I believe so, yes. I think I took it off when I went back out to look for Joe." He couldn't remember exactly when he had taken the coat off. That was the truth.

DS WILLMOTT: "And at no point did you see Joe in the sea?"

ANDREW: "No." His voice was both authoritative yet sad. DS Willmott remained silent. She let the tension build in the interview room. The soundproofed walls let in no noise. It was just her, Andrew and the faint whirring of the recording equipment. She was determined to get the truth.

DS WILLMOTT: "I have a couple of issues with what you have told me."

Andrew swallowed hard and looked down. What evidence had she got against him? What else could she have?

DS WILLMOTT: "When you were in the ambulance on the day of the incident, I asked you what had happened. I made a note of your answer to that question. You said "I couldn't get them both in." What did you mean by that? Why say that you couldn't get them both in if you only had the option of getting Maria in?"

ANDREW: "I…. Errrr…. Well, I guess I was in shock and wasn't thinking properly. That's the only way I can explain it." He was breathing a little bit easier now. If this was the only other evidence that DS Willmott had then he felt what he had said was defensible, given the circumstances. In no way did it prove that he had left Joe to die.

DS WILLMOTT: "So you only had the option of saving Maria? You didn't see Joe at any point in the water?"

ANDREW: "That's right."

DS WILLMOTT: "So why is his DNA all over the shoulder of your coat, then?"

She had him and she knew it. His eyes widened and he had the look of a guilty man. A bead of sweat trickled down his forehead, between his eyes, and rested on the bridge of his nose.

DS WILLMOTT: "Andrew? Any answer to that question."

ANDREW: "Well… I…. Errrr… What do you mean?' He was stalling for time, desperate to find a way of explaining it. Joe had been on his left shoulder in the sea, his face rubbing against Andrew's coat. Andrew didn't know much about DNA but he knew that it was good enough in court to get a conviction.

DS WILLMOTT: "It's a wonderful thing, DNA, especially now. Did you know that clothes can go through the washing machine a lot of times and still retain DNA that had been on them before they went in? It's the same deal with your coat. It doesn't matter that it was soaked by the sea. Joe's DNA was absorbed by the cotton. Pretty clever, don't you think?"

ANDREW: "I don't know, maybe, do you think, it might have been from earlier in the day maybe?" His voice was no longer authoritative and his sentences lacked structure. Clear signs of a guilt, thought DS Willmott.

DS WILLMOTT: "But it can't have been, can it? Joe didn't go into the beach hut. They got changed on the sand, remember? And he hadn't been there for weeks before."

ANDREW: "I don't know, maybe he brushed up against me at some point then." He was despairing in his attempts to provide an alibi.

DS WILLMOTT: "But you didn't put your coat on until they were already playing by the sea, Andrew. Then the dog jumped up at Sophie. Then they were gone." Again, she let the silence fill the room until it was screaming so loudly at Andrew that he had to break it.

ANDREW: "I just don't know."

DS WILLMOTT: "Would you like to clarify what you meant when you told me that you "couldn't get them both in" in the ambulance?" Again, a long and awkward silence hung in the air. "Andrew?"

ANDREW: "I think I'd like to speak to a solicitor now." He looked and felt defeated.

DS Willmott maintained her composure but internally she was elated. Her set up questions had left him absolutely no room for manoeuvre. She couldn't have scripted it any better.

DS WILLMOTT: "That is entirely your right. I'll stop the recording now so that we can arrange for a solicitor to attend."

She stopped the recording and sat in stony silence as she ejected and sealed the DVD discs. She was sure that the next time they were opened would be in front of a judge and jury. She looked at Andrew. He was looking at the ground and his head was slightly rocking back to front.

"I'll need to put you back into your cell until your solicitor gets here," she said. "Do you have any preference or do you want the duty solicitor?"

"I don't know," he replied. He was completely shell-shocked at how the interview had evolved. "I guess whoever will do."

DS Willmott led him back to his cell and shut the door. She softly put her ear up to it and heard very heavy breathing from the other side of it, followed by the sounds of a man trying to suppress tears. For the first time, she allowed herself a smile. There was almost a skip in her step as she walked down the corridor and arranged for the duty solicitor to attend.

The duty solicitor arrived about thirty minutes later. DS Willmott knew her well, having locked horns with her many times before, both in interviews and at court.

"Hi Jill," DS Willmott said as she walked into the Custody Suite. "Quite an interesting one for you today." While they may have been adversaries on a professional level, they got on well enough with each other on a personal front. "Come through and I'll give you disclosure."

DS Willmott and Jill went into a side room where DS Willmott laid out the evidence against Andrew. Jill rolled her eyes. She knew that it was overwhelming.

DS Willmott went and got Andrew from his cell for his consultation with Jill. His eyes were bloodshot and his cheeks red and blotchy. 'Checkmate,' was all that DS Willmott thought when she saw him. She was impatient to get him back into the interview room and to get him back on the record. The consultation lasted a lot longer than she thought it would, however. She thought that it would have been a very quick bit of advice - to hold your hands up and take it on the chin. The clock kept ticking though. Eventually, after about an hour, Andrew and Jill emerged. He looked happier than he had done when they went in.

The interview recommenced shortly after.

DS WILLMOTT: "This is a continuation of the interview with Andrew Wicks. Mr Wicks, please can you confirm that you have received the legal advice that you asked for during your previous interview and that you are happy to now proceed?"

JILL: "Having consulted with Mr Wicks, he is offering the following prepared statement. That I, Andrew Wicks, refer to and stick with my previous statements made in relation to the tragic death of Joe Jamieson. I do not know how his DNA got onto my coat but suggest it may have happened in the sea if he came across it after I had taken it off. For the avoidance of doubt, I did not come into contact with Joe in the sea. I will not be answering any further questions in relation to this matter."

DS WILLMOTT: "Andrew, are you really saying that Joe's DNA got onto your coat after you had discarded it in the sea?"

ANDREW: "No comment." He spoke quietly.

DS WILLMOTT: "And your statement about not being able to get them both in?"

ANDREW: "No comment."

DS WILLMOTT: "Tell me the truth, Andrew. They were both there, weren't they? You could've rescued them both, couldn't you?"

ANDREW: "No comment."

DS WILLMOTT: "This is going to eat away at you if you don't tell me what happened, Andrew. We know that he came into contact with your coat. Your explanation stretches the boundaries of credulity. Are you sure you don't want to tell me? Come on, Andrew, what happened out there. Don't you owe it to Chris?"

Andrew screwed his face up. He did owe it to Chris. He knew that. Chris had lost everything and didn't have any of the answers that he needed and deserved. Andrew had been managing to keep a lid on his feelings as the past week had gone by, but he was now suffering the dual effects of guilt and self-accusation. Should he say something, he wondered?

JILL: "My client is asserting his right to silence at this time. He won't be answering any further questions, DS Willmott."

DS WILLMOTT: "If that's the case, Andrew, then I'll end the interview. Is there anything else you want to say before I do?"

ANDREW: "No comment." He felt repulsed at his cowardice.

DS Willmott turned off the recording equipment. The interview had gone as well as it could have from her perspective. She had got everything that she had needed from it, and the only defence that Andrew had eventually provided seemed preposterous.

A brooding silence again filled the room. Andrew knew that the interview hadn't gone well. He closed his eyes and saw the image of Joe. His mind was taunting him.

"You're going to be bailed so I can speak to the CPS about all of this," DS Willmott said coldly. She was sure that she had sufficient evidence to charge him already but she wanted to put an appeal out to locate the dog walker before she sought charging advice from the local prosecutor. He might have further evidence to strengthen the case against Andrew, she thought.

Andrew looked to Jill for support but she avoided eye contact with him. Was she representative of society, Andrew wondered? Would he be shunned when word inevitably got out that he had refused to answer questions about Joe, and that Joe's DNA had been found on his coat? And how would Chris react? It was all a terrible mess - and one of his own making, he thought.

He was bailed and released from the police station. He walked out and breathed deeply. He was a free man but he felt condemned.

CHAPTER 16

Mike had stayed with Chris since Linda had been found, initially at the scene and then for the rest of the night at Chris' house. Mike was worried about Chris. Until Linda had been located, Chris had remained outwardly composed even though Mike knew of the inner turmoil he must have been suffering.

Linda had been found by the police helicopter shortly after it had arrived at the beach. The radio message would forever remain in Mike's memory.

"Hotel Charlie 11, visual confirmation of a body on the rocks."

It wasn't so much the words that had made an impression, more the instant reaction they had evoked in Chris. Mike could remember being mid conversation with him about search parameters when the message was delivered. Chris had immediately shut down. The conversation had come to a shuddering halt and Chris had stood frozen on the spot, either unwilling or unable to engage any further with Mike. There had been no tears or outburst, just what seemed to be a complete mental lockdown.

Amidst all the chaos and noise at the location, Mike had managed to walk Chris calmly back to their police car and had taken him straight home. There was no conversation and Mike had ensured that all of the police radios had been turned off. Linda was dead. There was no need for a running commentary relating to the recovery of her body or the initial stages of the investigation into her death. The journey passed in silence, but not an awkward one. It felt more like a necessary silence to Mike. Time for Chris to absorb the news of what had happened. Time for Mike to work out how he was going to get Chris through the process of dealing with the deaths of the two most important people in his world. Time for reflection for them both.

This was a unique situation for Mike. While he had dealt with officers who had lost family members before, he had never had to support someone through the death of a child and a wife. What was unthinkable twenty-four hours before had become unimaginable. How could he ensure the right support processes were in place to help Chris, he wondered. Was there even anything that could be done to help a man who had lost his child and his wife in such tragic circumstances?

Mike broke the silence as they pulled up at Chris' house. "I'm going to be here for you all the way mate. You've got my word on that." He was determined that this was not going to be an empty promise.

They went into the house and Chris sat upright on the sofa in the front room, still in full uniform and police kit. Mike sat with him. Chris appeared vacant and impassive.

"Chris, can you talk to me mate?" Mike asked.

Chris didn't acknowledge him or respond.

"I just need to know if you're still with me. I can't even begin to imagine what you're thinking or feeling mate, but I've got to be honest, I'm worried about you. Shall we get you checked over?"

Again there was no response.

Mike was genuinely worried for Chris' wellbeing. The lack of emotion being shown now meant that some form of outbreak would occur at another time, perhaps imminently. Mike wanted to have a plan in place to mitigate this. He walked out of the front room and into the kitchen where he quietly turned on his radio and tuned back in to the Havington frequency.

"Sergeant to control," he said.

"Go ahead," came the reply.

"Please can you ask Hotel Victor 25 to attend PC Jamieson's H/A?" Mike asked. Hotel Victor 25 was Tasha. Out of the whole team, Chris was probably closest to her. Mike wanted her there so that he could begin to put some plans into action while she sat with Chris.

"Hotel Victor 25, received that and on my way," Tasha replied almost immediately. The whole team knew what had been going on but there had been radio silence up until that point. Tasha was just relieved to hear the sergeant's voice and was more than happy to help in any way that she could.

"Sergeant to control, received and thanks. Please could you also arrange for the out of hours doctor to attend as well? I want PC Jamieson assessed here please."

Mike slipped back into the front room. Chris was still sitting in the same position with the same inscrutable look on his face. Mike held his shoulder and felt the tension flowing through him.

"I've got Tasha coming over mate," he said. "She'll sit with you while I sort a few bits out. I've also got the doctor coming just to have a chat." His voice was soft and calming, but his words finally elicited a response from Chris.

"I don't need a doctor," he replied. He spoke without agitation or hostility but remained sitting in the same position.

"What do you need then mate?" Mike asked.

The tension in Chris' shoulders seemed to fortify, before finally dissipating. He took a deep breath in, released it slowly and whispered "Can you get my dad please?"

"Of course," Mike said, overwhelmed with relief. He remembered speaking with Chris about his parents only last week. "It's just your dad, isn't it? I think you said your mum passed away a while ago? I just don't want to get anything wrong when I get there?"

"Yes it's just dad. You'll have to tell him what's happened. I wasn't totally straight with you about him before, Mike. We had an argument about ten years ago and I haven't seen him since. He's never met Linda or Joe. Wish he had. He'd have loved them." Chris' eyes filled with tears but he held them in. Mike felt some brewing in his own eyes, but he forced them away. He wanted to stay strong for Chris.

"Okay mate, as soon as Tasha is here I'll go and pick him up," Mike said. "You'll have to give me his address. Did you want me to cancel the doctor?"

"Yes please," Chris replied. "I really don't feel like chatting with someone I don't know."

It sounded reasonable to Mike. Chris was now engaging with him and it was likely that his dad would be able to offer another pillar of support for the hard times that were ahead. He again went out to the kitchen.

"Sergeant to control," had said into the radio. "Please can you cancel the on call doctor, PC Jamieson is now engaging with me. Full update will follow later." He again turned off his radio.

It only took about fifteen minutes for Tasha to arrive. Mike guessed that she had made her way on blue lights to get there that quickly - not something that was allowed, technically, but something that he understood and would happily turn a blind eye to. He met her outside.

"Thanks Tash," he said. "You know what's happened; it's absolutely hit him for six. I couldn't get anything out of him for a while but he's talking now. He's asked me to go and get his dad so are you alright to sit with him while I do that and then we can work out what's going to happen from there?"

"Yeah of course I will," she replied. "Go on, you go and get his dad." She walked into the house and shut the door, leaving Mike outside and alone for the first time since the events had unfolded, finally able to collect his thoughts. He had been struggling to think of any measures that he could have put in place sufficient to ensure Chris' ongoing welfare and was thankful that he had asked for his dad. Without that intervention, Mike had seriously been thinking of a medical resolution - if necessary, and if Chris hadn't started to engage - a mental health assessment. For the protection of his own relationship with Chris, he was so glad it hadn't come to that.

He got into his car and slowly drove to Chris' dad's house. It took ten minutes to get there and on his way he thought about what he would say and how he would say it. It was a tough proposition. He was going to tell someone that the daughter in law and grandson that they had never met - and possibly had never known existed - were both dead. There was no training manual for that.

The house was in darkness. Mike took a deep breath and knocked on the front door. He suddenly thought to himself that he didn't even know Chris' dad's name. He hadn't thought to ask that. He was about to call Tasha to find out, when he heard movement from inside. No time, he thought as the front door opened. A worried looking man had answered it and the resemblance to Chris was striking. Mike knew that he had the right house. Mike was concerned by his appearance, however. He appeared gaunt and haggard, just a slip of a man. He was unshaven and, to put it bluntly, Mike thought that he looked ill. Very ill indeed.

"Hello, are you Mr Jamieson?" Mike asked cautiously. He was wary of how the news would be received by Chris' dad.

"I am. Trevor, please. Is everything okay?" His voice was croaky and it seemed painful for him to speak.

"I'm sorry to have woken you, Trevor," Mike said. "Do you mind if I come in?"

"Of course," Trevor replied, gesturing for Mike to come in. "Please excuse the state of the place, I don't really have visitors."

Mike walked through the front door and into the front room. A solitary, threadbare armchair was in the corner of the room. There was no other furniture. Paint was peeling from the walls and there was mould and damp covering vast swathes of the ceiling. It was a scene familiar to Mike. He had been to many houses such as this where an ageing person lived alone and, in many cases, died alone.

"Has something happened to Chris?" Trevor asked. He hadn't seen his son for years yet he had no-one else in his life who would warrant a police visit in the middle of the night.

"There's no easy way to say this," Mike replied gently. "Chris asked me to come here. His wife and son have both died and he wanted you to be with him. I know you haven't seen each other for a long, long time but I'll take you to him now if you want me to."

Trevor stood still for a moment, and then stumbled over to the armchair where he sat down, his head in his hands. "I don't know what to say," he said faintly.

"I know how much of a shock this must be for you," Mike said. "If you want to go and get dressed then Chris is waiting at his house to see you."

Trevor stood up uneasily. His arms and legs were emaciated, almost to the point of atrophy. Mike didn't know if this was the result of illness or mal-nourishment.

"Is everything okay with you, health-wise?" Mike asked.

"Just a few issues," Trevor replied. "I'll go and get ready." He shuffled out of the room and made his way upstairs, the sound of his movements amplified by the apparent lack of carpet. Mike wondered if this had been the house that Chris had lived in. When and how had Trevor let it get into such a state of disrepair, he wondered? Had he simply given up on life?

Trevor's emergence was announced by the echoing thud of footsteps coming down the stairs. Mike walked into the corridor to meet him.

"Take me to see my boy, please," Trevor said, his voice still rasping.

Mike led him out of the house and to the police car. He was curious to establish the exact nature of Trevor's illness. It was clear that something was wrong with him and he had implied as much.

"Do you need any medication before we go?" Mike asked.

"I've got everything with me, thank you," Trevor replied.

"Is there anything I should know before we go to see Chris?" Mike asked. "He's suffering at the moment as you'd expect, and I just want to make sure that we can manage any issues that might arise."

There was silence for a moment. Trevor looked Mike up and down, a sad expression enveloping his face. "Cancer," he said. "I've got cancer. Not sure how long I've got. Now please, take me to Chris."

The journey back to Chris' house was silent. Each man was deep in thought, their minds separately occupied by recent revelations. Mike wore a placid expression but was now deeply concerned about what kind of impact Trevor's reintroduction into Chris' life would have. The wounds suffered from the loss of Joe had been intensified by the loss of Linda. To put it bluntly, Trevor didn't appear long for this world. How much more loss could one man take? Any other time, Mike would advocate and positively encourage the reversal of an estrangement. He just wasn't sure it was such a good idea in this particularly unique circumstance.

Trevor was quietly grieving. He was mourning the loss of a daughter in law that he had never known, a grandson that he would never meet. He didn't know their names, their faces, their voices or anything about them but he felt their loss intimately. The details would come later, he thought.

Mike pulled up outside Chris' house. They walked up the pathway side by side, Trevor ever so slightly unsteady on his feet and Mike positioned to assist him if he stumbled. Mike rang the doorbell and Tasha opened the door.

"Wait here, Tash," Mike said as Trevor walked in ahead of them.

Trevor slowly walked to the doorway of the front room, and peered around the corner, where his eyes met Chris' for the first time in many years. A sad, lonely and ill man was transformed into a protective and caring father. The years they had lost were forgotten, banished from thought as father and son were united in grief. The two men embraced.

Finally, the tears flowed.

Trevor stayed with Chris for the rest of the night. They spoke mostly about Linda and Joe, Chris sharing memories and both of them sharing tears. Despite the strength of his grief, Chris found comfort in talking about them. Neither man broached the cause of the years that they had been apart. There seemed to be a silent understanding that the past was gone and that they were now together, showing solidarity in the face of unimaginable tragedy.

Chris remembered his dad as a strong and able man. When Trevor had first walked through the door Chris hadn't noticed the obvious frailties that he was exhibiting. He was blinded by his presence, impervious to the physical decline caused by the cancer. The longer they spoke, the more apparent it became to Chris that something was wrong.

"Are you ill, dad?" He asked.

"I am son," Trevor replied. "I've got cancer. They've tried treating it but there's nothing they can do for me now."

"Why didn't you come to me, dad?" Chris asked.

"I honestly don't know son. The amount of times I wish I'd tried to find you. I didn't even know if you still lived in the area, to be honest. I've been on my own for so long that you just kind of get used to your own company."

"I always thought we'd bump into each other one day," Chris said. "I can't believe we didn't."

"I don't really go out," Trevor replied. "Just to the hospital for my appointments, that's it. Since you went… well… it's been a struggle. But that's gone now son. We're here now. That matters."

Trevor placed his hand on Chris' shoulder, radiating warmth through it. The paternal flame was reignited after years of being extinguished.

"I don't know what I'm going to do, dad," Chris said weakly. "How am I going to get through this?"

"With me by your side, that's how," Trevor replied. "Do you want me to move in for a while? Truth be told, I could do with the company, and I'm sure you could as well."

"Yes please," Chris replied, his voice almost inaudible.

The sun rose yet still they talked. Chris spoke so fulsomely of Linda and Joe that Trevor felt he knew them personally. He wished he had. The conversation slowly evolved to the events of the last week.

"I saw something on the news last week about it," Trevor said. "When something happens locally you tend to notice it. I had no idea that it was your boy involved. What happened son?"

Chris took a sharp breath in. His eyes narrowed. "I trusted someone with him," he hissed with venom in his voice. Andrew and Sophie hadn't crossed his mind until now. This whole chain of tragedy began with their negligence, he thought. "The police are looking into it," he continued.

"They'll get what they deserve."

CHAPTER 17

Prior to Linda dying, Chris had started to plan in his mind how Joe's funeral would look. His boy had been pure and innocent, and he had thought this would be best reflected by the colour white. He had visions of a white coffin adorned with six white roses, one for each year of his painfully short life.

Linda's death had made him revisit these plans. No longer would Joe be alone, Chris thought. Linda would be with him, side by side as they were laid to rest. She was a bright and vibrant woman and Chris felt that this should be reflected in the funeral planning. White for Joe. Red and pink for Linda. Colours that contrasted with those of a traditional funeral, but that complemented each other when celebrating the lives of a loving mother and her son.

Chris was happy to have Trevor with him in the aftermath of Linda's suicide. Not only was his company important for Chris' mental wellbeing, but his medical needs and regular hospital appointments gave Chris a focus that would others have been spent on dwelling on the why's and how's of both Joe and Linda's deaths. Internally, Chris was still struggling. At times, and normally in complete private, he would break down in tears, unable to contemplate life without his family. Crying himself to sleep became the norm, not the exception. Without Trevor there to share the burden of grief, Chris didn't think that he would have been able to carry on. The funeral planning had taken up a lot of his time and, while it intensified his grief, it also provided him with an outlet to channel that pain into something worthwhile. He was determined to do both Linda and Joe proud.

DS Willmott had made representation to the Coroner to have an interim death certificate issued for Joe and Linda so that the funerals could take place. Having heard the agonisingly sad circumstances surrounding their deaths, the Coroner had taken little time to decide that it was appropriate to do so. Chris had engaged the services of a local, family run funeral directors. They had laid his mum to rest all of those years ago and had offered for Chris to spend some time alone with Linda and Joe in the chapel of rest in the basement of their building on the day before the funeral. Chris had initially baulked at the idea, but as the days wore on he softened his stance. On the morning of the eve of the funerals his mind was made up. They were to have one last family meeting, just the three of them.

After a night of broken sleep, contemplating what he would say to them, Chris walked downstairs to find Trevor eating breakfast. Trevor had correctly guessed that Chris would take up the offer to visit Linda and Joe.

"You look great, son," he said. Chris was wearing smart jeans and a shirt that Linda had bought him for his 40th birthday. She had always loved that shirt. He was carrying Joe's favourite book. He had shaved for the first time in weeks and was wearing aftershave that Joe had chosen for Father's Day just a couple of months before.

"Thanks dad," Chris replied. His outward appearance of normality concealed the internal tension that was afflicting him. He knew that seeing Joe and Linda was going to be tough. He knew that the funerals would be even tougher. And then what? The inquests. A criminal case pending against Andrew and possibly Sophie. He couldn't even think about those names without feeling anger rising within him.

He couldn't eat breakfast. He hadn't eaten much since Linda had died and his weight had dropped noticeably. He looked at his dad. Trevor had actually begun to look better since he had moved in with Chris, as if being with company was a better medicine than the rounds of gruelling chemotherapy he was going through. He had put on the weight that Chris had lost. Chris paced the kitchen until it was time to go to the funeral directors, nervous energy suppressing the general feelings of malaise he had been suffering. He left thirty minutes early, sure that they would understand him being there before his appointed time.

It didn't matter that he got there early, however, as he sat outside in his car for twenty minutes, summoning up the courage to enter. His desire to see Linda and Joe was tempered by the fact that it was going to be his last time alone with them. He remembered all of the happy times that they had experienced as a family of three. Now he was alone. Sure, he was reunited with his dad, but for how long, he wondered.

It was now or never, he thought. He opened the car door and slowly walked towards the entrance to the Funeral Directors. His hand was shaking as he pushed the door open and he felt sweat forming on his forehead.

"Hi Chris," Lucy said. She was the funeral directors owner, and had been working closely with Chris on planning the funeral. It had been her suggestion for Chris to come in to see Linda and Joe, and she had made sure that there were no other appointments that morning to avoid any distractions or interruptions. "I've got everything ready for you and you've got as long as you need with them."

"Thank you so much," said Chris. He knew how much effort Lucy had put in to the preparations and he really did appreciate it.

"I've got to tell you, Chris, that Linda's coffin is closed," Lucy continued. "Her face and head took most of the impact from when she fell so I didn't want that image to be your last memory of her. Is that okay?"

Chris had already been warned that Linda's body had sustained terrible injuries during the fall. Mike had been providing him with regular updates about the investigation and it had fallen to him to provide Chris with the results of both of the post mortem examinations.

"I guessed it would be closed," he said sadly. "I guess it's better that way."

Lucy led him to the top of the stairs leading down to the chapel of rest and opened the door.

"They're down there waiting for you," she said. "I've put on some music for you. Just turn it off if you want to. And, honestly, please take as long as you need. When you're finished, you don't need to come and find me if you don't want to. Just make your way out if you need to." She leant towards Chris and squeezed his arm affectionately. Chris nodded and smiled weakly at her, then cautiously walked down the steps. Lucy shut the door quietly behind him.

Chris heard soft music playing in the background and the air was scented with a sweet perfume. Candles were flickering on the shelves around the room. It was perfect, he thought. Total and utter serenity.

And then he saw them. Two coffins, side by side. One open, one closed. One full length, the other half the size. His family. His feet seemed rooted to the spot but he forced himself to shuffle towards them. Tiny steps, but progress nonetheless, until he stood beside them. He looked at Joe. His boy. He looked entirely at peace. His face was so pale that his freckles seemed to shine. His hair had been washed and brushed, a side parting just how Chris had always liked it. There was no evidence of the trauma of the post mortem, and no signs of damage from how he had died. He just looked like he was sleeping. He had been dressed in his school uniform. He had always loved school and Chris remembered how smart he had always looked at the start of the school year. He had bought a new uniform especially for Joe to wear now. He looked every bit the boy who Chris had been so proud of in life.

Joe's hands had been placed on his stomach, his left hand covering his right, which in turn had a single white rose underneath it. Chris gently took hold of Joe's left hand. It was icy cold. Chris knew that it would be, but he still instinctively flinched. Rigor mortis had long since passed and Joe's hand fell softly into Chris'. It still fitted like a glove, Chris thought.

"Hi mate," Chris said quietly. "Daddy's here." Chris knew there wouldn't be a response, but he had so many things to talk to Joe about. He interlocked his fingers with Joe's, just how Joe had always done to him. He felt his eyes filling with tears but he was resolute in his determination to get through this without breaking down. He owed them that much.

"I'm so sorry mate. I'm sorry that you had to go through that on your own. I hope mummy has found you and that you're together somewhere now and that you're happy. You look after her for me, won't you mate?" He felt tears falling. He couldn't stop them. His voice quivered but he continued. "You look good mate, just like you're having one of those really nice naps that you love. Make sure you have sweet dreams, won't you? I've brought your favourite book with me. I know that mummy reads it best, but do you mind if I have a go?"

He gently placed Joe's hand back on his stomach, and took the book from his bag. He opened it to the first page and began reading. The words flowed, bringing back so many memories of him having read it to Joe on his bed, and also of hearing Linda read it many times as well. He didn't want it to end, but inevitably it did.

"I hope you liked that mate," Chris whispered softly to Joe. He leant over him and kissed him on his forehead. "Bye son. Daddy will see you soon."

He turned his attention to the closed coffin. A photo of Linda adorned the top of it. It was from their wedding and she had a glass of fizz in her hand, a huge smile plastered over her face. Exactly how Chris would remember her whenever he shut his eyes, he thought. He put aside any thoughts of the broken woman inside the coffin. He simply had a promise to make to her before he left.

"Hi love," he said. His voice was stronger now. "I know why you did what you did and I don't blame you. Look after our boy for me, won't you? I know you will." He stared at the photo. Their wedding day had been a special one, full of love and laughter. "The police are still looking into what happened. I promise you, Linda, I promise you that they won't get away with it."

He turned and marched out of the chapel. He had said what he needed to say and done what he needed to do. He didn't say goodbye to Lucy, instead he walked straight to his car and sat in the driver's seat, waiting for his heart rate to return to a normal level. He closed his eyes and pictured Joe lying there, so calm and restful. His life had been stolen from him. He breathed deeply, trying to quell the anger rising within. Eventually, he felt calm enough to drive.

He spent the rest of the day sitting on his bed, contemplating the funeral. He knew there would be a lot of people there. He wasn't sure that he could face a big group of people, but he knew that he had to. Trevor came in to see him several times but he could tell that Chris just needed time to himself, to be alone before he was thrust into the public glare where he would be looked at and talked about sympathetically. He knew it was going to happen. He just hoped that he could cope with it.

He slept relatively well that night, his mind allowing him temporary respite from the impending trauma of the funeral. He woke after dawn and walked to the bathroom where he stood with his eyes shut under a hot shower until his skin began to wrinkle. He shaved again. Twice in two days, he thought. He dressed in a beige suit, with a pink tie. No black today. Instead, innocence and vibrancy.

Trevor was already downstairs, dressed in a grey suit and also with a pink tie. He had been out to buy a new suit especially for the funeral, his old ones only fitting his pre-cancer physique.

"Good morning son," he said sombrely. While Chris had managed some sleep, Trevor had managed none and his eyes told the story of a cancer-ridden man suffering the effects of fatigue.

"Morning dad," Chris replied. He was trying to portray himself as a man in control, when really he felt anything but. He had asked for the funeral to be early in the day as he didn't want to spend the whole day waiting for it. He was glad he had. "The car will be here soon," he said.

They waited in silence, both of them welcoming the chance to collect their thoughts and prepare for what was to come.

Trevor hadn't known either Linda or Joe but his affection for them had grown without limit from all of the memories and stories that Chris had shared with him. He knew that today wasn't in any way about him, however. His self appointed mandate was to be there in a supporting capacity for Chris, to keep a close eye on him and to paternally guide him through the day as best he could.

The silence was interrupted by the front door bell. Chris took a deep breath in, and then walked out of the house with Trevor following closely behind.

Three vehicles were waiting for them outside the house. The hearse at the front was escorting Linda, the middle hearse Joe, and the vehicle at the back was there for Chris and Trevor. Chris took a second to look at Linda and Joe. It would be the last time that they would be at the house, and the last time that he would have with them without the intrusion of a crowd of mourners. He silently mouthed 'I love you' to them both, then went and sat in his appointed vehicle.

The journey to the Crematorium took only ten minutes. Again, silence. Nothing needed to be said between Chris and Trevor. Chris kept his eyes firmly fixed on the procession ahead of them, Joe's coffin visible through the rear window of the hearse in front of them. Members of the public stopped and stared as the cortege passed. Trevor noticed several people openly crying. It had been big news locally.

The Crematorium sat on public grounds, and the driveway leading to it was long and winding. As the three vehicles arrived, Chris was stunned to see that it was fully lined with people. Strangers. Well wishers. The tragedies had resonated with so many and they wanted to pay their respects. Amidst the depth of Chris' grief, he felt gratitude beyond compare.

The vehicles slowly approached the Crematorium and came to a gentle stop outside. Chris and Trevor got out of their vehicle and Trevor placed his arm around his son while they watched as the coffins were taken from the hearses. Chris began to silently weep, his head buried into Trevor's shoulder. Trevor led him inside the chapel, guiding his son to his seat at the front of the room. Chris kept his eyes shut. The utter silence told him that crowds of eyes were upon him. He sat and bowed his head, unable to lift it, unwilling to show himself until he had regained his composure. The Funeral March began and the congregation rose. The piercing chords of Chopin's masterpiece tore through Chris, so much that he grasped for Trevor's hand. His dad was right there next to him, waiting for exactly that.

The coffins were carried down the middle aisle of the chapel, Joe first, then Linda. Chris looked to his left as they drew level with him, and then kept them in his sight as they were gently placed next to each other to the left of the lectern where the celebrant was to speak from. Six white roses on Joe's white coffin. Linda in a beautiful oak veneer coffin, adorned with pink and red roses. Innocence and vibrancy. Chris shut his eyes again, and let the last few bars of music wash over him. He felt more at peace. After their journey to the Crematorium, Linda and Joe were now together again, never to be parted.

It was a short but beautiful service. Chris didn't look around once, but he could hear the muffled tears of many of those sitting in the rows behind him. He felt comforted by the thought that Linda and Joe had touched so many people. The words of the celebrant passed him by, so wrapped up was he in his own reflections and state of mourning. He did, however, hear one thing that resonated with him. "A candle that burns twice as bright, burns half as long." Appropriate for Linda, he thought. Not so much for Joe. Half a life would have been a blessing for him.

The funeral ended and the congregation was asked to stand. This was the bit that Chris had been dreading the most. He knew what was about to happen, and so it started. He watched with heavy tears as a curtain was slowly pulled across the entire width of the chapel, shielding the coffins from view as they made their way to be cremated. Chris couldn't bear to watch, but he refused to shift his gaze until it was done.

"Goodbye," he whispered, so softly that even Trevor didn't hear him.

Chris bowed his head and turned and walked out of the chapel, past rows of mourners who were looking at him sympathetically. He didn't make eye contact with any of them. He gulped down lungfuls of fresh air and took in the scene. It was such a tranquil setting. There were a lot of people around, but a feeling of peace permeated the air. Then, Chris saw him. Andrew. He was keeping his distance, but it was definitely him.

Chris stood for a few seconds, unable to believe that he was here. The feeling of tranquility and peace had been shattered. Chris ran towards him. All of the pent up anger and fury was in danger of spilling out. Chris got to within five metres of Andrew when Mike appeared and grabbed hold of Chris, forming a barrier between him and Andrew. Mike had been at the funeral out of sight, afraid that something like this might happen.

"What the fuck are you doing here?" Chris screamed. His eyes were crazed and his body shook with rage.

Andrew didn't say anything, and Mike was struggling to hold Chris back. "Get out of here, now!" Mike shouted at Andrew.

"I'm sorry," Andrew said softly. His eyes were bloodshot and his cheeks were red.

"GO!" Mike shouted. Andrew turned and walked away briskly.

"You did this you wanker, you murdered my family," Chris screamed as Andrew retreated. "You'll get what's coming to you!"

CHAPTER 18

Things had been tough for Andrew since he had been bailed from the police station. Following his arrest and interview with DS Willmott he had got home to face further questions from Sophie. He had explained to her what had happened at the police station, withholding nothing about the content of the interview. He knew that it would likely come out into the public domain anyway when it went to court or at the inquest. In his mind, he was going to be charged with an offence and would likely go to jail for what he had done. Still, he maintained his story that he had not seen Joe when he had been in the sea. His lie was too far developed to be able to change or retract it now.

Sophie had initially seemed sceptical but blind loyalty had persuaded her to accept his version of events as the truth, despite the DNA evidence to the contrary. She didn't want or need any more complications in her life. Things were hard enough as it was.

Andrew had gone back to work in the week following Linda's suicide. He had put it off for over a week and he needed to finish the extension on the bungalow that he had been working on. There was only a few days work left until the job was completed, and the money that he had earned had already been spent covering that month's outgoings. He had no other work scheduled and was worrying all the time about covering the next month of bills.

He had been struggling to sleep. Joe still haunted him when he closed his eyes. On the rare occasion when he did manage to fall into a deep sleep, he would inevitably wake in a sweat, dragged from his rest by a nightmare of the sea. Or of Joe. Or, more recently, of Linda.

Maria went back to school on the Monday after Linda had died. She had spent the week at home and, after the nightmares of that first night without Joe, seemed to have developed no ill effects as a result. Andrew and Sophie hoped that she had simply pushed the trauma out of her mind, that she had been too young and immature to process it so she had simply erased it from her memory. Sophie had been in close contact with the school to help facilitate Maria's reintegration back into school life, and plans had been put in place to manage any issues that might have arisen. None of them had needed to be implemented. It was like Maria had never been away. She seemed to have happily settled straight back in to the familiar and comfortable routine that school brings to a young child, content to be back with her teacher and her classmates. She didn't ask about or address Joe's absence. It was almost as if he hadn't existed.

Andrew had been keen to do the school run as much as he could, even though Sophie wasn't working and was available to do it. He wanted to spend as much time as he possibly could with his daughter, having seen how fragile and fleeting life was and how cruelly it could be extinguished. He knew it was likely that rumours had spread amongst the parents of the students and he had developed a sense that people were treating him differently. He wasn't sure if it was a mild form of paranoia or if it was genuine, but he felt as if people stopped what they were doing and looked at him when he passed them, sometimes whispering in hushed voices. He was sure that word couldn't have yet got out about the DNA or the interview, but if it hadn't then this was surely a taste of what was to come.

After Maria had successfully completed two weeks back at school without issue, Andrew collected her and took her home. He sensed that something was wrong as soon as he saw Sophie's face.

"Go and pop the TV on, princess," he said to Maria, ushering her into the front room. Sophie gestured for him to follow her into the kitchen.

"What's up, love?" He asked with panic in his voice. She wore an expression that he couldn't interpret and he was worried that something had happened to their unborn baby.

"I heard today, it's the funeral next week," she replied. "They're having it together, Linda and Joe."

Andrew sat down at the kitchen table. While he knew that the funeral was going to take place at some point soon, hearing that it had a firm time and place still took the wind out of him. He had agonised during those sleepless nights about how they should deal with the funerals. It hadn't occurred to him that both Linda and Joe would be laid to rest at the same time.

"What should we do?" He asked, almost rhetorically. He knew that he shouldn't do anything. He was on bail and still under investigation for his involvement in the death of Joe.

"I hadn't really thought about it until now," Sophie said. "Should we send flowers or something? I just don't know."

The question hung in the air, unanswered.

"Let's think about it," Andrew finally said. He got up and walked into the front room where he picked Maria up and held her in his arms, squeezing her just a little bit tighter than normal.

The funeral dilemma remained unspoken about. No flowers were arranged and no messages of condolence were sent. Neither Andrew nor Sophie could adequately form words to convey their sorrow at the loss of Joe and Linda, nor did they expect any words to be welcomed by Chris even if they could.

The morning of the funeral arrived and Andrew took Maria to school as usual. Work had completely dried up for him and he had planned to spend the day ringing around old acquaintances to see if there was any site work available. No work meant no money and things were becoming critical in that respect. At the school gate he noticed that a lot of the parents were wearing clothes with a distinct colour theme. White. Pink. Red. The hushed voices seemed amplified. The stares seemed more penetrating. The atmosphere, normally benign and with a sense of understating and sympathy, seemed more charged with emotion and tinged with anger. Andrew dropped Maria off and quickly made his way back to the car, keen to avoid speaking to, or looking at, anyone.

He locked the car doors and took deep breaths to slow down his racing heart. He took a tissue from his pocket and wiped the sweat from his forehead. A battle was raging between the rational and irrational parts of his mind, the irrational telling him that everyone knew what he had done, and the rational telling him that there was no way that they could know.

A conflict was also developing between his mind and his heart. His mind was telling him that there was no way that he should even think about going to the funeral. His heart was telling him that, if he ever wanted to get closure from this mess, then he simply had to go. He had to punish himself and see them laid to rest, to see the hurt that he had caused. Only then could he begin to atone for his actions. His heart was winning the battle.

He drove home, hoping that Sophie would bring some reason to the matter. He was sure that she wouldn't let him go, he thought. Her car wasn't on the driveway.

'Gone shopping, and then going for coffee,' the note on the kitchen table said. He was on this own.

He went upstairs and got changed into a light blue suit, and dug out a pink tie that Sophie had bought him years ago. He seldom wore smart clothes and the suit hadn't aged well. It needed an iron but he didn't have time. He put on a flat cap and sunglasses, hoping that this would be enough to disguise him from the people at the funeral who might know him. He had no intention of going into the chapel or even getting close to anyone else. Avoiding Chris was obviously essential. He just wanted to be in the grounds, to see Linda and Joe, and to hopefully begin the process of ridding himself of the grief and guilt that would otherwise eat him alive.

He parked a long way from the Crematorium and walked at a distance from other mourners, keeping his eyes firmly on the ground. He couldn't believe how many people were there. The road leading into the Crematorium was packed with people and vehicles, and the private driveway was lined with mourners. Many of them were sobbing, awash with emotion, consumed by grief.

He had caused this, he thought.

He slipped in at the back of a group of people of a similar age to himself, none of whom he knew, and walked behind them. He still didn't look up. He felt safer attaching himself to a group. Hidden in plain sight, he thought. The driveway safely negotiated, he separated himself from the group and found a quiet spot on the grassy area outside the chapel, close to a tree. A silence fell across the grounds. Andrew looked to his left and saw three vehicles approaching slowly, coming to a stop outside the Chapel of Rest.

He saw Chris get out of the third car, followed by an older man who he didn't know. He almost couldn't watch as Linda and Joe were unloaded from the other two vehicles. He forced himself to look.

This is what you're here for, he thought.

The older man had his arm around Chris, who was now crying. Andrew wanted to walk away. He wanted to scream. He wanted to do anything, anything, but be here to witness this. Instead, he looked on as Chris was escorted into the chapel by the older man, followed soon after by the coffins containing Linda and Joe. Andrew breathed uneasily.

An eerie atmosphere descended on the Crematorium grounds as the doors to the chapel were shut. Many people remained outside, unable to witness proceedings inside but keen to stay to pay their respects. Whispered conversations took place all around Andrew but he kept his head down, keen not to engage with anyone. So far he had remained anonymous.

He got lost in his thoughts, repeating the questions he had oft asked himself. Why hadn't he taken the coat off in the sea, why had they gone to the beach in the first place, why, why, why. Minutes passed by as he silently berated himself, working up such deep admonishment of himself that he felt the tears falling from behind his sunglasses. He momentarily forgot his surroundings and took off his sunglasses, then looked at his watch. Half an hour had passed.

The service must surely be over, he thought.

Then Andrew saw him. Chris. Staring right at him from just in front of the chapel doors. Their eyes locked on each other and Andrew felt his blood run cold.

CHAPTER 19

DS Willmott had to read the email several times before she was able to process the content of it.

CPS Charging Decision:

Case of Andrew Wicks:

Investigating Officer: DS Willmott

Deciding Prosecutor: Jenny Atherton

I have reviewed the case file in relation to the death of Joseph Jamieson and the associated paperwork relating to the arrest and interview of Andrew Wicks. I have given full consideration to the circumstances surrounding the death, and at present do not feel that there is sufficient evidence to charge the suspect. There is no evidence of wilful neglect when referring to the Prosecutor guide for public prosecutions. It is the opinion of this office that this was a tragic accident. The DNA evidence, while showing that the suspect and the deceased came into contact, does not in any way provide evidence of child abuse. It may show that his account is not true but it doesn't come close to meeting the threshold for charging with the offence for which he was arrested and interviewed.

Final Decision: No further action.

DS Willmott was stunned, though she wasn't surprised. She had spent several fruitless shifts on the beach trying to locate the owner of the dog that had jumped up at Sophie, questioning plenty of dog walkers but finding no witnesses. She had tried to arrange for Maria to be interviewed about the events surrounding Joe's death but had met with resistance from Andrew and Sophie, and she had managed to interview Sophie but it had not thrown up any other lines of enquiry. The issues surrounding interviewing Maria were complex. She was a six year old child who had experienced a traumatic event. DS Willmott could compel her to provide evidence, but it was to be used as a tactic of last resort. She had decided to seek CPS guidance prior to deciding whether or not to do so, but the email she had just received had resolved the issue for her.

Andrew Wicks was to face no formal sanction for his involvement in the death of Joe Jamieson.

DS Willmott pulled the case file onto her desk and flipped it open. She had affixed a photo of Joe to the underside of the file to remind her of the life that had been lost every time she opened it. His happy little face sent pangs of guilt racing through DS Willmott's body. She had failed him, she thought. She had made a promise to him and she hadn't made good on it. She had told him that she would find out what had happened. She hadn't. Instead, she had let a lie present itself as the truth, a lie that would now and forever remain unchallenged.

She buried her head in her hands, aware of the potential implications of this CPS decision. She had attended the funeral of Joe and Linda, something that was common practice for police officers investigating a suspicious death. She had been with Mike when they had seen Chris charge towards Andrew. She had been a bit slower than Mike to react, but had witnessed at close quarters the depth of anger that Chris had expressed towards Andrew. If Mike hadn't have intercepted Chris so quickly, she knew that the fallout would have been catastrophic.

There were two things that she needed to do: one of them, on the phone;. the second, in person.

She took out her mobile phone and dialled Andrew's number. He answered almost immediately.

"Hello Andrew, it's DS Willmott," she said, her voice emotionless and reserved.

"Hiya," he replied. He was due to return to the police station on bail that week and had been nervously waiting for any news relating to it.

"I'll keep this short, Andrew," she said. "The CPS have advised that you are to face no charges in relation to Joe's death. You don't need to come back to the police station later in the week and I will be cancelling your bail notice."

Andrew didn't say anything.

"There will be an inquest, Andrew," she continued. "I'll be presenting all of the evidence that I have gathered there."

She closed her eyes, and pictured Joe lying on the beach, a storm raging around him. Her voice lowered. "I know you didn't tell me the truth, Andrew. I know something else happened out there. You've got to live with that. Just a word of warning though..."

She paused to choose her words carefully.

"The truth always comes out."

She hung up without waiting for a response.

That was the easy job done, she thought. The next was going to be much more difficult. She hadn't had contact with Chris since the funeral. All investigation updates and welfare needs were being addressed by Mike. DS Willmott dialled his number.

"Hi Mike, it's Sue," she said. "It's bad news. CPS have NFA'd Joe's death. Can I come with you to tell Chris about it?"

Mike was on a rest day but had known that a result from the CPS was imminent. "I'll be with you in half an hour," he said.

He was in DS Willmott's office twenty-five minutes later. She drove them from the police station to Chris' house. On the way they agonised over what to tell him and how to frame the information. Mike hadn't told Chris anything about the DNA evidence, fearing that it would push him over the edge.

"What are we going to tell him then?" Mike asked.

"He deserves to know everything," DS Willmott replied. "It's all going to come out at inquest anyway. Why should we withhold it from him?"

"You saw him at the funeral, Sue," Mike said. He knew that Chris deserved the truth. He just didn't know if he would be able to accept it rationally.

Neither of them said anything and the rest of the journey passed in silence.

Mike knocked on the door. Trevor answered the door. Mike hadn't seen him since the funeral several weeks before.

"Hi Trevor, is Chris about?" Mike asked. Trevor looked like he had taken a turn for the worse. He had lost the weight that he had gained since moving in with Chris, and he looked even paler and more gaunt than when Mike had picked him up from his house weeks before.

"He's still in bed," Trevor said quietly. "Hang on, I'll go and get him for you. Make yourselves at home."

Trevor turned around and slowly made his way upstairs, each step requiring more effort than the last. Mike and DS Willmott went into the front room and sat down on the sofa. They could smell the stale aroma of a night of excess, and it hadn't emanated from Trevor. Five minutes later, Chris walked into the room. Mike maintained a placid demeanour, but he was shocked by the person standing before him. Chris appeared to be a shadow of the man he knew. He had two weeks worth of untidy stubble on his face, his eyes were red and bloodshot, his hair was wild and it was clear where the musty smell of alcohol was coming from. His clothes were stained and grubby. Trevor stood in the doorway, leaning uneasily against the doorframe.

'Hi mate," Mike said cheerily. He was there to deliver bad news, but he didn't want to speak sombrely.

"You're here to tell me something, I guess?" Chris replied. His breath smelt rancid.

"We are," DS Willmott said. Her tone was more businesslike. "And it's not good news I'm afraid Chris. The CPS have decided to take no further action against Andrew. We tried. I tried. But they have said that it is just a tragic accident."

Chris was breathing deeply. In his head, he was counting to ten. He got to four before he vented.

"How the fuck did they decide that?" He shouted. "He killed my boy and, what, he's going to get away with it? What evidence did you send them, for Christ's sake?"

DS Willmott felt conflicted. She had resolved in her mind that Chris should have the whole, unvarnished truth. He would find out about it eventually anyway. But was it appropriate for it to be disclosed to him in his current state? She had to make a decision on the spot.

"There was good evidence, Chris," she said softly. "I thought it was, anyway. This may come as a shock to you, and I really do want you to remain calm when I tell you this. Promise me, Chris?"

Chris sat down on the sofa next to Mike. He held his head in his hands, his fingers locked and his knuckles white. "Tell me," he whispered.

"Joe's DNA was found on the jacket Andrew wore into the sea. The basic explanation from our perspective is that Andrew came into contact with Joe in the sea. Andrew has denied it throughout. When I challenged him on it, he went no comment. As I've said, this will all come out at the inquest, it's just courtesy to you as a dad and as a copper that we're telling you now."

Chris pulled his hands slowly down his face, stretching his eyes open as he did. Mike noticed that he was shaking, barely perceptibly, but still shaking nonetheless.

"And Sophie? Maria? What did they say?" Chris asked.

"Sophie's account was nothing different to Andrew's," DS Willmott said. "Maria… Well, we haven't got a statement from her. Andrew and Sophie wouldn't allow access and now that CPS have said it was an accident I'm not going to be looking to do it I'm afraid. I know you don't want to hear that but I want to be honest with you."

Chris looked at DS Willmott, staring into her eyes. She could feel the burning sense of outrage within him, the perception of injustice that had befallen Joe. "I think you've said all you need to say," he said coldly. He got up from the sofa and marched out of the room. They heard him stomping up the stairs and a door slam. Trevor shuffled into the front room and sat in the seat just vacated by Chris.

"He's been drinking, you know," Trevor said. His voice seemed weak.

"Thought so," said Mike. "How have things been?"

"Up and down," Trevor replied. "Mostly down to be honest. He'll have a good day where we look at pictures and chat nicely them, maybe even get out for a walk or something. Then he'll have a couple of bad days to bring him right back down. Yesterday was a bad day. Looks like today is going to be as well."

You probably heard everything that we said to him," DS Willmott said. "It'll be a massive shock to him, obviously. What we don't need, for his sake, is or him to create any problems with Andrew or Sophie. The process isn't over yet. We've still got the inquest where the coroner will make a ruling and we don't want to jeopardise any of that. Do you think he'll be okay?"

"I'll keep an eye on him," said Trevor.

"Any problems then you just call 999 okay?" Mike said, as he stood up from the sofa. He said goodbye to Trevor and walked into the hallway with DS Willmott. They could both hear a faint, sobbing noise coming from upstairs. They quietly let themselves out of the front door and got back into the car.

"What do you reckon?" DS Willmott asked.

"I reckon he's on the edge," Mike replied. "The old man hasn't got long left either. What a mess."

"Any ideas?" DS Willmott asked.

"I'll get Andrew's address tagged for any calls to be treated as urgent," Mike said. "There's not much else we can do to be honest."

"Do you think he'll try anything?" DS Willmott asked, her voice quieter than before.

"Honestly?" Mike replied softly. "He's lost everything. Nothing would surprise me."

CHAPTER 20

Chris sat on his bed, brooding. Joe's DNA on Andrew's coat. Andrew refusing to answer questions about it. Hiding behind a 'no comment' interview. Chris had seen plenty of guilty people get away with things in the past - it was the nature of the British judicial system that guilty people sometimes went free in order to ensure that innocent people weren't wrongfully convicted. But this was different. The CPS were effectively saying that no offence had been committed, that Andrew and Sophie had not neglected Joe. Something had happened in the sea for Joe's DNA to be on Andrew's coat - DS Willmott had made that clear. As it stood, however, conjecture and speculation were all that Chris could rely on. He seemed to have no route to the truth, and that was the most bitter pill for him to swallow.

His mind was working overtime with different thoughts and theories developing apace. He realised there was no rational explanation for the DNA that fitted with Andrew's account of what had happened. None at all.

Chris couldn't provide himself with an answer to what had happened, so he resolved to go and find one.

He peeled off the clothes that he had been wearing for days and went to the bathroom where he looked at himself in the mirror. His reflection sent a chill down his spine. He turned on the shower and spent an age under the scalding water, almost burning his skin in an attempt to cleanse himself of the grime that had accumulated since he had last washed. He couldn't remember when that was. He eventually finished showering, and then closely shaved away the weeks of untidy growth that had amassed on his face and neck. He again looked in the mirror. Better, he thought. By no means good, but better.

Back in his room, he dressed himself. Dark chinos and a short sleeved shirt, and a pair of sunglasses in his pocket. He pulled out a winter coat from his wardrobe and put it in a rucksack. He'd need that but he didn't want to stand out. His chinos were now so loose that he needed to punch another hole in his belt to keep them up. He brushed his hair back. It needed a cut, but now that it was clean it looked presentable, he thought. He shouldn't have any trouble getting there.

He stood on the landing, waiting for his dad to go to the kitchen. He needed to get out of the house without Trevor obstructing his path - he didn't want any conflict with him. He knew that Trevor's health was rapidly deteriorating and he didn't want to put him in harm's way. After a few minutes he heard Trevor filling up the kettle. Perfect timing.

He almost ran down the stairs and burst through the front door, not stopping as he made his way down the pavement and disappearing before Trevor had even had a chance to react. Time to get those answers, he thought. He didn't take his car with him. He knew that there were ANPR cameras en route to his destination. It was a journey better taken on foot. Besides, a walk would give him a chance to strategise.

A sense of calmness washed over him, something that he hadn't felt for weeks. He was going to find out what had happened to his boy. Where DS Willmott had failed, he was determined to succeed.

In the distance behind him, he heard his name. It was his dad, screaming for him to return. He felt guilty, knowing the amount of pain it must be causing his dad to scream like that, the amount of energy it would take out of him and the toll it would take on his wellbeing. But Chris knew that he had to find out what had happened. Everything else was secondary.

Trevor had been sitting in the front room, shocked at the information that had been provided by DS Willmott. He had known that the merest hint of foul play in Joe's death was something that Chris would be unable to deal with. DS Willmott had pretty much said that it was definite. He didn't know how Chris was going to react, but he knew that a reaction was inevitable. He heard movement upstairs. Chris, walking to the bathroom. He heard the shower turn on and he felt relief. Relief that Chris was showering. Trevor had not said anything to him, but Chris' hygiene had been poor and the whole house was beginning to smell. His shower seemed to last an age, so long that Trevor was walking up the stairs to check on him when he heard it turn off. He quietly slipped back downstairs and into the front room, waiting to hear the familiar creak of the floorboards directly above him, indicating that Chris was back in his room. He'd make them a nice cup of tea when Chris was dressed, he thought.

Soon after, he heard that creaking. He heard drawers being opened and closed, and Chris' wardrobe doors sliding shut. He waited a minute and then stood up, making his way slowly to the kitchen where he filled the kettle and turned it on. He was hoping that a new man would come down the stairs shortly and that they could sit down together to confront the tragedies that had befallen them.

Instead, he heard Chris thunder down the stairs and storm out of the front door, the door slamming with such force that the reverberations echoed around the kitchen where Trevor was standing. Trevor froze momentarily. He rushed for the front door as fast as his cancer-ridden body would allow him, but when he opened it there was just silence. No sign of Chris. His car still on the driveway, and no indication of where he had gone.

Trevor tried to call for him, but his voice felt weak and ailing. He breathed deeply, calling on reserves of strength that he had long since felt had been lost. He dug deep within himself, and somehow found conviction and power in his voice. He screamed for Chris to come back. He begged for his return, fearing for Chris' safety and, to a much lesser extent, Andrew's. His cries hung in the air, but ultimately remained unanswered.

Chris was gone.

Trevor rushed back inside. DS Willmott and Mike had not been gone for more than half an hour and their advice was still ringing in his ears. He took out his phone and dialled 999.

Chris heard the wailing of sirens in the distance as he walked. He guessed correctly that Trevor had called the police, but also surmised that patrols would be dispatched to Andrew and Sophie's house. That suited him. He wasn't going there. He continued walking, happy in the knowledge that the sirens weren't getting any closer to him. He pulled his sunglasses out and put them on. Having seen himself in the mirror earlier, he doubted that anyone would recognise him anyway, but he didn't want to take any chances.

Finally, he reached his destination.

Beachbrook Primary School. No sirens here.

It was break time and the sound of children playing made Chris' heart ache. Joe used to be one of them. Now, he was just a memory, a footnote in the school's history. Chris stood and watched, scanning the playgrounds for one child in particular. One who might be able to give him the answers that he needed. Someone who might've witnessed first-hand exactly what had happened in the sea. And someone, with the pure mind of a child, unable to distort the truth in the cynical way that Andrew had. He was looking for Maria.

And then he saw her. She was playing on her own in the playground, at the furthest point from him and close to the school building.

He took the thick coat from his rucksack. School security had been beefed up nationwide following a number of high profile incidents, and Beachbrook Primary School had been no different. In addition to automated gates controlling access to vehicular traffic, large fences with anti-intrusion measures similar to barbed wire had been erected around the perimeter of the school. A simple way to breach these, Chris knew, was to throw a heavy coat over them and then climb over that. No injury to your hands that way. He knew, however, that he needed to be quick. It was likely to cause a commotion very quickly.

He expertly slipped over the fence, and silently stalked his way to Maria. He was confident in his stride, trying his best to blend in as a school employee and not as a trespasser. He was yards away from her. Feet away from her. Then, inches away.

Maria looked at Chris. She knew who he was, and the look on his face scared her. She began to shake.

"Hello Maria," Chris said calmly. He may have been composed but his voice was ice cold. He knew he didn't have much time to get what he needed.

Maria didn't reply. She was still staring at him, a look of terror spreading over her face. Her mind was starting to connect the dots. Vague memories of the sea were beginning to seep into her subconscious.

"What happened to Joe, Maria?" Chris asked directly. His voice was still soft and he allowed himself a glance around. There was still no adult activity near him. He had, so far, not been noticed.

An explosion of images were filling Maria's mind. A mixture of these memories and the emotions that she had kept repressed for all of the weeks leading up until this point were suddenly combining to wreak havoc on her unprepared and immature psyche. She didn't answer Chris. Instead, she lost control of her bladder. Urine began to seep down her legs.

"Answer me," Chris said to her. His tone was now both menacing and desperate.

"Excuse me, what are you doing?" A voice from the other side of the playground shouted. Salvation for Maria. Too late, however, to stop the mental damage that had been inflicted on her. She was crying now.

Chris knew his chance had gone. He turned and marched back across the pavement, his head bowed and his pace quick. Various teachers were congregating in his path. In the distance, he could hear the wailing of a siren, and it was getting closer. He broke first into a jog, then a sprint as he made his way back to the boundary fence where he had gained entry. His coat was still on the fence, his exit seemed as assured as his entrance had been. He mounted the fence as the sirens grew louder and harsher. They were close now.

He clung to the top of the fence, his coat protecting his hands from getting savaged but also marginalising the amount of traction he could gain to hoist himself over. He scrabbled to pull himself up. The sirens were deafening now.

He dragged himself up until his upper torso was clear of the fence line. He got no further. The congregated teachers had sprung into action and collectively pulled him down from the fence. The police car arrived on cue, screeching through the school gates that had been left open for them, two police officers bursting from the doors and pinning Chris to the floor. He didn't resist. He had played his hand and, on this occasion, he had lost. Handcuffed and brought to his feet, he looked over to where Maria had been. She wasn't there now, but she knew something. Chris was sure of it. She knew what had happened.

CHAPTER 21

Andrew put the phone down from DS Willmott and sat at the kitchen table, breathing heavily.

"What is it?" Sophie asked. She had been with him when he had answered the phone and had seen the impact that the content of the phone call had had on him.

"They've decided not to prosecute me," Andrew murmured. A range of contrasting and powerful emotions surged through him. Elation. Guilt. Joy. Sorrow. He was happy that he wouldn't be separated from his family through the judicial process, but he had a hollow feeling - that somehow, he was escaping the punishment necessary for him to truly be able to atone for his actions both in the sea and beyond. In many ways, it felt like a pyrrhic victory.

"That's great news!" Sophie said with genuine happiness. It felt like a weight had been lifted from her shoulders. She had been carrying the strain of a pregnancy, a husband under suspicion and the grief of losing her best friend and her son. That grief, albeit in exceptional circumstances, still felt very real. Now that one of the pillars that had been the source of her stress had gone, she hoped the others would be toppled as well. Their future looked brighter now than it had at any point over the past few weeks, she thought.

"I just need a moment," Andrew said, and he got up and went out to the garden. Life had been weighing heavily on his shoulders for weeks now as well. Following the funeral, he had struggled to get out and about. Whereas previously he had only suspected that people had been looking at him and talking about him, now they actually were. Chris' attempts to attack him had been a very public spectacle, one that had been the talk of the town and one that had gathered momentum. It seemed like everyone knew about it and everyone had an opinion on it. Not many of those opinions were in Andrew's favour, and this was before the extent of the evidence even came out.

He was sure that this public sentiment was behind the fact that he hadn't had any work for weeks. It seemed churlish to worry about money when much bigger things were going on in his life, but the bills still needed paying and they were behind on pretty much everything. Reminder letters had started to come in and they couldn't be ignored forever. He just hoped that he could find something in the short term to tide him over. So far, none of his old contacts had seemed willing to give him work on any sites and most of them had seemed short with him when he had contacted them. They knew, he thought.

Sophie came out to join him in the garden.

"Come on, we're going out for breakfast," she said. "You can't hide away forever."

Andrew knew that she was right, but he dreaded the thought of the stares and the whispers. Still, this was his town, he thought. He had to get through it.

They drove to the High Street and parked on the top floor of the multi-storey car park. It was close to their usual cafe of choice. Andrew wore the same sunglasses and flat cap that he had worn to the funeral, keen to avoid being noticed by anyone. It wasn't sunny out.

"Take them off," Sophie instructed, sternly. It wasn't a matter up for discussion. Andrew reluctantly removed both items and threw them in the back of the car. They walked across the car park to the stairs that would take them down to the ground floor. Another couple were standing there, waiting for the lift.

"We'll get the lift," Sophie said. She wasn't doing it to torment Andrew. She was trying to get him used to being around other people. Andrew didn't see it that way. He didn't want to be trapped in a little box with others, even if it was for only seconds.

"Can't we just take the stairs, it'll be quicker?" He pleaded.

"No, the baby is playing up a bit," Sophie replied. The baby wasn't but she knew that he wouldn't be able to argue against that.

Andrew stood in a moody silence until the lift door opened. The couple in front of them were of a similar age but neither Andrew or Sophie knew them. They walked into the lift first and then turned around. Until that point, they hadn't seen Andrew's face. As they did, both of them almost imperceptibly did a double take. They then both immediately averted their gaze, keen to look anywhere apart from in the direction of Andrew and Sophie. Sophie ushered Andrew into the lift and pressed the button for the ground floor.

It was only a journey of three floors down. It took less than thirty seconds. There were only four of them in the lift, two couples that were apparent strangers. The atmosphere that developed in the confines of that metal cube, however, was extraordinary. It was almost tangible, so much that Andrew could nearly taste the resentment and bitterness being emitted from the strangers. He forlornly grabbed Sophie's hand, his palms sweating so much that their hands slipped apart initially. In his panic he squeezed too tightly, causing her to flinch and recoil. She looked at him and saw his distress, but she seemed oblivious to any issues.

The lift doors opened and Andrew burst out, almost hyperventilating.

"He's not good in lifts," Sophie said to the other couple, who both laughed nervously before walking away quickly. The truth was that she had noticed their reaction to him. She knew exactly what had happened but she also knew that if he didn't confront it head on then their life would never get back to any kind of normality.

"Calm down," she said to Andrew gently, while rubbing his back. He was bent over and trying to catch his breath, to regulate his breathing and get his racing heart under control. "I know what happened," she continued. "We'll get through this, I promise you. Would you rather go home?"

"Yes," Andrew blurted out as soon as she had asked the question. He had no appetite, either for food or for socialising.

They slowly walked up the stairs and back to the car. Andrew slumped in the passenger seat as Sophie drove home.

"We'll try again tomorrow, okay love?" She said to him.

Andrew didn't reply.

He sat in the garden, alone, speculating if this was going to be the new normal for him. He wondered if he would forever be the man who everyone looked at and spoke about under their breath, the one who was responsible for the loss of a child. He closed his eyes. Joe stared back at him.

His phone rang. An unknown number. He didn't feel like talking to anyone at the moment. If it was important then they would leave a message. Two minutes later, his voicemail notified him of something in his inbox. It was a message from Mike.

"Hi Andrew. It's Sergeant Adams. This is a courtesy call to tell you we have been to see Mr Jamieson and have told him that you aren't to face any further action in relation to the death of his son." Mike paused for a few seconds and then continued. "We have no indication that anything untoward is going to happen but, after the incident at the funeral, I am advising you to call 999 if Chris turns up at your house or if you feel threatened in any way." Mike had hung up without saying goodbye. He was determined to remain professional but this didn't extend to being personable with Andrew in any way.

Andrew listened to the message several times. There was no indication as to what they had said to Chris, only that he had been informed that there would be no further action taken against him.

The silence of the garden was gently interrupted by wailing in the air. A siren. The noise grew louder as the siren drew closer and closer. The siren was turned off, but was replaced by the noise of tyres squealing as a car skidded to a halt outside the front of Andrew's house. He couldn't see it, but he knew that it was a police car, and he knew why they were there. He just wondered how they had got there before Chris.

Confusion reigned in Andrew's house. Four police cars had turned up but there was no sign of Chris and no-one had any idea where he had gone. DS Willmott and Mike arrived shortly after, having heard the call go out over the air following Trevor's 999 call.

"Have you heard anything at all from Chris?" Mike asked, his voice strained with urgency.

"Nothing," Andrew replied. "I wouldn't expect to, would I?"

"Sarge, you've got to hear this," a Police Officer shouted from out in the street. DS Willmott and Mike both turned around, as the chaos turned to silence. Radios were turned up. The Operator was diverting patrols to another incident.

"Control to all patrols, please respond immediately to Beachbrook Primary School. Subject has been seen at that location and is trespassing on site. No further information."

Everyone in the house heard the call being broadcast. Andrew looked at Sophie, his eyes widening in fear.

'MARIA," he screamed. He ran from the house, grabbing his car keys from the shelf by the front door and joined at the back of the procession of police cars that were making their way on blue lights to the school. He didn't have emergency lights or a siren, but he maintained pace with them, jumping red traffic lights and speeding beyond his driving abilities. Only one thing mattered to him. He had to get to Maria. He hadn't even taken the time to wait for Sophie to join him. She was left to make her own way there, distraught and pregnant.

A sea of blue lights greeted Andrew on his arrival at the school. He got out of his car and ran aimlessly without knowing where he was going. DS Willmott had arrived shortly before him, having jumped in one of the marked police vehicles back at Andrew's house.

"Andrew, over here," she called to him. She was standing at the main entrance to the school building, not far from where Chris had confronted Maria. Andrew ran over to her.

"Where is she?" He shouted. Tears were streaming down his cheeks and he didn't even know if Maria was safe. All he knew was that Chris had been at the school, trespassing.

"Calm down," DS Willmott said firmly. "She's in there," she continued, pointing into the building.

Andrew didn't wait for any further explanation. He barged past DS Willmott and ran into the reception area of the school. He looked around. No sign of Maria. He breathed deeply, and heard someone saying her name.

"Maria, are you alright love?"

The voice was coming from beyond a door that was ajar to the left of him. He ran towards the door and pushed it open.

Finally, he saw her.

The other people in the room seemed to melt into obscurity. All Andrew cared about was Maria, and she was now in front of him, sitting on a chair.

He stepped towards her and then faltered. Something had happened to her. She had a towel wrapped around her legs and he saw her skirt and knickers discarded on the floor behind her. She looked terrified beyond belief, wearing an expression of abject fear that Andrew had not seen before.

"Hiya Princess," Andrew whispered. "Daddy's here now."

"Cuddle Daddy," she whimpered, reaching out her arms to him.

Andrew scooped her up into a tight embrace, squeezing her close to him. He could feel her rapid heartbeat thudding against his chest. He stroked her hair and, slowly, her heart rate began to normalise. He continued to hold her, indifferent to the eyes that were staring at both of them from the growing number of people gathering in the room.

"Andrew, can I borrow you for a minute?" DS Willmott said eventually. Her voice, softer now, was measured so as not to alarm Maria.

"Can it wait?" Andrew replied gruffly. He didn't turn to look at DS Willmott, his attention utterly absorbed by the emotional needs of his daughter.

"Meet me outside when you're ready," DS Willmott said. "Take your time," she added. She recognised the importance of the moment, both to Andrew and Maria.

Andrew did take his time. He continued to hold his daughter until her breathing had calmed and the tension had dissipated from her tiny muscles.

"Andrew, what happened?" Sophie shouted, bursting into the room. She had arrived well after Andrew, not having taken the risks on the road that he had. Andrew put his finger up to his lips. The atmosphere in the room was calm and he wanted to maintain that.

"Look sweetheart, Mummy's here," he whispered to Maria. "How about a big cuddle with her?"

Maria looked around, and stretched her arms out to Sophie. Despite the growing bump in her tummy, there was still plenty of room above for a cuddle with her daughter.

Andrew quietly slipped out of the room. It was his turn now to feel a burning rage inside, to want answers to questions relating to his child. He met DS Willmott in the corridor.

"Where is he?" Andrew asked, his voice shaking with anger.

"Chris has been arrested to prevent a breach of the peace at the moment. It doesn't look like he's actually committed any criminal offences," she replied, knowing that this wouldn't placate Andrew.

She was right.

"Nothing criminal?" He shouted. "Have you seen my daughter? And why the hell is she wearing a towel? Did he try to touch her or something?"

"Trespassing on a school site is a civil offence, Andrew," DS Willmott said. "He was seen talking to Maria. We don't know what about, but she wet herself. He didn't touch her. I can assure you of that."

Andrew leant in close to her. "You're telling me that he can leave her in a state like that and it's not criminal?" He whispered menacingly.

"Steps will be taken to make sure that something like this doesn't happen again," DS Willmott said.

Andrew was still standing close to her. She leaned in even closer. "I guess he's trying to find the truth. Like I said, it will come out eventually." She spoke so quietly that Andrew barely heard her, but her words registered loudly with him.

He stepped away. The confidence and anger that he had confronted DS Willmott with had now gone, replaced with a growing sense of anxiety. He wondered what other depths Chris would sink to in order to get to the truth. If even Maria wasn't off limits, then how far would he go? He turned and walked away from DS Willmott.

"If you get any more problems you know where we are," she called after him. Her voice sounded reassuring, but Andrew knew that her words were hollow.

This was something that he would have to sort out himself.

CHAPTER 22

Chris' shoulder hurt from where he had been pulled down off the fence, and his wrists ached from where the handcuffs had been awkwardly applied behind his back, but as he was taken from the school and escorted to Beachbrook Police Station he felt strangely satisfied that he had achieved something. He had established in his own mind that Maria knew something about what had happened to Joe, something more than Andrew was letting on. Now he just needed to convince DS Willmott to reopen the investigation and to compel Maria to be spoken with about it.

Even though he didn't work in the district, Chris knew Beachbrook Police Station and the staff there well. He remained in handcuffs as he was taken into the Custody Suite, where he stood before a Sergeant who he had dealt with many times before professionally. The Sergeant seemed unaware that it was Chris standing in front of him.

"Name?" The Sergeant said, disinterestedly.

"Christian Jamieson," he replied. The Sergeant suddenly looked interested.

"Chris, is that you?" He asked, squinting at him. Despite Chris having shaved earlier, he looked so gaunt and scruffy haired that he hadn't recognised him.

"Yeah, it's me," Chris replied solemnly.

The Sergeant sighed. Like all of his colleagues, he had followed the events of Chris' life with increasing sympathy over the weeks gone by and he wanted nothing more than to put an arm around Chris and offer him all the support in the world. Unfortunately, he knew that he had a job to do, and that was to remain impartial until the matter for which Chris had been arrested was dealt with.

"Circumstances of the arrest, please," he said to the arresting officer.

"We were called to Beachbrook Primary School following reports of a trespasser on site," the officer began. "Upon arrival, the male here had been detained by staff at the school having confronted a child there about something as yet unknown. Tensions were running high and he has been arrested to prevent a breach of the peace."

The Sergeant looked at Chris. "I don't know why you were there, Chris, but you know that I've got to authorise your detention here so that we can get to the bottom of what has happened and to work out what happens next. You know all of your rights and entitlements so I won't bore you with those. How are you feeling?"

"I've been better," Chris replied. "It was his daughter, the guy who lost my boy. I just wanted to know if she knew anything. He wouldn't let her talk to us officially so I just wanted to ask her."

"You know the score Chris," the Sergeant said, cutting him off. "We can't talk to you about it now. If they need anything from you then they'll interview you but you've only been arrested to prevent a breach of the peace. I'll have a chat with someone and work out what the plan is, okay?"

Chris nodded. He was led to a cell and the door was closed. It was a taste of policing from the other side of the fence to that which he had become accustomed. He looked around the four walls. Graffiti adorned them. A basic metal toilet was in the corner, no toilet seat though. He knew all of this, of course. He had been in many cells all over the county, but it was only when one became your temporary home that you really took notice of the features of it. It felt claustrophobic beyond compare and Chris resolved that he would never again be in a police cell in this capacity. If he was to do anything in the future that might attract police attention, it would have to be done in a different way.

He sat on the plastic mattress and waited. He imagined that discussions were being had at a senior level about him and what he had done. He knew that he hadn't crossed the line in committing a criminal offence. All he had done was enter a school site as a trespasser and spoken with a child who he knew. He did not have any weapons with him, nor had he committed any public order offences by being threatening or abusive. There had been no damage to the fence and he had not assaulted anyone. He had been very careful to ensure that he had committed no offences. The very worst that they could do was to bind him over to keep the peace. That would mean a trip to court the following morning, but arrests for breaches of the peace rarely ended up there. Normally, once everyone had had chance to calm down and the 'breach' had gone, the arrested person would be released with no further action. That was what Chris was anticipating.

He had no point of reference to determine how much time had passed. He tried to lie down and shut his eyes but sleep was impossible. The adrenaline that had been coursing through his veins had not yet totally left his system, he thought. Besides that, his arm and wrists still hurt. He bore no grudges against any of the school staff who had detained him - they had simply been doing their job, just as he had done hundreds of times.

Footsteps echoed throughout the Custody Suite and Chris' cell was on the main corridor. Finally, he heard some of those footsteps stop outside his cell door. The heavy clanking of metal indicated that it was being unlocked. DS Willmott entered the cell, accompanied by a uniformed Superintendent.

"Chris, this is Superintendent Murphy," DS Willmott said. "She needs to speak to you about a couple of things."

"Hello Ma'am," Chris said, turning to the Superintendent. He needed to speak with DS Willmott about his suspicions that Maria held vital information, but he didn't want to do it in front of the Superintendent. He knew why she was there.

"PC Jamieson," Superintendent Murphy said. "I'm from the Professional Standards Department, and I need to give you formal notice that you are suspended from duty, effective immediately. You'll understand that your behaviour today wasn't acceptable and we need to look into it fully." She remained totally professional as she completed the necessary paperwork with Chris. The formalities completed, her tone and demeanour noticeably softened. "DS Willmott has filled me in on everything that has been happening, Chris. Firstly, I'm so sorry for your loss. If you have any welfare needs, you'll still have full access to anything required. I understand that Sergeant Adams has been dealing with that. If you need anything, anything at all, then please do get in touch with him."

"Thank you Ma'am," Chris said. "Would you mind if I speak to DS Willmott alone?"

"Of course," Superintendent Murphy replied, turning around and walking out of the cell.

DS Willmott left the cell door open but pushed it until it was only just ajar. "What the hell were you thinking, Chris?" She hissed at him. "Do you know the shit storm that you've created?"

"Well you weren't going to speak to Maria so I had to," Chris replied. "She knows something. I could see it in her eyes, Sue. She's covering up for her dad."

"She's six years old, Chris!" DS Willmott said, raising her voice. "Covering for her dad? That's just ridiculous. Now listen to me and listen to me good. Andrew and his family are off limits for you. That means no contacting them, no accidentally bumping into them in the street, nothing. I promise you that if something like this happens again then I'll put the papers in to the court myself to get you charged with something. You scared that poor girl half to death today." She instantly regretted her choice of words.

"Half to death?" Chris shouted. "HALF TO DEATH!? My boy is fully dead and you've got the gall to spout that to me? How about you investigate what happened? You know, why my boy died?"

DS Willmott didn't want this to turn into a shouting match. "I'm sorry for saying that, Chris," she said. "I really am. You need to understand that the investigation is over, though. The CPS said there isn't an offence there. It wouldn't matter what Maria said and I wouldn't be able to justify forcing her to give a statement, especially after the way she reacted to you today. It's tough to say, but you've got to let go." She turned and walked out of the cell without waiting for a response, closing the cell door behind her. She puffed out her cheeks. If the whole situation was a mess before, then disarray now reigned. Her head began to ache. Superintendent Murphy had instructed her to provide a full report on the whole incident, including the background to it, by the end of the day. She would have to disclose that she had told Chris the full extent of the evidence against Andrew, and her rationale behind the disclosure. She knew that it was going to be a long day.

DS Willmott walked down the long corridor and approached the custody desk, where she spoke with the Custody Sergeant.

"What are we doing with him, then?" The Custody Sergeant asked.

"Give him a couple of hours to calm down and then let him out," DS Willmott replied. "If there's any sign that he's not going to play ball then send him to court tomorrow for a bind over." There wasn't a lot else that she could suggest.

Chris had no interest in going to court and he knew that it was essential that he said and did the right things to get out of the police station as soon as possible. Those couple of hours took an age to pass by, so much so that Chris began to wonder if he was actually staying in his cell to go to court the next day. Finally, his cell door opened. The Custody Sergeant was standing in the doorway.

"Hi Chris," he said. "How are you feeling?"

"Hiya," Chris replied. "Better now, thank you. I don't know what came over me earlier. Just trying to work out in my head what happened, I suppose. I really hope the girl is okay, I never meant to upset her." Excellent words, he thought. That should work. He flashed his best look of contrition to complete the act.

"I need to be sure that there are going to be no further issues, Chris," the Custody Sergeant said. "I'm trusting you on this."

"I promise you nothing will happen," Chris said, unsure himself if he was even telling the truth. It didn't matter. The Custody Sergeant had heard enough and showed Chris out of the Custody Suite. As he did, he looked him in the eyes and shook his hand. Each man nodded slightly at the other, the Custody Sergeant in sympathy and solidarity, and Chris in appreciation and respect. Chris was offered a lift home but he said he'd walk. He wanted to be alone with his thoughts, to breathe some fresh air and to contemplate what he would do next.

DS Willmott may have closed her investigation, but his was very much active.

CHAPTER 23

Andrew put Maria to bed and lay with her until she fell asleep. She had clung to either him or Sophie since they had come home from the school, not wanting to be put down or separated from them. Andrew and Sophie hadn't had a chance to discuss what had happened between their daughter and Chris as they hadn't had any time alone to do so, and it had hung in the air for the remainder of the day, festering in both of their minds. Maria hadn't said anything about it and, by the time that bedtime had arrived, she seemed to be back to her normal state. Still, she wouldn't let Andrew leave her until sleep arrived. When it did, Andrew gently pulled her duvet over her, kissed her on the forehead and looked at her for a few minutes. His beautiful, precious daughter had been subjected to something that had caused her such mental trauma that it had caused her to wet herself and withdraw emotionally. He had suppressed his anger all day, keen to provide the support that she had needed from him. Now, he felt fury like he had never felt before. Any feelings of remorse or guilt towards Chris had gone. In their place was pure, unadulterated rage. He knew that Chris had been released from the police station without any sanction, having received a phone call from Mike a few hours before. He hadn't stayed on the phone long enough to listen to the reasons why.

He tiptoed across Maria's room and closed the door gently behind him, waiting for a few seconds to check that she didn't wake. She didn't. He walked downstairs and found Sophie in the front room, quietly sobbing. She had kept her emotions in check all day, now she was letting them go.

"What did he do to her?" She asked Andrew in between her tears. She knew that he didn't have the answer.

Andrew shook his head. "I don't know. But I'm going to find out," he replied. "Do you trust me?" He asked Sophie.

"Of course I do," she replied. "What do you mean?"

"I'm going out for a while," Andrew said. His voice was calm and measured. "Don't call the police, I'm not going to do anything to him. I just need to know what happened."

Sophie thought about what Andrew had said to her. They had been told in no uncertain terms by both DS Willmott and Mike that they were to have no contact with Chris, yet she was also incandescent with rage at what he had done to their daughter. This rage blinded her to the obvious fact that a confrontation could only ever end badly.

"Do it," she said. "Just don't get in trouble."

Andrew turned and walked out of the house. In truth, he didn't know what he was going to say or do. He just knew that he had to do something - that Chris needed to know that he had overstepped the mark and to make sure that nothing like this would ever happen again.

Andrew drove the route that he had taken many times before, and arrived in Chris' road still unsure of his plan of action. He parked away from the house, and slipped out of his car. The double beeping sound indicating that he had locked it seemed louder than normal, such was the silence in the street. It was dark and there were no street lights. The moon was hidden by a thick layer of cloud and the only thing guiding Andrew along the pavement was his knowledge of the street and the faint illumination provided from behind the curtains of the houses that he passed. He felt nauseous, but he didn't know why.

He stopped short of Chris' house. Downstairs, darkness. Upstairs, lights on and curtains pulled. Both Chris and Linda's cars were on the driveway. He waited for a minute, trying to work out his opening line. Nothing sounded right to him. It'd come, he thought. It was time.

He ghosted up the pathway to Chris' front door. To knock on the door or to ring the doorbell, he wondered. A knock on the door sounded better, he thought. A good, loud rap of the knuckles on wood. That'd show confidence. He knocked purposefully four times. No response, and no sounds of movement inside. He knocked again, louder this time. He heard it echo inside. No-one could've missed that, he thought. Sure enough, a sound of shuffling down the stairs. Andrew's feeling of nausea intensified.

The front door opened and Andrew took a step back. It was Chris, although it wasn't. The face was like a badly aged caricature of him, the body wasted away and the voice hoarse and rough.

"What are you doing here," Trevor hissed at Andrew. He knew who he was. Andrew had seen Trevor from a distance at the funeral but only now made the connection that he was Chris' dad. The resemblance was obvious.

"I need to speak to Chris, right now," Andrew said, suddenly flush with confidence.

"You've got no right to be here, none at all," Trevor replied gruffly.

"Who is it dad?" Chris called from upstairs.

"Nothing to worry about, son," Trevor replied. "Just someone at the wrong house."

"Get down here now!" Andrew shouted.

Silence hung in the air for a couple of seconds, until a door slammed shut loudly upstairs and footsteps stomped across the landing. Chris almost launched himself down the stairs. He had expected some form of comeback from Andrew, but he hadn't expected it this quickly. He had promised the Custody Sergeant that nothing would happen, but he hadn't instigated this. Andrew had turned up on his doorstep. The man responsible for the deaths of his son and wife was calling him out and he was furious.

He stormed out of the front door and stood in front of his dad, eye to eye with Andrew, their noses almost touching. Their eyes were locked, neither man willing to look away or even blink first. Chris' eyes were wide and wild and white speckles of foam were forming on the outermost creases of his mouth. Andrew saw at close range the impact of weeks and weeks of emotional turmoil. He blinked first, and then stepped away.

"You ever go near my daughter again…" he said, not finishing his sentence, leaving the threat implied. His voice carried less bite than it had done with Trevor, his confidence diminishing with every word.

"Your daughter is still alive you fucking prick," Chris screamed. "You killed my boy and you fucking know it."

Chris didn't wait for an answer. He threw himself at Andrew, tackling him to the floor and sitting astride him. "What about the fucking DNA!" He bellowed, raising his right hand, his fist clenched tightly. Andrew struggled and managed to push Chris away, both men rising to their feet and again staring each other down.

"Pack it in you two," Trevor called from the doorway. Neither man listened to him as they closed in on each other until they were again face to face.

"There's nothing to fucking say about any DNA," Andrew spat out as he jabbed Chris in the cheek with his finger. "If you want to have it then let's go, right now."

They both heard a siren in the distance. The commotion had attracted the attention of Chris' neighbours, and groups of them were congregating on the street. Someone must have called the police, Chris thought. They'd be here soon.

"Right now," Chris said in agreement, violently shoving Andrew in the chest.

Trevor was watching the confrontation unfold and felt helpless. His breathing felt laboured, so concerned was he by the situation that was developing in front of him. They're going to fight, he thought. He had to stop them.

Chris and Andrew circled each other on Chris' front garden as boxers would at the start of a bout. A few drops of rain began to fall.

"Chris, come back inside," Trevor shouted weakly.

"I'm never going to give up without knowing what happened," Chris said, looking at Andrew. "Never."

More rain fell, and the sirens grew louder. There was more than one of them on the way, Chris thought.

"Chris, please" Trevor begged.

"Maybe if you'd been there for Joe a bit more, then this wouldn't have happened," Andrew shouted. He wanted to hurt Chris and knew that those words would cut deeper than anything else.

"Chris," Trevor pleaded.

He either wasn't heard, or was ignored. Chris and Andrew rushed at each other, throwing punches, grabbing, gouging and doing anything they could to harm the other, both of them fighting to defend the honour of their child. They fell to the floor, clinched together in combat.

Trevor could watch no more. His chest was pounding and his breathing felt shallow but he couldn't stand by while this was happening. He needed to intervene. He tried to pull them apart but they were oblivious to him. He tried to get help from the neighbours, but they all just watched on. He tried everything, he really did.

He couldn't do any more. His chest was just too painful. His breathing was just too hard. He stumbled backwards, gasping for air. He knew what was coming and his eyes filled with tears. It wouldn't be long now. He fell to the floor. The rain was lashing down, stinging his cheeks with its intensity. He thought of his life, of the wasted years without Chris. To his last breath, he would still grieve for the daughter in law and grandson who he had never met. That last breath was almost upon him.

Dad?" Chris cried out, jumping to his feet and running to Trevor. He sunk to his knees, cradling his dad in his arms. "Someone, get an ambulance," he screamed. His voice was swallowed up by the sirens that were echoing in the road. The rain intensified further, and the whole road was bathed in a sea of blue. "Come on dad," Chris begged, "not now."

"On your feet," a voice behind Chris said sternly. Chris heard the words but it didn't register that they were aimed at him. He didn't move. "I said, on your feet," the voice said again, this time harsher in tone.

Chris was roughly pulled from his dad's side and his arms were held behind his back while he heard the familiar ratcheting noise of handcuffs being applied.

"Help him," he shouted at the police officer.

The police officer looked on in bewilderment. He had been sent to an anonymous report of a disturbance, and was now confronted with a chaotic scene and a man lying on the floor, apparently unconscious and deeply unwell. He released his grip on Chris and kneeled over Trevor. He couldn't find a pulse and couldn't establish if he was breathing.

Another police car screamed down the road, more sirens announcing their arrival. Two police officers ran to assist their colleague with Trevor, commencing CPR in an attempt to maintain blood flow around his body. One of them broadcast a message over his radio, his voice brimming with panic and urgency.

"We need an ambulance to our location now. Unconscious and unresponsive male, not breathing. Urgent assistance required."

CHAPTER 24

Andrew checked his rear view mirror repeatedly. He had seen Trevor fall to the floor and had melted away from the scene as Chris had rushed to his stricken father's aid. He had heard the sirens and knew that the police would have been turning up imminently. He didn't want to be a part of the fallout. He didn't want to be there to see Chris dealing with another potential tragedy. He didn't want to explain why he had gone there. He didn't want the blame for what had happened to fall at his feet. He knew, however, that it was likely.

The last thing he had seen as he drove cautiously away from the location had been Chris in handcuffs and standing over Trevor's prone body. He had been trying to blend into the background, to be anonymous amongst the cacophony of noise and mayhem that was ongoing in Chris' road. He needn't have worried. All efforts were focussed on Trevor and, to a much lesser extent, Chris. It seemed that no-one had noticed his departure and subsequent absence.

Andrew drove into his road, half expecting to see a police car outside his house waiting for him. There was no-one there. He pulled onto the driveway at his house, and walked through the front door quickly, locking it behind him. Sophie had been looking out of the upstairs window, awaiting his return and was waiting for him in the hallway.

"What the hell has happened?" She asked. Andrew hadn't thought about his appearance. He was covered in mud, his clothes were soaking wet and he had a few abrasions on his face that were slowly developing into bruises.

"I need to sit down," he replied, walking into the front room and falling onto the sofa. The enormity of what had happened was gradually registering with him. He had seen Trevor fall and had seen the look of impending doom on his face. Why had Trevor collapsed? He had been trying to stop Andrew and Chris from fighting. Why had they been fighting? Because Andrew had gone to Chris' house to confront him. He didn't need anyone to join the dots together for him. He knew that his actions had led to this, and he knew that this was exactly how Chris would interpret it as well.

Sophie sat next to Andrew and held his hand. "Well?" She asked.

"It all went wrong," Andrew said wistfully. "I don't know what happened. We argued, then we were fighting, then his dad went over."

"His dad?" Sophie said. She knew that Chris had long been estranged from his dad.

"I saw him at the funeral," Andrew replied. "I only realised who he was tonight. He was shouting at us to stop and then he fell down." He searched for words to convey to Sophie what he had seen, to impress upon her the gravity of the situation. He found none.

"I think he's dead," was all that he could murmur.

Chris sat on the back of a police car, also soaking wet and covered in mud. The chaos that had descended upon his road had now subsided, replaced by an uncomfortable calmness. An ambulance had been and gone. Chris had watched the paramedics work on his dad and had seen him loaded into the ambulance as they continued to do so, but it had seemed that there was no hope. He knew the little gestures to look for with paramedics and he had seen them in abundance. The almost imperceptible shaking of a head, the decrease in effort with CPR, the sense of going through the motions just so they could say that they had tried everything.

"So what happened?" A police officer asked. They had been knocking on doors up and down the road but no-one had been willing to give them a statement. It was common for people to not want to say anything if it involved their neighbours, normally in pursuit of maintaining a harmonious neighbourhood. No-one liked a grass. Chris knew this and had no intention of incriminating himself. He hadn't seen Andrew depart but he knew that he hadn't been there when the first patrol had arrived, or he would have been in handcuffs as well.

"My dad fell," he said quietly. He recognised the police officer, but didn't know him well. "You know who I am, don't you?" He asked.

"Yeah I do," the police officer replied, his voiced tinged with sympathy. The story of Chris' losses had spread throughout the force. "Tell me what happened, we might be able to help out."

Chris thought long and hard about what he was willing to say. From a purely legal perspective, having a fight is classed as Causing an Affray and he could be arrested for it. He didn't know what to do for the best so decided to stall for time.

"My Sergeant has been helping me a lot through all this," he said. "Do you think you might be able to get him here? It's Sergeant Mike Adams."

The police officer looked at him with a pitying smile. "I'll see what I can do," he said.

Mike arrived half an hour later, dressed in jeans and a t-shirt. He walked into Chris' house then emerged about five minutes later. Chris saw him talking animatedly with the police officer whose handcuffs he was still wearing behind his back, but - from inside the police car - couldn't hear what was being said. Mike eventually stomped over to the police car and opened the door. He had a face like thunder, although Chris didn't know if that was aimed at him, the police officer or the whole situation.

"Why is he still wearing bracelets?" Mike barked at the police officer. "Get them off him, now," he instructed.

The police officer fumbled for his handcuff key as Chris awkwardly got out of the police car. Chris turned around silently and presented his wrists for extrication. He knew that he was going to have to explain himself to Mike, but he wanted to do it without any other ears listening. As his hands were finally freed he realised just how much his wrists were hurting, having been in handcuffs twice in the space of a day.

"I'll deal with this from here," Mike boomed, ushering Chris towards his front door. They both entered the house and Mike closed the front door behind them.

"In there," Mike said to Chris, directing him to the front room.

Chris walked in and saw DS Willmott sitting on the sofa. He hadn't seen her arrive, and she didn't look amused.

"Sit down, Chris," she said coldly. It was an instruction, not a request, and Chris felt compelled to comply without questioning it.

"Listen, I…" Chris started to say, before DS Willmott cut him off.

"No, you listen Chris," she began. "Before we start, you're going to tell me the truth. Mike has promised that he'll arrest you himself if you don't. You're lucky you're not in a cell already. Do you understand?"

Chris looked at the floor. "Yeah," he replied meekly.

"Right then," DS Willmott continued. "Did Andrew come here?"

"Yeah," Chris replied quietly. "He came to have it out with me about what happened at the school."

"And did you have a fight?" DS Willmott asked.

"I wouldn't call it a fight," Chris replied, taking time to choose his words carefully. He didn't want to lie. "Just a difference of opinion. It might've got a bit out of hand." He didn't really care about any of that, though. Just one thing was occupying his thoughts. "Has there been any update on my dad?" He asked. While he feared and expected the worst, even the merest slither of hope was something that he was willing to cling to.

"They were still working on him a few minutes ago," Mike said. "I'll go and see if I can get an update." He got up and walked out of the house to speak to one of the patrols who were still at the scene, conducting house to house enquiries.

"That's why I'm here," DS Willmott said to Chris. Given the nature of the incident, and the fact that a death may be involved, it was standard practice for a DS to attend the scene to assess if there were any suspicious circumstances. "What happened with your dad?"

Again, Chris took some time to think about his response.

"I don't really know," he replied. It was the truth. He had been vaguely aware of his dad calling out to him and Andrew to stop, but it was peripheral noise. The adrenaline that had been coursing through his veins at the time had drowned out the pleas of his father. "He just went down. You know he's terminal, don't you?"

"I do," DS Willmott said. "I think you know what I'm asking, though, Chris. Did he get in the middle of you and Andrew? Did he get a whack on the head or something?"

"No," Chris shouted instantly. This was the whole, unblemished truth.

"You know I've got to ask," DS Willmott said, as Mike walked back into the room.

Chris tried to read Mike's face but it was expressionless. If he had an update on Trevor's condition then we wasn't letting on.

"Can I have word outside," Mike said to DS Willmott. She looked at him quizzically and then joined him in the front garden. One patrol car remained at the scene now, and they had only remained at the behest of Mike.

"House to house has thrown up a witness, Sue," he said. "Pretty much confirms that Trevor went down on his own and he wasn't assaulted. Off the record, they'll tell us that Chris and Andrew were fighting but they won't put pen to paper. No-one else is saying anything."

"And what about Trevor?" DS Willmott asked.

"They're still working on him but it doesn't look good," Mike replied. "If you're happy there's nothing suspicious then I'll take Chris to the hospital?"

DS Willmott took stock of what evidence she had in relation to Trevor's situation. He had no injuries consistent with an assault, and an independent witness had now said that there had been no third party involvement. She wasn't there to investigate if Andrew and Chris had been fighting - that had been the responsibility of the patrol officers. She was there solely to investigate the circumstances surrounding Trevor's collapse and the reasons for him being rushed to hospital. She was satisfied that, based on the current information, no crime had occurred.

"Sue?" Mike said.

"I'll write this one up," DS Willmott said. "Take him to see his dad. You know you've got to warn him, though, don't you Mike? This can't go on."

"I'm on it," Mike replied.

On the way to the hospital he made Chris aware in no uncertain terms of how serious the situation could have been.

"You know you should be in a cell right now, don't you?" He said, his voice simmering with anger. Mike found himself in an impossible position, stuck between the ongoing need to manage Chris' welfare, and the obligation he had as a police officer to ensure that lines weren't crossed. "This is the last straw, Chris. I promise you that if something like this happens again, I won't be there to bale you out."

His words were like white noise to Chris. He heard them, but he didn't listen to them. Just one thing was consuming him, and it was eating him up inside. Andrew. He had caused this. He had turned up, uninvited, and had set in motion the chain of events that had led to his dad's collapse. Andrew. Directly responsible for Joe's death. Joe's death directly caused Linda's suicide. Andrew. He'd decimated Chris' family. Andrew. Andrew. Andrew. It rang through his head until he could hear and think of nothing else.

We're here," Mike said.

Chris didn't respond. He had shut out all background noise.

"Chris?" Mike said, louder now.

He gently bumped Chris' arm with his elbow, jolting his passenger back into the present. Chris looked out of the window and saw the familiar surroundings of the Accident and Emergency Department.

They made their way inside and Mike went to speak with the receptionist while Chris stood in the waiting room.

"Through here, Chris," Mike called out to him, gesturing towards the side door. Chris thought back to the last time he had gone through that door. It had been weeks before, when he had been searching for answers about Joe. Back then, he still clung to hope that his boy was alive. His wife was still alive. A forbidding sense of deja vu swept over him as he stumbled clumsily into the inner sanctum of the A&E department, where he was directed to the Family Room. He had been in there countless times before. No good news ever came in this room, he thought.

"The doctor will be in soon," Mike said. He said it several more times as they waited and waited for news. Chris wasn't in the mood to talk. Eventually, an exhausted doctor came into the room. Her voice was calm, but she only managed three words.

"I'm really sorry…" was all that Chris needed to hear. He turned around and left the room, making his way through the A&E department and outside, Mike in quick pursuit.

"I'm really sorry, mate," Mike said. He had nothing else to say. He knew that any other words would be pointless.

"Take me home, please," Chris said quietly. He had felt grief for the loss of Joe. He had felt tormented at the loss of Linda. Now, he felt anger at the loss of his dad. He closed his eyes and swore silently that, somehow, and in some way, retribution would be his.

CHAPTER 25

He expected a visit, but it never came. He expected a call, but the phone never rang. In many ways Andrew was more unnerved by the lack of contact from the police than he would've been had he been arrested for his involvement in the incident at Chris' house. He had hurried to search the internet to see what the ramifications were for having a fight, and found that he could have been arrested for it and that a conviction for Affray could have actually resulted in a jail sentence. Still, the knock on the door didn't materialise. The phone remained silent. He tried to put it out of his mind and tried to focus on the future, hoping that the nightmares of the months gone by were finally behind him and his family.

The truth was that DS Willmott didn't have the stomach to tell him that he had got away with something again. Off the record, she knew that Andrew had instigated the confrontation. It had been he who had gone to Chris' house and caused the fight, which in turn had indirectly caused the death of Trevor. It was a bridge too far to link the two things formally, however. No-one was willing to give her a statement and so her hands were tied. She could do nothing, and it pained her.

Maria had reintegrated back into school as she had when she returned after the incident with Joe. It was like she had never been away, and she appeared to be suffering no ill effects from Chris' incursion onto the school grounds. Security measures at the school had been ramped up and, in an effort to placate Andrew and Sophie, the headteacher had agreed that a dedicated member of staff would be responsible for monitoring Maria at a discreet distance for the foreseeable future. It had been a weight off their collective minds that the school had taken the incident so seriously, and they were both satisfied that her safety was being treated as of paramount importance.

If the recent past had been bleak, then the immediate future was looking brighter for the Wicks family. Sophie was finally relaxing into the midterm of her pregnancy. Her bump had now fully popped and, day by day, she felt less and less burdened by the events that had cast a dark shadow over her family. She was still struggling to get Andrew out socially. He had still not fully got over the experience with the couple in the lift, but she was testing his resilience more and more as the days passed.

In any case, Andrew had a reason to be getting out of the house more. He had finally managed to secure some work, a local project that would at last ensure that the household bills could be paid. He had been contracted by a local Estate Agent on behalf of a Landlord to renovate a large rental property while it was in between tenants. His initial assessment of the property told him that this was going to be a long term job and that a complete overhaul was required, such was the state of disrepair present within. He had been given free rein to bring it up to spec, and a handsome budget to go with it. Life was indeed looking up.

Mike had tried his best to maintain links with Chris, but it had proven increasingly difficult as the days turned into weeks. In Chris' new, post-family world, days and nights blended into one solitary juncture where he existed according to his needs rather than to the conformed structure of a day. He slept when he needed to sleep. If that was in the middle of the afternoon then so be it. He ate when he felt the urge. If that was in the middle of the night then it didn't matter. He had given up on living according to societal norms.

The impact of the three deaths on Chris was beyond comprehension. In the space of a few weeks he had lost his son, his wife and his father to unnatural deaths. One death in such a manner could crush a person's spirits. Three, in such close proximity, seemed to extinguish all hope of Chris' spirits ever being restored.

Mike faced two main problems with Chris. Firstly, he wouldn't answer the door to anyone, instead choosing to live his life in a moody darkness behind pulled curtains and drawn blinds. Secondly, his phone was forever out of battery and Chris rarely had any inclination to charge it up. On the odd occasion when he did, he would be greeted with numerous old answerphone and text messages, all of which were from Mike who, to his credit, hadn't given up on Chris when it would have been easy to turn him over to the force welfare department.

After a few weeks without contact, Mike began to feel more and more uneasy. He was being chased for an update on Chris from his Inspector who was, in turn, being pressed for information from the district Chief Inspector. Despite his suspension, Chris was still a warranted police officer, still in the employ of the force and still universally well thought of by his colleagues. His well-being was still a priority. The familiar voicemail message greeted Mike every time he tried to call. A wall of silence was all that responded to his booming knocks on Chris' front door. Mike decided that enough was enough. It was time for him to speak to Chris, face to face.

Mike was on an early shift and had spoken to his Inspector about his concerns and the apparent resistance to contact that Chris was exhibiting. It had been agreed that Mike was to attend his address and force entry if necessary in order to conduct a welfare check on him. It was justified in law - there is a specified legal right for a police officer to enter a property in order to save life and limb. Chris had been out of contact for weeks and it was time to check up on him. Other officers were to attend but, if all was in order, they were to withdraw so that Mike could address any issues that presented themselves. A simple but effective plan, Mike thought.

He briefed Tasha and Jim, the two officers who were to attend with him. He had chosen them as they were the two members of his team who were closest to Chris. He really wasn't expecting any trouble but, if something did happen, then a friendly face was more likely to defuse a bad situation than a stranger. They drove the twenty minute journey in convoy, Mike leading the way in the Sergeant's car and Tasha and Jim following behind. Mike was apprehensive about what he was awaiting them behind the front door. The last time he had seen Chris was when he had dropped him home from the hospital following the news of Trevor's death. Despite his efforts, there had been absolutely no contact since.

Mike slowly pulled into Chris' road. The chaos that had descended there a few weeks before had been replaced by a sense of calm. Still, the neighbours' curtains seemed to twitch. One police car in a quiet, residential street could be passed off as general patrolling. Two police cars, however, indicated that something was going to happen.

Both police cars rolled to a gentle stop directly outside Chris' house. The blinds and curtains remained in the same position they had been for weeks, allowing no light in and letting no signs of life out.

"Okay, guys?" Mike asked.

Tasha and Jim both nodded anxiously. They were concerned for their colleague and friend.

Mike led them up the path. He removed his extendable baton and rapped the butt of it on the heavy, wood-panelled front door. He placed his ear to the door and heard the echoes from his knocking reverberating inside. No response came. He repeated the process, only louder. Still, no response. He pushed open the letter box and propped it up with his baton, peering inside as light penetrated the gloom. He saw an accumulation of letters and mail gathering on the floor just the other side of the door.

"Go and get the Enforcer, Jim," he said quietly.

Jim went to his police car and returned moments later with a big, red lump of metal, shaped like a battering ram. The 'Enforcer' is what the police use, not very subtly, to ram open a door.

"Chris," Mike called through the letter box, "if you're in there then please open the door. We're going to force it if not." His words weren't answered. "Last chance," Mike pleaded. Still, nothing.

Mike moved out of the way and nodded Jim past him. The door offered little resistance. Two hefty swings from Jim with the Enforcer and it was off its hinges and lying on the floor. Mike led them tentatively into the house.

"Carefully, guys," he said. "Slow and steady wins the race."

Mike had been dreading crossing the threshold into the house, knowing that the smell would dictate to him what he was likely to find. He had dealt with enough dead bodies over the years to have a sense of smell finely attuned to the odour of expiration. To his relief, he didn't detect it there. What was obvious, however, was that Chris had been drinking, and drinking heavily. Aside from the strong stench of alcohol, bottles had been discarded with abandon and patches of dried vomit stained the floor in several locations. Mike held his nose. He hadn't detected death, granted. What he had detected, however, was hideously offending his nasal cavity.

Mike looked at Tasha as they searched the ground floor, both of them with raised eyebrows. They had both been there just a few weeks ago, but the orderly home from then was now transformed into the kind of squalor they normally associated with squats and crack houses. The walls were stained with alcohol and, unless Mike was very much mistaken, faecal matter. Shattered glass crunched under his feet as he walked slowly up the stairs, using his baton as a makeshift stick to remove soiled items of clothing that had been discarded in his way.

"Chris?" He called. "It's Mike, I just need to know if you're okay." Again, no response.

More empty bottles lined the upstairs landing. There were four doors leading into different rooms. Two were open and two were closed. Mike could see that the two open doors led to the bathroom and what appeared to be a spare room. A cursory check of them revealed nothing. Mike knocked gently on one of the closed doors and then opened it slowly.

A child's bedroom. Immaculate, Mike thought. Almost like stepping back in time, back to a time when this specific room was full of love, laughter and life. Joe's room. Preserved in exactly the way that it had been left, untouched by the mania that seemed to have taken root in the house. Mike suddenly felt like an intruder, a trespasser invading the private sanctum of grief that Chris had established. He quickly closed the door and took a step back, as the feeling passed.

"Alright Sarge?" Jim asked. He had joined Mike on the landing as Tasha watched on from the top of the stairs.

"Yeah mate," Mike replied. "Just this one to go," he said, pointing to the other closed door.

"WHO'S UP THERE?" A voice boomed from downstairs.

A stunned silence greeted the enquiry. The voice may have been loud, but the three police officers knew immediately who it was.

"Chris, it's me," Mike called. "I'm here with Jim and Tash. We're coming down."

They hastily made their way down the stairs, taking care not to stumble on the glass or other trip hazards as they did so, and found Chris standing in the hallway. Mike widened his eyes.

"Chris?" He asked incredulously.

The man standing before him bore no resemblance to the man he knew, not only in the physical change of appearance but also in the air of menace that he presented. Everything about him was different. His hair was matted and greasy, his beard held remnants of food, his skin was a pale shade of yellow and his eyes were bloodshot and wired.

"What's going on?" Chris asked, breathlessly. He was sweating. Mike noticed the back door was open behind him. It had been closed when they had gone up the stairs.

"We've been worried about you mate," Mike said, trying to ratchet down the tension that was building between them. "I haven't heard from you for weeks now, I just needed to know how you're doing. From the looks of it in here, not too good."

"I'm doing fine," Chris snapped back.

"Listen mate, I'm worried about you," Mike said placidly. He really didn't want to turn the situation into an argument. "Is there anything we can do for you? How about a cup of tea or something?"

"I don't need anything," Chris replied coldly. "I'll deal with things my own way and at my own pace. Now who's going to fix my door?"

Mike sighed. He desperately wanted to help Chris, but it was obvious that now wasn't the time to be pressuring him to accept it. He knew Chris well. He knew that he was a good man, and that - in time - he would hopefully accept and maybe even embrace the idea of help. Now wasn't that time, however. He was alive. He was coherent. He was cognitively aware. There was nothing more that Mike could do.

"I'll get it arranged," Mike said. "If you need anything, you know where I am."

Chris stormed up the stairs and a door slammed shut.

"Let's go guys," Mike said, turning to Jim and Tasha.

Both of them were crying.

CHAPTER 26

Mike knocked on Inspector Sullivan's door. He had always got on well with his boss, but knew that this was going to be a difficult conversation. Inspector Sullivan was on the phone but gestured for Mike to come in and sit down. He had been waiting for Mike to return from Chris' house. Mike had briefly updated him by telephone but he wanted to speak about it in person.

"I've got to go," Inspector Sullivan said into his phone, "I'm just about to get a full update now." He hung up and then turned to Mike. "The Chief Inspector is chasing me," he said. "So go on then, what happened?"

Mike relayed what had happened, leaving nothing out. He spoke of the smell in the house and the squalid living conditions. He described Chris' haggard and emaciated appearance. He conveyed his concerns, hoping that interventions could be arranged to help Chris return from the brink.

Inspector Sullivan leaned back on his chair and chewed the end of his pen while he considered a response.

"Honestly, guv," Mike said, "it was horrendous. He's going downhill fast. We've got to do something or he's going to crash and burn."

"What would you suggest, then?" Inspector Sullivan replied. He wasn't trying to shift the burden of responsibility onto Mike's shoulders, he was just having a difficult time working out exactly what measures could be put in place to help Chris.

"I'm not sure," Mike replied. He had been hoping for inspiration from his boss, but none appeared to be forthcoming. The problem was that, in a situation like this, a person needed to want help and actively seek it. To use police powers in such a case was a last resort and fell within Mental Health legislation where a person was a clear and present danger to themselves or others. Chris had been cognisant, coherent and - although gaunt - not apparently in need of immediate medical intervention. The state of his house was immaterial in this regard. How someone chose to live their life in the confines of their own four walls was not something that the police could dictate or interfere with.

"Well, we can't section him," Inspector Sullivan said, confirming what Mike had thought. "We can't force him to engage with us if he doesn't want to. Do you think he'd speak with a doctor or a counsellor?"

"No," Mike replied quickly. These were all suggestions that he'd been through over and over again in his own mind. "He's too far gone, boss. I honestly struggled to recognise him."

"Then I don't think there's much we can actually do," Inspector Sullivan said. "Where are we with the inquests?"

"No dates yet," Mike replied. "I really don't know how he's going to cope with them."

"And the school investigation?" Inspector Sullivan asked. "Any update from Professional Standards?"

"Nothing yet," Mike replied. "Everything's up in the air still."

Inspector Sullivan sighed loudly. He was annoyed, but not at Mike. "The Chief Inspector is waiting for me to get back to him with an update," he said. "Basically, there's no good news, is there?"

"No," Mike replied. "And I can't see it getting any better."

Andrew was riding high on the crest of a wave. All of his recommendations for the renovation had been accepted without question and he had even managed to secure more money for the project than had initially been granted. The Final Warning bill reminders had stopped being delivered and the family was finally solvent again. They had managed to do it without

Sophie having to go back to work and Maria was still getting on well at school.

He still hadn't heard anything from the police and had compartmentalised thoughts of Joe, Linda, Trevor and Chris in a portion of his mind that that was inaccessible during his conscious hours. The image of Joe still plagued him when he slept, but he accepted it as part of his penance. His waking hours were largely free from internal wrangling, and he was less conscious of others when he was out and about. People still stared and whispered. He was just learning to deal with it better.

It had been three months since Joe had died and Andrew had settled into a daily routine. It began with him dropping Maria at school in the morning. After the school run, he made his way to his renovation project, normally arriving any time around 09:20. Every time he opened the front door, he was welcomed by a mass of junk mail. He hadn't known the previous tenant, but the sheer volume of catalogues and circulars bearing the name of Rosina Janice Smith made him feel like he knew her well. He had asked the Estate Agent what the landlord had wanted done with all of the mail and if there was a forwarding address for her, but he had been told to just put it to one side. The trouble was, that 'one side' was now two, three and four sides. It was everywhere. He'd have to chase it up again, he thought.

He found he was at his most productive for about six hours per day, so he worked until school pick up time. It suited him perfectly. He could do both of the school runs and still have a good day at work in the middle. For him, it was the perfect job and he intended to eke out every single day that he could on it.

Andrew doing the school runs meant that Sophie had more time to spend concentrating on her pregnancy, which was now into the third trimester. She had managed to put the events of the past few months firmly behind her, and was concentrating on savouring every moment that remained of her pregnancy. Both she and Andrew were amazed that she had come through it unscathed, given the amount of stress and strain that had been placed on her body and mind. It just reinforced to Andrew what a special woman she was. Many others would've buckled, but she had remained steadfast in the face of adversity. He had always known that he had married well. Her support of him over the past few months had reaffirmed to him just how right he had been. He just hoped that he could repay her for the faith that she had shown in him.

Sophie was shopping in the High Street when she saw him. At least, she thought it was him. She hadn't seen him since the day that Joe had died, when he had turned up at Maria's hospital room in search of answers. She squinted to check. He was about thirty metres away from her and was looking in a shop window, apparently oblivious to her presence. She ducked into a shop doorway and peered out from the side. Gone. She scanned the street, searching for him, anxiety growing within her. Was it him? Had she imagined the likeness? From behind, she wouldn't even have looked twice, such was the spindly and withered stature of the man. But she had seen his side profile. His face was drained, almost cadaverous, but she recognised it. She was sure it was him. And now she saw him again, walking in her direction. His bloodshot eyes shifted around, his head twitching in all directions. Was he looking for someone? Was he looking for her? She quickly pushed open the door and entered the shop, not even aware of where she was. She watched as he skulked past her. It was definitely him and he definitely seemed to be looking for someone. He looked hostile, somewhere between a vacant entity and one filled with malevolence. She melted into the background, trying to make herself as anonymous and inconspicuous as possible. Being heavily pregnant didn't make it easy, but it seemed to work. He was gone, but his presence had evoked recently forgotten feelings of angst within Sophie. She took her phone out of her bag, but her hands were trembling so much that she struggled to unlock it. Eventually she managed to call Andrew.

"I've just seen Chris," she said, her voice gripped with trepidation. "Can you come and get me?"

Andrew was on his way before she could say another word, arriving in a state of panic a while later. He held her tightly, manoeuvring his body to accommodate her bump. He could feel her shaking, prompting him to hold her even tighter. He tried to slow his own thumping heart in an effort to impart a state of calm into his wife.

"Come on love, let's get you out of here," he said quietly. He led her out of the shop and looked both ways up and down the High Street before walking along the building line with Sophie directly behind him. Hiding in plain sight, he thought.

They couldn't see him anywhere.

"He's gone, love, don't worry," Andrew said, trying to reassure his wife. "It's just a coincidence. We live in the same town, we're going to see him at some point."

He had his back to her so couldn't see her shaking her head in response. She knew that he had been looking for something. Or someone. It had unnerved her to such an extent that she decided there and then that the remainder of her pregnancy would be spent at home, away from any social setting. She didn't want to feel like this again any time soon.

Back in Andrew's car, she locked the door and felt marginally better.

"So what happened?" He asked gently as he drove away.

Sophie explained what had happened and, on the face of it, it sounded like an innocuous, chance encounter. She couldn't explain why she had been so spooked. She couldn't describe adequately the look of malice that had been present on his face. She couldn't portray his twitching, bloodshot eyes, searching and scanning his surroundings. It would make no sense to Andrew, but it made perfect sense to her.

"Take me home," she said, her confidence shattered.

Andrew drove home in silence, not knowing if he should say anything. Instead, he rested his hand on her leg, trying to impart a feeling of unity and reassurance. She placed her hand on top of his. She didn't normally sweat, but her palm was warm and moist.

"Come on, I'll make you a cup of tea," Andrew said as he pulled into their road.

He helped her into the house and sat with her in the front room while the kettle boiled.

"It'll be okay, love," he said, clasping her hand. It was still sweaty. "I'll stay with you now and then we'll go and get Maria together later."

"Okay," Sophie murmured. She wasn't as convinced that everything was going to be okay. She had seen his face. She had seen the anger. She felt that something was brewing. She just couldn't articulate why.

Andrew took a few days off from the renovation to be at home with Sophie. He was under no time pressure to get the work done and knew that she needed him at home with her. Seeing Chris had really knocked her. She was still unable to say what it was that had caused her so much turmoil. The closest she could get was to suggest that the aura he carried that day was wicked and that she had felt threatened by his presence, even if he hadn't been aware of her being there. They did the school run together, something that they hadn't done for a long time. Despite the reasons for him not being at work, this was time together that he actually enjoyed, in stark contrast with the endless days of turbulence that they had recently experienced together.

Now, Andrew felt, it was his turn to build Sophie up. She had spent the past few weeks and months trying to get him in a position where he felt mentally strong enough to face the world. Now the roles were reversed and she needed the confidence to get back out. The stares and whispers were background noise. He had a focus now, to help his wife regain the self-assurance that she had possessed prior to the chance encounter with Chris. That is how Andrew had interpreted the situation. It was a coincidental encounter with a person who lives in the same town. Nothing more, nothing less. It would likely happen again and both he and Sophie needed to build up their resilience levels to be able to deal with it.

It was Friday morning. Andrew and Sophie had dropped Maria off at school and waved to her as she went in as normal. Andrew was taking one last day off work before he went back in on the following Monday. He was satisfied that Sophie was on the right path now and that she would be okay at home while he worked.

"Fancy a coffee, love?" He asked.

She took a few seconds to answer. "Okay," she replied, unsure if she wanted to but knowing that she needed to.

Andrew drove to the multi-storey car park where the incident in the lift had occurred. He didn't drive to the top floor this time, instead parking on the ground floor in a parent and child bay. He was sure it was acceptable given Sophie's heavily pregnant state. As he locked the car he noticed his flat cap and sunglasses sitting on the back seat, still discarded there from a few weeks before when he had intended to use them to disguise himself. He realised how much his mental fortitude had strengthened now that he hadn't even thought to reach for them.

"Wait there love, I'll help you out," he called to Sophie as he walked around to the passenger side of the car. He offered her his hand and gently eased her to her feet. She couldn't really remember the latter stages of her pregnancy with Maria but she didn't recall Andrew being as caring as he was now. He held her hand as they walked into the High Street. Sophie's hand instinctively tightened when they walked past the spot where she had seen Chris, but she tried to push any negativity from her mind. Andrew had convinced her that it was a coincidence and, despite her reservations, she had persuaded herself to accept that as the truth.

A few people stopped and gawped at them as they walked but Andrew refused to even acknowledge their presence, instead concentrating on escorting his wife to their first real appearance in public together in months. He felt untouchable. The seal of anxiety that had stopped them from going out had been broken and it felt like nothing was going to stop them now.

They sat in their favourite cafe and realised how much they had missed each other's company. Sure, they had been in each other's presence for months, but it had been lacking the familiarity of emotion and connection. They had merely been existing. Now, it felt like there was a chance they could start living again. They spoke to each other in ways they hadn't done for a long time, both realising that the love they felt for each other still ran true and deep. To anyone taking a snapshot of the day, it would just look like a husband and wife having a morning coffee together. To Andrew and Sophie, it signified a new beginning, the rekindling of a passion that had all but been extinguished by a series of tragedies. They had survived.

They had one coffee, then a second, then by the time they had a slice of cake and a cold drink it was past midday. Time had flown by and neither of them had realised.

"Look at the time," Sophie exclaimed. "We'd better get back, you've got washing to do."

Andrew laughed. He was trying to be a lot better at doing things around the house and had recently learned how to use the washing machine. He had been quite embarrassed at how simple it was to use. He had always thought it would be a complicated process. "Come on then," he said. He looked at Sophie, gazing into her eyes as they got up. "Thank you, love," he said quietly. "For everything."

She flashed him a smile then grabbed his hand and led him outside and all the way back to the car. Whereas she had walked slowly and timidly on the way to the cafe, on the way back she strode with confidence. Andrew felt warm inside. Whatever had afflicted her the other day, she was now back to her normal self, he thought.

He drove home, his hand in its familiar place on Sophie's leg. She held her hand over his. Her palm wasn't sweaty now, he thought.

They arrived home and Andrew parked on the driveway. He looked at Sophie and saw that she was staring at him. They both knew why, and both burst out laughing.

"You can't do it once and not again," she said. "Come on, help me out. I'm carrying your child!"

"I've made a rod for my own back here, haven't I?" He replied with a grin. "Alright, alright, I'm coming."

He got out of the car and began to make his way around the rear of it to help Sophie up, when he stopped dead in his tracks. He had looked casually into the back of the car and saw that his flat cap and sunglasses weren't there. He thought back to when he had parked up in the car park. Had he moved them? He hadn't. He had specifically thought about them and their relevance to his current mental health state, and he could remember exactly where they had been. Without trying to alert Sophie, he discreetly peered through the rear window, this time intentionally and with purpose. They must have fallen into the footwell. No matter how hard he looked, they weren't there. They had gone.

"Come on, that washing isn't going to wash itself," Sophie called in jest.

"Coming love," Andrew replied, forcing cheer into his voice. He didn't want to alarm her but he had a deep sense of foreboding growing within him.

He walked around to her and summoned the best fake smile that he could muster as he helped her from the car. It must've been good, as Sophie didn't say a thing.

"Thank you my hero," she said with a laugh, as she planted a kiss on his lips.

They went into the house and Andrew put the kettle on.

'I think I dropped my wallet in the car," he called to Sophie. "I'll be back in a minute." He couldn't rid himself of a sense of something not being right. There had been no sign that anyone had broken into the car and, in any case, why would they have taken his hat and sunglasses. It made no sense unless, he realised, it was meant to make no sense. He turned the car up-side down trying to locate the missing items but they weren't anywhere. He looked in the centre console, which was still full of the loose change that he threw in there. If this had been an opportunistic thief then they would have taken the money, Andrew thought. But he wouldn't have noticed that. Whoever had taken the hat and sunglasses hadn't done it for any kind of gain. They had done it just to show Andrew that it could be done. That he could be got at. And, maybe, that he was being watched. He tried to force those thoughts from his mind, trying to convince himself that it was a sense of paranoia that was taking root within him that had no basis in reality but he just couldn't shake the feeling of unease. He walked back into the house with a lot less swagger than he had been displaying earlier in the day.

"Did you find it?" Sophie called.

"What's that?" He replied.

"Your wallet," she said.

"Oh, yeah, down in the footwell," he replied.

The weekend passed without further incident and Andrew returned to work the following Monday. He had spent a couple of nights feeling troubled by the theft from his vehicle, but had taken the time to rationalise what had happened. Something had been stolen. It happened up and down the country every day. He concluded in his own mind that he had been over-thinking things and tried to forget that it had happened.

Sophie took Maria to school on the Monday. Andrew had a meeting arranged for some time in the morning with the Estate Agent and the land-lord so he wanted to get there early to tidy a few bits up before they arrived. He had been absent from the renovation for a few days and the build-up of post behind the front door was such that he had to gain entry to the prop-erty via the rear access He had never really taken the time to admire the size and scale of the property that he had been working on, more the gen-erously sized grounds in which it was situated. He surveyed the gardens, with various derelict outbuildings plotted about and masses of overgrown weeds and foliage. So much potential, he thought. If he had the money, this kind of project would be perfect for him and his family. He declut-tered the area around the front door, adding volumes of junk mail to that already set aside for the previous tenant. Rosina Janice Smith had a lot to answer for, he thought to himself with a chuckle. He'd have to chase it up again with the Estate Agents.

He settled in for a solid day's graft, keen to make progress. He knew that giving a good account of himself here might lead to further work, especial-ly if the landlord had a portfolio of properties. He had just knocked up some plaster when his phone rang. He looked at it. Sophie. He couldn't answer as his hands were covered in dust, so it rang through to answer-phone. When it immediately rang again, he knew something must be wrong.

"What's up love?" He asked.

"Someone's been in the house," she screamed back at him.

"What!? Are you safe?" He replied helplessly.

"I'm outside the house…" she said, before being cut off by Andrew.

"Hang up and call 999," he said to her. "I'm on my way."

CHAPTER 27

Andrew arrived at his house before the police did. He heard the sirens getting closer and knew that their arrival was imminent. Sophie was pacing the pavement outside the house and in a state of shock.

"What's happened?" Andrew asked as he ran from his car to console his wife.

"The photos," Sophie replied distantly, "photos and newspapers, the kitchen."

"I don't know what you mean, love," Andrew replied.

"In there!" Sophie screamed, pointing into the house.

Andrew looked at the open front door, and listened to the sirens that were getting louder by the second. He didn't know what had happened, and wasn't getting any sense out of Sophie. Acting on pure instinct, he ran up the garden path and into the house, making his way straight to the kitchen. He saw immediately what had agitated Sophie to the point of stupor.

She had been right. Photos and newspapers. Emblazoned all over the back wall of the kitchen. Linda and Joe staring at him. Clippings and cuttings relating to their deaths. The words jumped out at him. "Death." "Suspicion." "Local man." "Arrested." A morbid mosaic dedicated to a departed mother and son, deliberately placed to strike fear in Andrew and Sophie. It had worked.

Andrew heard voices shouting in the house.

"Front room clear!"

"Dining room clear!"

The kitchen door burst open.

"Kitchen cle.... Are you Andrew?" A police officer shouted, wielding his extendable baton and wearing a look of aggression. Andrew nodded. "Kitchen clear," the police officer shouted.

They methodically searched the rest of the house while Andrew remained in the kitchen, staring at the wall in quiet disbelief. He had felt a sense of foreboding when he had noticed the theft from his car the previous week. Now, the same feeling threatened to overwhelm him. The theft hadn't been a coincidence.

It had been a message.

They were being watched. The break in to the house had made that abundantly clear. Andrew always took Maria to school. It was only because he had a meeting that morning that Sophie had needed to do the school run. Someone had been watching, and knew that the house was empty.

"House is clear," the police officer said to Andrew as he walked into the kitchen. "What's all this then?" he asked, pointing to the wall.

Andrew sighed. He didn't want to recite the events of the past few months again.

"Please can you call DS Willmott?" he asked wearily. "She knows all about it."

She knew before she picked up the phone what it was going to be about. She had been following the progress of the call both on the radio and the control room computer system.

"DS Willmott," she said with her eyes shut.

"Sarge, we've got a bit of an odd job here," the Police Officer at the scene said. "Fella says you'll want to know about it. Any chance you can come and have a look?"

"I'm on my way," she replied.

"Do you want to know the address?" The police officer asked.

"Don't worry, I know it well," DS Willmott replied.

She slowly stood up from her desk. She had always thought that further incidents were likely, perhaps even inevitable. She just didn't know how far they were going to escalate. If a home invasion was the first step, then who knew how far it would go before this whole thing played out to a conclusion?

As she walked to her car, she reached for her phone and dialled Mike.

"Hi Sue," he said with trepidation. Phone calls from her had rarely borne good news recently.

"Mike, we've got a problem," she said.

"I'm jumping in the car now," he replied. "Where am I going?"

"Andrew's house," she said. "Get on hands free and I'll fill you in on the way."

DS Willmott arrived before Mike, but waited in her car at the end of the road until he arrived. She had told him over the phone about the unfolding incident at Andrew's house, but wanted to speak with him face to face before they attended the scene.

"Have you seen Chris recently?" She asked when he arrived.

"Not a thing," Mike replied. "We put his door in a few weeks ago and he was in a right state, but nowhere near bad enough for him to be sectioned. Haven't heard from him since. To be honest, I think they're going to look down the unfit for work route and bin him."

"It sounds pretty disturbing, what's gone on this morning," DS Willmott said. "What do you reckon? Could it be him?"

Mike raised his eyebrows, but said nothing. He didn't need to.

"Come on then, let's go and see it for ourselves," DS Willmott said, leading Mike down the road and towards the Wicks's house.

Crime scene tape had been placed around the front garden of the property and a police officer stood guard, supervising access to the property. DS Willmott and Mike stepped inside the house and walked into the kitchen, where they both stopped in their tracks, mouths agape at the scene that presented itself to them. It was a harsh clash between the photos full of life, and the articles full of death. Colourful pictures of Joe and Linda in the prime of life interspersed with dull, black and white words announcing their demise. It took them a full, few minutes to appreciate the scale of effort that had gone into collating this and erecting it. That someone had managed to do it in the time it took for Sophie to do the school run beggared belief.

"I think there's one missing," DS Willmott murmured, not sure if she was talking to herself or sharing a thought with Mike. Either way, he walked over to her. Sure enough, there was a gap in the collection of photos and clippings, right in the centre. It was photo sized.

DS Willmott and Mike walked out of the kitchen. They had both seen enough.

"Can we get CSI here please," DS Willmott said to the police officer standing guard. "If they can't get some fingerprints or DNA off that lot then they're in the wrong job." She looked around. "Where are Andrew and Sophie?" She asked. It hadn't occurred to her until now that they weren't at the scene.

"Back at the nick giving a statement," the police officer replied. "Proper shaken up, they were," he added.

Sophie tried to drink her tea, but her hands were trembling too much to be able to hold it to her lips without it spilling. Andrew looked at his heavily pregnant wife and was worried for the safety of both her and the unborn child inside her, such was the stress that she was suffering. He tried to quieten his own feelings of anxiety in order to assist in soothing hers, and took hold of her trembling hand, clasping it between his palms. A detective in plain clothes walked into the side room at the police station where they were sitting. It was the same room that Andrew had been interviewed in for the first time months before. Now, he was the victim. Now, he was being given tea and asked how he was.

"I'm going to take your statements, but I need to do it individually so that you don't fill in the gaps for each other, okay?" The detective said. "I'll do Sophie's first, then yours after, Andrew. If you want to go outside and get some fresh air that'll be fine but it might take a while with both of you, okay?"

Andrew didn't want to leave Sophie, but he looked at her and she nodded for him to go. He stood up and walked out reluctantly, and paced the floor of the front counter area before going outside to get some fresh air. It was clear to him who had done this, and he was sure that it would be clear to any rational, sane person as well. What was distressing him was what else Chris would do. He had confronted Maria, broken into their home and maybe broken into his car as well. He felt violated. He felt sick. And he knew that it wasn't over yet.

The minutes turned into hours. The detective hadn't been lying when he said it would take a while, he thought. He went back into the front counter reception where he sat on a wooden bench.

"Hello Andrew," a familiar voice said, awakening him from his thoughts.

He looked up. DS Willmott was standing in front of him. He scrambled to his feet.

"Have you got him yet?" he asked, assuming that efforts were being made to arrest Chris.

"Come with me and I'll take your statement," DS Willmott replied, leading him to another, smaller room.

"Well?" Andrew said.

"Well what?" DS Willmott replied. She felt no sympathy for Andrew. Of course, she would investigate any offence diligently and to the best of her ability, regardless of who had committed it and who the victim was. Comfort and consolation were not things she was willing to afford him, however.

"He's going to be arrested, isn't he?" Andrew asked.

"We'll get to that," DS Willmott replied. "We need to look at this from all angles. At the moment, we have lots of photos and newspaper clippings. Of course, Chris would be the logical suspect, but this whole case has affected a lot of people and there are lots of people angry with you out there. I'm sure you know that."

Andrew had been living with it for months. Of course he knew that.

"I thought you might say that," he said, almost with a sneer. "Well how do you explain this, then?"

He threw a photo down onto the table. The photo that had been missing from the wall when it had been inspected by DS Willmott. She looked at it and knew straight away that there was no disputing the fact that her list of potential suspects had instantly been reduced to just one.

"I took it just in case you tried to look the other way," Andrew said softly. "I've got a photo of it on my phone and I've emailed it to myself as well. Now, tell me, who else other than Chris could have taken this one then?"

DS Willmott looked at the photo. Joe. Lying peacefully in his school uniform. His hair in a side parting. His skin pale and his freckles shining. His hands grasping a white rose. In a white coffin. In the background an oak veneer coffin. Linda. The candles of the funeral home glowing.

And the words scrawled on the photo in thick, red ink 'YOU DID THIS'.

CHAPTER 28

Mike's phone rang in his pocket. He had pre-empted the content of the call and was already sitting at the end of Chris' road with Jim and Tasha.

"Hi Sue," he said. "What's the plan?"

"I've just taken Andrew's statement," she replied. "It got worse. Chris had put a picture of Joe and Linda from the funeral home on the wall as well. Andrew had taken it before we got there and showed it to me when I was taking his statement. It was definitely Chris, Mike."

Mike had been in no doubt that Chris had been responsible for breaking into the Wicks' house, but this merely confirmed it. He didn't say anything.

"There's something else," DS Willmott added. "Andrew thinks that his car was broken into the other day. He thinks that Chris has been following them. He needs nicking ASAP."

"So what are we looking at?" Mike asked.

"Harassment as a minimum at the moment," DS Willmott said. "Burglary if we can make it stick. Either way, he needs lifting soonest."

"I'm parked in his road now," Mike replied. "Give me ten minutes and I'll update you." He hung up and turned to Jim and Tasha. He explained the extent of the new evidence against Chris and watched as their expressions turned from inquisitiveness to the pained realisation that they needed to arrest their friend and colleague.

Mike felt a strong sense of deja vu as he led Jim and Tasha along the road as they made their way to Chris' house. They had made trodden this path before. Then, to check on Chris' welfare. Now, to start his journey through the criminal justice system. He felt sad that he had watched helplessly as Chris descended into the shadow of a man that he once was. He knew that he had to put personal feelings aside, but it was a hard thing to do having lived through every step of it with Chris.

The curtains and blinds were still pulled as they had been permanently for the preceding months. There was a new front door, the previous one having been destroyed by Jim when they had forced entry weeks before. It was cheap and flimsy and wouldn't put up much resistance to the Enforcer, Mike thought. The cars were still on the driveway. Chris must be there, Mike thought. He knocked on the door with his baton. No reply came.

"Chris, we need to talk" he shouted through the letter box. Again, no reply. The pile of letters that had accumulated last time they had been there had grown substantially. He stood away from the door, then turned to Jim. "Same as before, mate," he said quietly.

It only took one, half hearted swing at the front door for Jim to gain entry. Mike led them as they cautiously made their way into the house. Last time, the risks posed upon entry had seemed lower. Now, the stakes had been raised and Chris was wanted for criminal offences. Mike was worried about how he would now react to them.

The rancid stench that had welcomed them previously had intensified in both odour and strength. It hit all three of them like a wall as they crossed the boundary from public place into private dwelling. Even more bottles, both intact and smashed, were strewn on the carpets. More vomit stains. More evidence of Chris using anywhere other than the bathroom as a toilet. More confirmation of a life that had plunged into mania.

They searched downstairs but there was no sign of life. Mike opened the fridge in the kitchen and immediately regretted it, closing it as quickly as he could to stop the whiff of rotten food adding to the already fetid smell. He retched, but the feeling passed before he was physically sick.

"Chris, if you're upstairs then come out,' Mike called authoritatively, having made his way to the bottom of the stairs. "We're coming up."

Piles of soiled clothing blocked his path. He gestured for Jim and Tasha to move from the bottom of the stairs as he fished the items out of the way with his baton and threw them down there. Once a path had been cleared, the three of them slowly proceeded to the upstairs landing, batons drawn and ready for anything. Mike remembered the upstairs floor plan well. Previously, he had felt like he had been intruding when he had entered Joe's bedroom. Now, he felt like he was performing his duties as a police officer with diligence. He pushed open the door. It was still immaculate and untouched, a haven of peace in stark contrast to the chaos of the rest of the house. Mike felt a familiar pang of sympathy at Chris' plight, but quickly suppressed it. He was there with a job to do. He gently shut the door, hoping to keep the forbidding atmosphere of the rest of the house out of Joe's unsoiled room.

The bathroom was in a grim state with the toilet blocked and close to overflowing. A cursory check showed that Chris wasn't in there. The spare room remained untouched and, again, there was no sign of Chris or evidence that he had been in there. Only one room remained unchecked. Chris' bedroom. The only room in the house that Mike hadn't entered the last time they had searched the property. He gestured to Jim and Tasha that he was going to enter, and silently mouthed to them to be ready. All three of them braced themselves for a confrontation as Mike quietly opened the door and pushed it ajar with his baton.

"Chris, are you in there?" Mike asked. His voice trembled with nerves. Silence greeted his query.

He pushed the door open and stood in the doorway. His hands dropped to his side as he stood with his mouth agape.

"Oh my God," Tasha whispered next to him. Jim remained silent.

Mike pulled out his phone and dialled DS Willmott.

"Sue, you've got to see this," he said.

"I'm on my way," she replied, dropping onto her desk the paperwork she had been looking at and heading out of her office immediately.

She arrived at Chris' house a little over fifteen minutes later and was met in the front garden by Mike, Jim and Tasha. The smell of the house had been too much for them to stay in there any longer.

"So what's going on?" DS Willmott asked.

"Well, he's not here," Mike replied. "The house is even worse than before. There's something you need to see upstairs." He had a strange look on his face, one that DS Willmott couldn't read but one that she could tell didn't bear good news.

"Come on then," she said. "Show me where."

Mike led her into the house.

"You'll have to mind the smell," he said. He didn't need to worry. DS Willmott had smelt it as soon as she had arrived at the scene.

He led her upstairs in silence, cautioning her to mind the broken glass and discarded items along the way. Mike had closed all of the doors upstairs, and slowly opened the one leading into Chris' bedroom. DS Willmott stood completely rooted to the spot as she looked inside.

Not an inch of wall space had been spared. Every available surface was plastered with an array of photos, newspaper clippings, and scrawled messages. The scale of it made the assembled collection of similar items placed at the Wicks's household appear trivial in comparison. DS Willmott stepped cautiously into the room, mindful of the need to preserve evidence but drawn like a magnet to the sheer volume of material present. It was a macabre shrine, she thought. How long must it have taken Chris to assemble this? Why had he done it? She delved further into the room, taking the time to look at some of the photos. Joe as a baby. Linda on their wedding day. Holiday photos. Family photos. School photos. She saw the same image that had been presented to her by Andrew earlier in the day of Joe in his coffin. Blown up newspaper clippings brought context to the photos, most of it from local media but some that the national tabloids had printed in the initial, chaotic stages of the investigation. She hadn't realised that so many column inches had been devoted to the tragic events. Random articles and photos had been scrawled over by Chris in thick, permanent pens - mostly in red ink, but sometimes in black. Some articles relating to Andrew bore the word 'MURDERER' and a death sign had been drawn next to him on various newspaper articles reporting his involvement in the events.

The bedroom was the manifestation of so many of the emotions that had been plaguing Chris, DS Willmott thought. Grief. Anger. Pain. Wrath. As she surveyed the furthest wall of the room she added vengeance to the list.

"Mike..." she called, unaware that he was standing behind her, looking at the same thing as her.

A whole portion of wall space, dedicated to photos of Andrew, Sophie and Maria. But not normal photos. These were surveillance photos, taken without the knowledge or consent of the subjects. And there were masses of them. Maria at school. Andrew in his car. Sophie in the High Street. Various photos of the Wicks' house, both in daylight and by night. Enhanced images of the bedroom windows and front door. And next to it all, a written itinerary detailing a typical day for Andrew. He had been stalking them, and it had been going on for a while.

"What the fuck…" Mike said, echoing the thoughts of DS Willmott.

"Have we got any idea where he is?" DS Willmott asked. She was normally unflappable in a professional capacity but her voice was strained with tension.

"No," Mike replied. He didn't have anything else to offer. Chris and Linda's cars were still on the driveway. He had no family in the area. He didn't have anywhere else to go.

"Can you get a patrol to Andrew's house until we get there," DS Willmott said, prompting Mike to immediately get on his radio and relay the request to the control room. The operator could hear the urgency in Mike's request and resourced it immediately.

They both walked out of the bedroom, shutting the door behind them.

"No-one goes in there until it's been examined by CSI," DS Willmott said to Jim and Tasha who were waiting for them at the top of the stairs. "As of now, this is a crime scene. Everyone out, please, and get a scene log started." DS Willmott felt haunted by what she had seen, but couldn't put into words why. On the face of it, she had evidence of harassment - a serious offence, but not one that would normally warrant a crime scene for forensic analysis being established. Having seen it with her own eyes, however, she knew that it was so much more serious than that. These were the actions of a seriously unwell, mentally unhinged man. And also, a man who knew how the police played the game.

And a man with vengeance on his mind.

CHAPTER 29

"What's going on?" Andrew asked, his exasperation growing with the lack of answers being provided.

"I've told you," the police officer replied, "we've just been asked to come here until someone comes to explain everything. I don't even know what's going on myself."

Andrew was pacing up and down in the front room. They hadn't been home from the police station for long when a police car had screamed to a halt outside their front door and two police officers had nearly knocked the front door off its hinges in their attempts to gain entry quickly. Andrew had thought they had come to arrest him for something, such was their haste. He looked at his watch.

"I've got to go and get my daughter from school soon," he said.

"That's taken care of," the police officer replied. "Someone has gone to get her for you."

"So you know THAT, but you don't know what else is going on?" Andrew replied in a disbelieving tone. It was the truth, however. The police officer had been listening to the various urgent messages being broadcast over the radio and was aware that something huge was brewing, but didn't have the most important bit of information that Andrew desired. Why?

"DS Willmott will be here soon," he replied. "That's all I can tell you because that's all I know."

A stony silence filled the air. Andrew didn't believe the police officer and the police officer, being aware of Andrew's involvement in the events leading to the tragedies that had afflicted his colleague, didn't care what Andrew believed.

Maria arrived home soon after. She ran into the front room and cuddled Andrew, apparently oblivious to any tension in the air and excited that she had got a lift home from a real policeman in a real police car. Sophie came in and took Maria upstairs to get changed out of her school clothes. They had been warned to pack a bag in case they needed to go somewhere else for a few nights, but still no-one could provide them with any explanation.

Andrew walked out of the front room and into the kitchen. The photos and newspaper clippings had been taken away by the police, but the image of them still burned in his memory. Someone had been in his home. No, Chris had been in his home. He didn't know why everyone kept referring to the intruder as 'someone'. It had been Chris.

As he filled the kettle up with water he heard a knock at the front door. He went to answer it but saw that the police officer had got there before he could. In the doorway stood DS Willmott and Mike. Finally, Andrew thought.

"Can we come in, Andrew?" DS Willmott asked. She spoke in a tone that he was unfamiliar with. Generally, she had treated him with disdain. Now, she seemed almost humane.

"Yes," Andrew replied. "I need to know what the hell is going on." He gestured for DS Willmott and Mike to go into the front room where they sat on the sofa. Andrew sat down next to DS Willmott.

"We need to talk about Chris," DS Willmott said.

"So it was definitely him, then?" Andrew replied.

"There's more to it than that," DS Willmott said. "Not to put too fine a point on it, but we have evidence that he has been stalking you and your family." She leant in closer to Andrew and lowered her voice. "It's serious, Andrew. Very serious. I don't use the word obsessed lightly, but it appears that he has some kind of fixation on you and your family."

"But you've arrested him, right?" Andrew replied. His belligerence had gone.

"No," DS Willmott replied. "We don't know where he is." She was barely whispering.

Andrew felt his stomach tightening as a feeling of nausea grew within him. "You must have a plan though, right?" He was almost begging for DS Willmott to provide him with some comfort, a strategy to show that something - anything - could be done.

DS Willmott was prepared for this and had already arranged for measures to be put in place to ensure the wellbeing of the Wicks. "That's what we're here to discuss," she replied. "I appreciate how scary this must feel but threats of harm aren't uncommon to the police and there are a range of things that we do to deal with them. Someone from our technical team will be coming here to install a panic alarm that links directly to our Control Room. Until that's done, a patrol will be parked outside permanently. After it's done, your house will be a priority tasking for high visibility patrolling. In the meantime, we'll be doing everything we can to find Chris."

It was a lot of information for Andrew to take in. Panic Buttons. Priority tasking. Technical team.

"Have you any idea where he might be?" Mike asked. Despite Chris' current state of mind he had been friends with Andrew for years. Any ideas would have been welcomed.

"No," Andrew replied.

They sat in gloomy silence, each of them searching for inspiration but all of them drawing a blank. Andrew eventually stood up and went upstairs to update Sophie on what had happened. When he came back down shortly after, DS Willmott and Mike had gone. The uniformed patrol was still there.

"Tech team will be here soon," the police officer said. "We'll wait in our car until they're done," he added as he walked out of the front door.

Andrew felt his eyes filling with tears. He walked into the front room and dropped onto the sofa where he held a cushion to his face to muffle the sound of his sobs.

DS Willmott sat in her office and agonised over what else she could do to locate Chris. His phone hadn't shown any signs of activity for a while and so couldn't be traced. He didn't have any social media accounts and no other friends of note in the area. The family vehicles had remained on the driveway and hadn't been moved. His bank cards hadn't been used recently. He had simply vanished.

She had already circulated him as a wanted person and updated the Professional Standards Department regarding the events of the day. His career was over. That being said, she still felt a personal obligation to him. She had made a promise to his son that she felt she had broken, and was determined to resolve this situation without further incident.

Mike was sitting opposite her, both of them nursing cups of tea that had long since gone cold.

"Can we get a plain clothes patrol sitting up on Chris' house?" Mike asked. "At least then we can see if he comes back and nick him before anything else happens."

"Already in hand," DS Willmott replied. "I'm just waiting for the Superintendent to sign the surveillance authority." She had already selected four officers from her team to work rolling twelve hour shifts sitting outside Chris' house in the hope that he would eventually go back there. They had been briefed and were ready to go as soon as the Superintendent gave them the go ahead.

They both sat in silence as daylight gave way to the auburn glow of sunset.

"Superintendent has signed the authority, Sarge," DC Harris said as he walked into DS Willmott's office, waving a piece of paper.

"Right, let's get moving then," DS Willmott replied. "You're up first, Tom. One of you at the front and one of you at the back. Keep it nice and tight please, and report anything out of the ordinary."

"Who's signing the overtime?" DC Harris replied with a smile on his face, trying to bring a bit of levity to the situation.

"We'll worry about that another day," DS Willmott replied. The gravity of the predicament facing them had sapped any reserves of humour within her.

DC Harris turned and walked out of her office, knowing that it was going to be a long night ahead. He walked quickly over to DC Flanagan's desk, where she was trying to finish a case file before they were deployed for the night.

"Got to go, Amy," DC Harris said. "The sarge is in a foul mood and she wants us plotted up ASAP."

They made their way to Chris' house, making sure to park a few roads away so that they could walk the last part of the journey on foot under the cover of darkness that was rapidly falling. The air was still but they both felt the chill of the crisp, autumnal evening.

"Front or back?" DC Harris asked.

"Back," DC Flanagan replied. "Swap half way through?"

"Deal," DC Harris replied. "Back to back on Channel 21?"

"On it," DC Flanagan said, as they both set their radios to a private channel so that they could maintain a dialogue without using the main, operational channel.

They touched knuckles as DC Flanagan disappeared into an alleyway that led to the rear of Chris' house. Darkness had totally enveloped the street, making covert surveillance a lot easier. In many ways, DC Harris was glad that he was doing the night shift. He knew how difficult it was going to be to remain undetected during the hours of daylight. He walked along the line of cars parked on the side of the road until he saw Chris' house, fully in darkness. He tracked away from the house until he found a row of bushes, where he was able to secrete himself comfortably while still maintaining a direct and unobstructed view of the target premises. Satisfied that this was his optimum location in terms of proximity and concealment, he turned off the backlight on his radio and settled down for the long night to come. He looked at his watch. It was 19:46.

"Tom to Amy," he whispered into his radio.

"Go," she replied quietly.

"Are you set up?" he asked.

"Yes yes," she replied. "In target's garden, behind shed. Unobstructed view. No signs of life. You?"

"Received," he replied. "I'm in some bushes opposite his house. Nothing this end either. Check in again soon."

"Will do," DC Flanagan replied. Shifts spent doing surveillance could be tedious, but this felt different to her. There was a crackle of tension, an anticipation that something out of the ordinary was happening. "Tom, what's the plan if he does turn up?" She asked.

"Arrest him," DC Harris replied. "Then call in the cavalry."

CHAPTER 30

The Technical Team completed the installation of two static panic alarms at the Wicks' house in a matter of minutes, such was their expertise. One was located in Andrew and Sophie's bedroom, the other downstairs in the lounge. Not much instruction was needed on how to operate them - they were simple devices equipped with a large red button that were mounted on the wall, high enough to be out of Maria's inquisitive reach.

"Hit the button and a patrol will be here in minutes," were the parting words of the Technical Officer who had fitted them.

As he walked out of the front door, the patrol car that had been guarding the house drove off without saying goodbye. Despite the knowledge that efforts were being made to locate and arrest Chris, and that he now had a direct link to the police control room by means of hitting a button and waiting for help, Andrew felt exposed and vulnerable. He quickly closed the front door and double locked it, then walked around the house checking that all of the windows were secure. Finally, he locked the back door and bolted it both at the top and at the bottom. He was not taking any chances with the safety of his family.

He sat in the kitchen looking out of the window, watching as day turned into night. He didn't know what he was looking for, but he just sat there, watching. For anything out of the ordinary. For anything that didn't look right. For anything that seemed like a threat. For anything that might harm him or, more importantly, his family. For Chris.

Sophie took Maria to bed yet still Andrew remained in the kitchen, a captain manning his post and protecting his troop. His eyes felt heavy. He closed them momentarily, only to be confronted by the familiar image of Joe that plagued him in moments of stress. His eyes shot open. He couldn't sleep. The risks were too great. Sophie hadn't come back downstairs, he thought. She must've stayed in bed with Maria. They were safe. That was what mattered.

The clock on the oven showed 22:38.

DC Harris looked at his watch. 22:38. He'd been in position for just under three hours and the base of his back was starting to go numb. He tried to manoeuvre himself into a more comfortable position but he was unable to do so without making too much noise. Instead, he put weight onto his legs to try to get some blood circulating through the parts of him that he couldn't feel any more.

"Still there, Amy?" He whispered quietly into his radio.

"Confirm," she replied faintly. Then, ominously, "standby, movement."

DC Harris extricated himself from the bush as quietly and as quickly as he could, having decided in an instant that the risk of exposing himself was justified if Chris was in close proximity to Amy.

"False alarm, cat or fox," DC Flanagan murmured into the radio.

"Received," DC Harris replied. He melted back into his hide, hoping that no-one had seen him and that his cover was intact. The brief bit of excitement had at least alleviated the numbness to his back, he thought, as he positioned his body in a more suitable pose for the hours ahead.

The radio remained silent and the road traffic dried up as the night wore on. DC Harris had been at work since 08:00 and had been working extended shifts all week to keep on top of his workload. Suddenly it seemed that the hours of toil and graft were catching up with him. He felt his mental capacity diminishing, such was the intensity of concentration demanded from this surveillance detail. He fought to keep his eyes open, he really did. Alas, he couldn't do it. His fight with sleep was lost and his eyes closed.

Chris' house was vulnerable from the front.

Andrew woke, disorientated by the noise. He looked at the clock on the oven. Through the smoke he could see it was 01:15. Thick smoke. The noise of the smoke alarm screaming in his ears, invoking clarity in the midst of his state of confusion.

"SOPHIE, MARIA!" He screamed, words that caused him to choke as he inhaled lungfuls of acrid smoke.

He stumbled from the kitchen and saw flames licking the front door, the heat coming from it forcing him away. The smoke was thicker in the hallway. His panic caused him to breathe in instinctively despite his intention to hold his breath. He could feel the grip of panic as the smoke choked him. Holding his throat and down on his knees, he crawled and scraped his way into the front room where he shut the door and wedged a cushion in place at its base. Less smoke, but still too much. He reached for the panic alarm and hit it numerous times, desperate to register the state of emergency that he found himself in. He needed air. He urgently, gravely needed air. Unable to find an implement to smash the lounge window, he used his fists. The adrenaline was flowing and it only took one punch before he had his head outside and was sucking in litres and litres of only mildly smoke filled air. Still, it cleansed his lungs and gave him the strength to do what needed to be done.

He could hear sirens in the distance but they were too far away. He needed to do it himself. He pulled off his jumper and tried to use it as a makeshift mask to protect against the smoke. It was too smoky. He pulled off his t-shirt, now naked on his top half, and used that instead. Much better, he thought. Then, back into the fray.

"SOPHIE, MARIA," he screamed as he ran back into the hallway, his words not now choking him but muffled from behind the t-shirt mask. The fire around the front door was now intensifying and taking hold in the hallway itself. Not much time, he thought. Upstairs, the thick smoke dulled out the sound of the smoke alarm. What had been a penetrating noise downstairs was suppressed and almost strangled in intensity on the first floor. Maria's door was shut. Andrew charged through it, screaming for his wife and daughter as he did. He'd got there before the smoke and fire and saw his two girls sitting bolt upright in Maria's bed, shaken to consciousness by Andrew's arrival with a look of collective terror spread over their faces.

"There's a fire," Andrew shouted while coughing. "It's spreading quickly." He grabbed the first thing that he could find on the floor, a towel that Sophie had used to dry Maria after a bath earlier in the evening. He wrapped it around Maria's head, covering her mouth and nose. It was still damp.

Perfect. He thrust his t-shirt into Sophie's hands, gesturing for her to cover her mouth face with it, as he scooped Maria up in his arms. He didn't need a mask. He had his hands full and was going to get them out without taking another breath.

"We're going NOW," he shouted to Sophie. He could hear the lick of the flames taking hold downstairs. "Hold on to my belt," he called, and felt Sophie tugging at his midriff. No more words, he thought. Time to go.

He took a breath in, wondering if it would be his last. He moved quickly, aware that the flames that were now engulfing the stairs were the enemy but mindful that Sophie and his unborn baby were clinging to him and needing guidance to get out of the property. If he lost her now, he doubted he'd get her back. He could feel and smell the hairs on his back singeing as flames kissed his skin, only stiffening his resolve to lead his family to safety. The heat intensified on each step down the stairs until it was almost unbearable at the bottom. Still, he fought on. He held Maria tighter, willing the inferno to burn him and not her. His lungs were empty. He needed to breathe. He turned and marched quickly down the hallway away from the front door, arriving at the back of the house and blindly unbolting and unlocking the back door. Sophie was still clinging to his belt. Maria's head was still wrapped up in the towel. Then, fresh air. He'd never been so happy to see his garden. Sirens and the smoke alarm competed for attention as the emergency services closed in on the house. Andrew unwrapped Maria's towel and pulled Sophie in close to him as he embraced his family, his eyes stinging from the smoke but streaming from the tears that were flowing.

"Tom, are you there?" DC Flanagan whispered into her radio. Silence greeted her. "Tom?" She said, louder this time. Still, silence.

She looked at her watch. 01:27. She had heard a chorus of sirens in the distance as an army of emergency service personnel had been dispatched to an ongoing incident, but she was not tuned in to the local radio frequency and so didn't know what was going on.

"Tom?" She said, louder still. As before, radio silence was all that came back.

She didn't know what it was at first. It began as a slight glow through the cracks of the blinds covering the windows at the rear of the house. She couldn't be sure. Then, she could smell it. Then, she was sure.

"Tom," she called into the radio, the fear of being exposed now completely gone.

In the bushes, DC Harris was awoken by the last transmission. The fear in DC Harris' voice had awoken him.

"I'm here," he said as he gathered his senses and rubbed his eyes. He checked his watch, ashamed that he had fallen asleep. Then he saw the cost of his negligence. He rubbed his eyes to check that they weren't deceiving him and then furiously scrambled to change his radio channel. He heard the chaos of a house fire erupting over the airwaves and wondered where the cavalry were, if not here. Then it dawned on him. There were two fires.

"Control from DC Harris, we have a house fire, repeat, a house fire at our location." He managed to cut in during a brief pause in transmissions with an emergency message. Panic was obvious in his voice. "Fire is taking hold quickly here. Send anyone you've got."

He jumped from his hide and ran across the street and saw DC Flanagan emerging from the alleyway.

"Did you see him?" She screamed as they ran towards the front of the house.

"Didn't see a thing," DC Harris replied, unwilling to disclose that he had fallen asleep.

As they reached the front garden the intensity of the heat beat them back, but a strong smell of petrol permeated through the air. The fire was spreading quickly and raging furiously.

"He's been here," DC Flanagan shouted as the inferno roared behind them. "How did you miss him?"

DC Harris shrugged his shoulders. He had no answer.

CHAPTER 31

DS Willmott had left strict instructions that she was to be called if anything of note happened overnight. She wasn't the Night Duty cover, but she had left her phone on and told DC Harris in no uncertain terms that she was to be the first call that he made in case of an emergency. The events of the night certainly fitted that criterion.

The phone only rung once before it was answered.

"What's happened, Tom?" DS Willmott asked. She was awake and alert. DC Harris wondered if she had actually been sleeping.

"It's all happening Sarge," he replied breathlessly. "Arsons at the Wicks' house and here at Chris'." He paused for a moment. "He's in the wind again," he added quietly.

DS Willmott didn't want answers over the telephone. DC Harris had been right in assuming that she hadn't been sleeping. In fact, she was still fully dressed in anticipation of the phone ringing at some point in the small hours.

"I'm on my way," she said, hanging the phone up and cutting DC Harris off before he could get his excuses in.

She was standing next to DC Harris and DC Flanagan within twenty minutes of the phone call. The fire was still raging behind them as firefighters fought to bring it under control. Fire crews and police patrols had been mobilised from across the County to assist local personnel at the two resource intensive crime scenes. Fires generate interest and interest can bring about chaos. Many patrols were required at both scenes to establish cordons and to evacuate neighbours from vulnerable properties nearby, as well as to manage the growing crowds. It may have been the middle of the night but a swell of people were gathering at both fires. All of these patrols being tied up in these essential duties meant that no-one had thought to start coordinating a search for the perpetrator. Chris had gone. DC Harris knew it. DS Willmott knew it.

"Well?" DS Willmott hissed. She didn't need to expand. DC Harris knew exactly what she was asking.

"I don't know," he replied. "There was just a fire. I honestly don't know how he did it without me seeing." He knew that lying to a superior officer was grounds for dismissal under gross misconduct rules, but he thought that telling the truth would have left his career in ruins as well. Stuck between a rock and a hard place, he had chosen stalling tactics.

"We haven't finished this conversation," DS Willmott said abrasively. She had put the players in position but they hadn't executed the game plan. She was not happy as she turned around and made her way back to her car.

Five minutes later, she arrived to a scene almost identical to the one that she had departed. A fire. Emergency service personnel working hard. Crowds gathering and being marshalled by police officers. The only difference was the addition of two ambulances, which is where DS Willmott headed immediately upon arrival. She knew that she owed an explanation to the Wicks family.

She peered around the rear door of the first ambulance. It was empty. She made her way to the second ambulance and heard raised voices coming from inside. She recognised one of the voices and knew that Andrew was inside. The rear door was ajar so she pulled it open and then stood wide eyed at the commotion inside. It was a regular sized ambulance, but was crowded with people. Maria was sitting in one of the passenger chairs with a seatbelt over her lap, apparently well but with a vacant look on her face. Andrew was standing over Sophie, who was lying prone on the trolley while a paramedic strapped her in. She was conscious but her face was covered by an oxygen mask. Even so, DS Willmott could see it was contorted with pain.

"What's going on?" DS Willmott said. Her voice didn't penetrate the havoc unfolding inside.

"Andrew?" she called, her voice louder this time.

Andrew looked in her direction, his expression changing from one of concern to one of outright rage.

"You call this protecting us?" he shouted, his voice laced with venom.

"Andrew," Sophie called from the trolley, pulling the oxygen mask away from her face to get his attention. "It's coming, I can feel it coming."

"Excuse me love," one of the paramedics said to DS Willmott, "can you shut the door. A bit of privacy if you don't mind."

"I'm a police officer," DS Willmott said, showing her Warrant Card.

"I don't care if you're the Chief of Police," the paramedic replied. "If we don't get her to hospital soon then the baby will be born in here. Now move, please."

DS Willmott stepped back out onto the street and shut the ambulance door. The air was still thick with smoke. It was no place for a baby to be born.

She surveyed the scene. Mayhem. The criminal investigation would come, of course. She intended to be at the front of the queue to be in charge of that. In the back of her mind she knew that a parallel investigation would soon begin as well, one that would be conducted by the Professional Standards Department and that would examine if every possible step had been taken to prevent this from happening. A serving police officer had likely committed some of the most serious offences possible and was still at large. The ramifications would be immense and it gave DS Willmott a headache just thinking about it.

The ambulance moved slowly away from her, navigating a tricky path around emergency service vehicles and personnel in order to transport Sophie to hospital. DS Willmott hadn't established if the baby was at risk or if Sophie was in a natural labour. It suddenly dawned on her that the gravity of the crime could escalate dramatically if a baby's life was in danger. She needed to be at the hospital, and she needed to be there now. She ran back to her car and drove as quickly as she dared, arriving at the Accident and Emergency Department in good time. She burst through the doors and approached the receptionist.

"Sophie Wicks, I need to check on her," DS Willmott said breathlessly, again flashing her Warrant Card.

The receptionist tapped on her computer. "No-one here by that name," she said.

"She must be," DS Willmott replied. "They've just brought her in. She's having a baby."

The receptionist flashed half a smile. "Then she'll be in the Maternity Unit love," she said.

DS Willmott silently cursed herself for not realising this. The Maternity Unit was on the other side of the hospital. She didn't acknowledge her mistake and just turned around and ran back out of the A&E doors. She knew where the Maternity Unit was. She had given birth there herself.

It took her ten minutes to navigate the dark and empty corridors of the hospital. The Maternity Unit was a ward that didn't run by the normal conventions of time. It was fully functional and fully active twenty-four hours a day. As DS Willmott was buzzed in, it was a hive of activity. She approached a receptionist who looked tired and stressed.

"I'm here for Sophie Wicks…" she began, before being cut off.

"Visiting begins at 10am," the receptionist said.

"I'm a police officer," DS Willmott replied sternly. "She's been brought in by ambulance and I'm here to check on her welfare. Now where is she?"

The receptionist rolled her eyes and looked at her computer. "She's in delivery," she said. "You can't see her."

"And her husband?" DS Willmott asked. "Where is he? They came in with their other daughter." Her patience was wearing thin.

"If he's not in delivery then try the Family Room," the Receptionist said, pointing down the corridor. She turned on her chair and started leafing through a pile of paperwork in front of her, indicating that the conversation was over.

DS Willmott made her way to the Family Room and gently held her ear to the closed door, trying to hear if anyone was inside. She heard a familiar voice talking in hushed tones. Andrew was in there. She quietly knocked on the door and pushed it open. Andrew was sitting on a chair with Maria asleep on him, her head cradled in his lap.

"Keep dreaming princess," he said quietly. "Daddy's with you." He had seen DS Willmott enter the room, and gestured for her to come and sit next to him.

"I've just got her off," he said, his voice calm and soothing but his face etched with rage.

"I'm so sorry about what happened," DS Willmott whispered, mindful to keep her voice hushed. She could see the anger on Andrew's face and knew that he was doing everything he could to suppress his feelings while Maria was sleeping on him. "How's Sophie doing?"

"I don't know," Andrew replied. "There's no way I was going to leave Maria on her own."

DS Willmott felt a pang of sympathy at Andrew's plight. He had been forced to choose to be absent from the birth of his child in order to ensure that his daughter was not left alone. Silently, DS Willmott applauded his decision.

"Go and be with Sophie," she said. "I'll stay with Maria."

Andrew looked at DS Willmott and the fury melted from his face. "Are you sure?" He whispered. "What if it takes a while?"

DS Willmott smiled. "Go on, I'll be here," she said.

Andrew gently manoeuvred Maria onto DS Willmott's lap. She had fallen into a heavy sleep and didn't wake.

"Thank you so much," he said as he walked out of the door.

"My pleasure," she replied, stroking Maria's hair much as she did with her own daughter. She turned her phone onto silent mode and then closed her eyes as a warm sense of familiarity spread across her. She was reminded of the number of times that she had spent on her sofa at home, rocking her child to sleep. She had been on an adrenaline high for much of the past hour, but now that it had passed through her she felt fatigued beyond compare. Her eyes remained closed as she drifted off to sleep.

“Sue,” Andrew said quietly. She was snoring gently. Maria hadn’t moved at all. “Sue,” he repeated, squeezing her leg softly. Her eyes opened and darted around. It took her a few seconds to remember where she was.

“What’s happened?” she asked. “Is the baby okay?”

Andrew smiled. Any traces of ill temper had been vanquished from his face. “He’s fine,” Andrew replied. “Sophie’s fine. Everything is fine.” His smile turned into a grin.

DS Willmott was pleased for Andrew and Sophie, but the feeling that overwhelmed her was one of relief. The investigation into the handling of the entire affair was going to be intensive, but if anything had happened to either Sophie or the baby then it would have been in an entirely different stratosphere.

“We’re calling him Lewis,” Andrew added.

DS Willmott heard him, but didn’t listen. She didn’t know how long she had been asleep but one look at her phone told her that the events of the night were far from over. Twenty-two missed calls. Three answerphone messages. One text message from DC Harris, sent fifteen minutes before.

“Sarge, we’ve been trying to reach you but no-one can. Not sure if you’re at home but you need to call me ASAP. Please, it’s urgent. Tom.”

CHAPTER 32

"Tom, what's going on?" DS Willmott asked. She hadn't listened to the voicemails.

"I'm just arriving now," DC Harris replied. "Get to Beachbrook Beach, there's another fire there."

DS Willmott was already in her car and, now that she had a destination, she accelerated from the hospital car park. The adrenaline was again rampant within her.

Dawn was just breaking as she pulled up at the beach. She jumped out of her car and ran towards the steps leading down to the beach, past an officer holding a scene log and onto the main sands. She could smell the fire in the air but the smoke wasn't as thick or harsh as it had been at the two houses earlier in the night. There were no fire engines here. There had been none available as they were all engaged at the other incidents and it hadn't been deemed a high enough priority to pull them away.

While en route to the beach from the hospital, DS Willmott had speculated in her mind what had been set fire to. Her guess had been correct. A smouldering debris was all that was left of the Wicks' beach hut and its contents. It hadn't been used since that tragic day months before, and would never be used again.

"He's burning it all down, isn't he?" DS Willmott said wistfully as she walked up to DC Harris. "Only question is, what's next?" DC Harris remained silent. He was unsure if she was actually asking a question.

They looked around for anything that could point to a source of ignition or an accelerant, but any evidence that could be deduced by the naked eye had long since gone, incinerated by the strength of the fire. Crime Scene Investigators were going to have their hands full with the two house fires so a forensic examination of this scene was unlikely.

"Let's get out of here," DS Willmott said, turning away from the smoky remnants of the beach hut.

DC Harris followed as they trudged back towards the steps. The sun was making its slow ascent up from beyond the horizon. The black of night had given way to the first light of dawn. The full length of the beach could now be seen, no longer hidden under the cloak of darkness. In the distance, DS Willmott could see a police officer running towards her.

"Sarge, wait," echoed through the air as the police officer got closer.

She waited.

He arrived by her side, breathless from running but with something he had to say. "Sarge, I've got a witness." He was struggling to get his words out. "Saw the fire then came down to have a look." He was still breathing heavily. "Saw him strip naked and walk out to sea. Said he was carrying something heavy over his shoulders, like a rucksack with bricks in it or something" He took some deep breaths, willing his heart rate to come down. "There's a note, Sarge. You'd better come and see."

DS Willmott pursed her lips and then puffed out her cheeks. This was the longest night, and it wasn't over yet. The police officer turned and jogged back in the direction from which he had come. DS Willmott looked beyond him, and saw a person standing in the distance next to something dark on the sand. Chris' clothes, she presumed. She turned to DC Harris. He was staring at her intently, looking for direction.

"Let's go, then," she said and walked briskly after the police officer.

She had been right. It was a pile of clothes. A jacket, a jumper, a pair of jeans, underwear, socks and a pair of trainers. All of them were dirty and stained. An opened envelope sat on top of the pile. On the front of it bore one word.

'Police'.

"I opened it, Sarge," the police officer said. "There's a note in there." He handed DS Willmott some gloves before she handled the document.

She put on the gloves and looked at the envelope. "Have you read it yet?" She asked the police officer.

"No Sarge," he replied. "I saw you and put it back."

She carefully picked up the envelope at the edges, mindful of the need to be forensically aware. It flapped open, inviting her to examine the contents. She meticulously removed the note. A single piece of A4 paper, folded in half. She unfolded it, revealing a handwritten message. Black ink. Probably a biro. Barely legible, but just enough to be able to read it.

'If you're reading this then I am gone. Don't try to find me. I'm with my family now. Peace at last. I hope he burned with his lies.

Christian Jamieson'

DS Willmott looked out to sea. The place where it all began. And the place where, now, it had come to an end.

EPILOGUE: HAPPILY EVER AFTER

Every day, he followed the same routine. Get up with the kids. Drop Maria to school. Continue the renovation. Pick Maria up from school. Go home. Play with the kids and embrace their family life. Cuddle up to Sophie. Sleep. Wake. Repeat.

A month had passed since that night. Time had healed some of the mental wounds, but the psychological scars would remain forever. Andrew held his children just a tiny bit tighter than normal each night, his kisses lingered for a nanosecond longer than before. He knew how close he had been to losing Maria, how real the prospect of never meeting Lewis had been.

Sophie had thrown herself back into motherhood with aplomb, her way of coping with everything that had been thrown at her. Excursions from the house were taken warily, but she was building up her confidence. Time. It would take time.

They were living in rented accommodation. The damage from the fire had been severe and their house was uninhabitable. It wasn't clear when, or even if, they would be able to move back in there.

The renovation was going well. So well, in fact, that the Estate Agents had received a message from the landlord asking for Andrew to see if any work could be done on any of the outbuildings to potentially convert them into other accommodation. They had called him late in the afternoon asking him to come in and see them first thing in the morning so that they could discuss some plans. Be there at 9 sharp, they had said. The landlord had some big plans apparently. Sophie would have to do the school run in the morning.

He kissed Sophie goodbye then gently stroked Lewis on the head, still marvelling at the miracle that they had created. He pulled Maria in for a cuddle and then walked out of the door and headed for the Estate Agents. He was in there for an hour, going over plans and deciding how they could best utilise the space in the outbuildings. They had always been locked and he had never been in them but had seen from the outside how big they were. The potential was massive.

He made his way to the house. Even now, months after the previous tenants had moved out, junk mail still arrived. Rosina Janice Smith. Every day, more mail. He chuckled as he looked at the piles that had been building up. He had given up trying to get it taken away. Now, it was just a game to see how high the piles could grow before they came crashing down.

He had the plans with him. No time like the present, he thought. He made his way outside. Not a breath of air. But a sound familiar to him. A distant sound of a baby crying. Autumn had stripped the trees of their leaves, and the crunching of his footsteps drowned out the sound. He stood still. The noise was louder. The baby was closer. He took a few more steps towards the outbuildings. The crying turned to a scream. Definite distress. Then, silence. A neighbour must've had a baby.

He walked to the door of the first outbuilding. Brick structure, boarded windows and a decent roof. Good potential. He had been given a key by the Estate Agent, but the door was unlocked. He opened it to darkness and fumbled for the light switch that was next to the door.

Light brought terror.

A scene he had seen before. Newspaper clippings. Photos. Joe. Linda. Sophie. Maria. Himself. Lewis. Lewis. Lewis. Photos taken after Lewis had been born. After Chris had walked out to sea. After Chris had apparently died. All stuck to the walls.

He found himself drawn into the room. A desk with piles of photos on it. Heaps of newspaper clippings. His hat and glasses that had been taken from his car. And a bundle of letters. All addressed to Trevor Jamieson. All with the same address on them. This address. Chris' dad's house. He had been renovating Chris' dad's house. He had never met the landlord and now he knew why.

The crying started again, only this time it was close. It was in the building. From a distance it had sounded like an anonymous, crying baby. At close quarters, it sounded familiar. Horribly familiar.

He forced himself to follow the cries, not knowing what it was leading him into, but knowing he had to do it. A closed door leading to an adjoining room. He cautiously opened it. A living space. Tins and tins of food and gallons of water. Surveillance equipment. A bed. On that bed, a baby. His baby. Lewis. Instinct drove him to run to Lewis. He had walked into the trap and the door slammed shut behind him.

"I've been waiting for you," Chris said.

Andrew didn't have time to turn around. The knife, already wet with the blood of Sophie, penetrated him at the top of his spine.

Then, darkness.

JOE'S DAY

He woke up needing his Mummy. He shouted out for her. His Daddy never came, it was always his Mummy. She came in looking tired, but he knew that she was always happy to see him, even if it was in the middle of the night. He wanted to play but she said they could read a book instead. It sounded like a fair compromise to him. He loved reading. They read for longer than he thought he'd be allowed to and eventually his Mummy told him that he needed to get some sleep. He was going to see Maria for the day. He was excited about that. He secretly loved Maria.

His Mummy cuddled him and he eventually fell asleep. He woke up and walked into his Mummy's bedroom but she wasn't in there. He liked investigating things. He decided he would investigate where his Mummy had gone. He looked in the bathroom but she wasn't there. He looked in the spare room but she wasn't there. He went downstairs. She wasn't in the kitchen. Eventually, he found her. She was asleep on the sofa.

"Mummy?" He asked. She didn't reply. "Mummy?" He repeated, a little bit louder.

His Mummy opened her eyes but she didn't look like she knew where she was.

"What are you doing here Mummy?" he asked.

She told him that they had to get ready quickly otherwise they were going to be late. He was worried about this as he didn't want to miss out on seeing Maria. They rushed to get ready and didn't even have time for breakfast or for him to get dressed before they were in the car and on their way to Maria's house.

On the way there, he thought about Maria. He really did love her. Maybe today would be the day that he would ask her if she loved him as well.

When they got to Maria's house he had breakfast and got dressed. He didn't know what they were doing to do for the rest of the day, but he knew that it would be fun because he always had a good time when he was with Maria. He asked Maria's Mummy what they were doing. She said they might go to the beach.

Maria and her Daddy came downstairs while he was eating his breakfast. He told them that he was looking forward to going to the beach. He knew that Maria loved the beach. If she loved it then so did he.

After breakfast he went with Maria to play in her room. They were playing soldiers and Maria was the Captain. She was in charge. He liked it that way. He didn't like to make decisions and would happily do what Maria told him. Her Daddy came in and told her that she had to tidy up the room. When her Daddy walked out, Maria was still their Captain and she told him that he had to do what the Captain said. The Captain said to tidy the room, so he followed the orders.

They went to the beach a little while after. He chatted with Maria in the car. He was happy chatting to Maria. They chatted about funny things that they could see and told each other made up jokes. He laughed at Maria's. They were really funny.

It started raining when they got out of the car. He noticed quite a few spots of rain landing on him as he chased Maria down the steps and onto the beach. There was no-one else there. It was cold and windy, but it was still fun.

"Come on," Maria said, "let's get our wetsuits on and go in the sea."

He didn't know if he wanted to go in the sea. It looked scary. The waves were really big and frightening.

"You're not scared, are you?" She asked.

"No," he replied. He wanted to find out if she loved him. She wouldn't love him if he was scared.

They went over to the beach hut to get changed. Maria's Daddy tried to talk them out of it but Maria was adamant that they were going in the sea. Then they came to something called a compromise, where they would only go in the sea to paddle. This made him happy. He really didn't want to go in the sea but he didn't mind paddling.

Maria's Daddy told him that he didn't have to go in if he didn't want to, but he knew that it would make Maria happy if he did.

"Maria wants to paddle so I'll go with her to make sure she's OK," he said. He fist bumped Maria's Daddy. He liked it when they did that.

They ran down to the edge of the water. He didn't actually mind being near the water, it was only going in that he found a bit scary. He couldn't swim properly. He didn't mind going in the sea when it was calm but it was anything but that today. Maria started kicking water at him, so he kicked some back at her. They both laughed. They ran further along the beach, still trying to get each other wet. Maria called out to her Mummy and Daddy. She called them Mum and Dad. He found that a bit weird. He waved to them as well, but was starting to get a bit cold. They got a bit closer to the water and heard Maria's Daddy shout for them to not go any further. Maria waved back at them. He didn't. He was really cold now.

"Can we go back?" he asked. He was shivering and his voice was trembling. The water was up to their ankles.

"No!" Maria replied abruptly.

"Please," he asked.

"Stop being afraid," she said.

He looked at her. He knew that he loved her. Maybe if he told her, then she would say that she loved him as well and they would be able to go back and get warm. It was worth a try. The water was now over their shins.

"I love you, Maria," he said.

They had been standing next to each other, but she took a step back. Her face changed. He didn't know what expression it was, but she didn't look happy. He hadn't told anyone that he loved them before and didn't know what he was supposed to do now.

"Do you love me?" He asked. The water was over their knees.

"NO," she shouted then pushed him really hard.

He stumbled backwards into the sea just as a wave broke. He fell and it crashed over him, sucking him underneath and pulling him away from the shore. He couldn't swim. He couldn't float. He couldn't breathe.

Maria found him. She was next to him and held his hand as he came back above the surface. He was scared for himself and scared for Maria. She was screaming "DADDY, DADDY." He was too scared to join in.

Maria's Daddy did come to them. He was happy that he was there. Adults could solve anything, he thought. He climbed onto Maria's Daddy's back and buried his face into his shoulder. They didn't make any progress. The sea was just too strong to fight against. If anything, they were going further out to sea. Maria's Daddy asked them if they could swim against it themselves. Maria couldn't, and he certainly wasn't able.

He loved Maria so much. He was sure that she loved him too, even if she had said that she didn't. She hadn't meant it. So when her Daddy told him that he was sorry, he knew why and he didn't mind. As long as Maria was safe. Then they were gone.

He was tired. He felt the sea taking him away. He thought of his Daddy. He thought of his Mummy. He thought of Maria.

Then, darkness.

THE END

ACKNOWLEDGEMENTS

Having never written a book before, I expected this page to be akin to an Academy Award acceptance speech.

I haven't as yet obtained representation, so I can't thank an agent. Nor have I got a publishing deal, so I can't thank my publishers either!

What I can do, and will happily do now, is thank a few people who have been reading this novel as I have been writing it. They don't know it yet, but I will be asking them to re-read it again and again to find any significant plot holes, continuity errors, grammar and spelling mistakes and anything else that comes with being a proof reader! So thank you to my 'gang', my Dad, my sister Nicki, Helen and Debs.

To my beautiful wife for putting up with me while I spent hours, days and weeks trying to put this together. Thanks Wifey.

To my two amazing kiddies for allowing me to have the parental insight necessary to write from the heart about things no parent should ever bear. You're both my inspiration and my reason.

And finally, to Rosina Janice Smith. You don't exist. In fact, I made you up and your name only appears three times in the body of this book. As an anagram of Christian Jamieson, however, you are perfect.

ABOUT THE AUTHOR

Gary was a police officer for ten years before a hereditary heart condition caused him to retire at the age of 29. He now owns a coffee shop in Ramsgate, Kent, where he lives with his wife and two young children. He has always loved to play with words and used a winter off in the COVID-19 crisis to finally put pen to paper on an idea that had been formulating for years.

This is his first novel.

He hopes to write many more.

Content Warnings:

Child death

Suicide

Mental illness

Death at sea

Violence

Printed in Great Britain
by Amazon